House of Secrets

Lynda Stacey

Where heroes are like chocolate – irresistible!

Published 2017 by Choc Lit Limited
Penrose House, Crawley Drive, Camberley, Surrey GU15 2AB, UK
www.choc-lit.com

A CIP catalogue record for this book is available
from the British Library

ISBN 978-1-78189-374-6

MIX
Paper from
responsible sources
FSC® C104740

Printed and bound by Clays Ltd, Elcograf S.p.A.

To Haydn

I want to thank you for being both my husband and best friend for the past 25 years, for the life we've spent together, for always loving me, and for taking me to Wrea Head Hall on so many wonderful occasions.

I love you so very much xx

Acknowledgements

I'd like to wholeheartedly thank Mr Gerald Aburrow and Dr Mark Giles, the true owners and Keepers of Wrea Head Hall. They've been amazing, enthusiastic and so very supportive right from the very first moment that I asked for permission to use the hall as the backdrop to my novel. I love the hall so much and couldn't have wished for a more beautiful and inspirational setting. Wrea Head Hall is my favourite place to go in England. I always feel very spoiled when I stay there. It's a fantastic hotel, with the most beautiful food, open log fires and exquisite rooms. The whole team at Wrea Head Hall makes every visit the most wonderful experience and I'd encourage anyone to go and stay ... you wouldn't be disappointed.

A huge thank you goes to my husband, Haydn. Who not only took me to Wrea Head Hall for a birthday treat, but has continued to take me back on a regular basis (and he pays for it). He's the anchor in my life, the one person in the world I could not live without and even though my writing means that he ends up spending many evenings watching TV without me, he's been understanding and encouraging throughout.

Thank you to my brother, Stuart Thompson, who has been the one constant person in my life. Not only did he buy me an Audi TT, for which I'll be forever grateful, he also bought me my very first word processor and said to me, 'You keep saying you're going to write a novel, get on with it.' Well, thank you, I finally did ...!

I'd like to thank the amazing author Jane Lovering, who has mentored me for the past three years. She's pulled me along, kicking and screaming (on some days) and celebrated with me on others. Thank you for everything, you've been an amazing friend x

To both Kathy Kilner and author Victoria Howard who have read my manuscript repeatedly. You've both helped me, critiqued my work and supported me daily. It's friends like both of you that keep me going on days when it would be easy to do other things. Thank you.

To Jayne Stacey, Cynthia Foster, and Vivien Norton. You have all read my work over and over, you've all believed in me, supported me and encouraged me to continue. Thank you.

To my amazing editor, I loved every minute of working with you. You were the best and I couldn't have wished for a better editor. You helped me add the sparkle and shine. Thank you.

To the Romantic Novelist Association. Being a member of this association has changed my life. I've met some of the best authors in the world, spent time with them and what's more, I get to call them all my friends. I'll be forever grateful that this group exists, and thankful that I was accepted onto their New Writers Scheme in 2014. I'm sure that without them I'd have never become an author.

And finally, I'd like to thank the team at Choc Lit for believing in me and giving me the opportunity to fulfil my lifelong dream. Special thanks goes to the Tasting Panel readers who passed the manuscript: Claire W., Jenny M., Lizzy D. Jo O., Sigi, Linda W., Alma H., Ann C., Gill L. and Jenny K. Thank you so much, I can now call myself an author xx

Author's Note

Whilst Wrea Head Hall, the hotel described in this book, is a real place *House of Secrets* is a work of fiction. Any names, characters, events or incidents are fictitious and any resemblance to actual persons, living or dead, or actual events is purely coincidental.

Chapter One

Madeleine covered her eyes in an attempt to shield them from the early morning sun. It burst in through a tiny slit in the bedroom curtains and shone directly at her. She lay for a few moments, waiting for her eyes to become accustomed to the light before peering across to where Liam slept.

She took a deep breath and inched her body between the crisp white sheets towards the edge of the bed in an effort to widen the gap between herself and her naked lover. Then she lay as still as she could, not daring to move, as she watched him sleep. She used to love watching the steady rise and fall of his chest, his deep, slow, untroubled breaths and the way he slept on his back with his arms spread outward, as though surrendering in a childlike, unconscious state. But he'd changed. Now, she didn't know whether to love him or to hate him, at any given moment.

Holding her breath, she noticed his eyes flicker and knew that as soon as he woke, she'd have to quickly judge whether he was in a good mood or bad. Whether he'd want to make love or argue and, right now, she was tired and didn't feel in the mood to do either. Closing her eyes, Madeleine lay back against the pillows, only to feel Liam's hand pushing the sheets down to uncover her.

'You awake, Maddie darlin'?' his soft Irish tone mumbled in her ear.

Liam's hand started to move over her body in soft, gentle, caressing strokes. Madeleine felt herself relax. This was Liam in a good mood. For a moment she enjoyed the simple feeling of tenderness, along with the feel of his hand moving sensuously over her body. It was what she'd enjoyed so much at the beginning of their relationship and a small part of her wondered if he could change, if they could both change, and if once again she could have the loving and caring Liam, without the nasty side she'd experienced of late.

She inhaled deeply and then caught her breath as Liam's hand travelled down to her thigh. There had been a time when she'd have felt waves of excitement, times when she'd wished for him to be closer and, more often than not, it had been her that had instigated their lovemaking. But that was before. Before she'd moved into his house with her daughter and before he'd taken control of everything she did. Madeleine thought back to when she had first met him, how generous, caring and loving he'd been, which made her wonder why he had changed, if the arguments were her fault and whether it was her that made him angry. Maybe he regretted allowing her to move in, or perhaps he simply didn't like the fact that she was a mother, with a very young daughter.

Madeleine glanced up, staring directly into Liam's sleepy green eyes that were now just centimetres away from hers.

He flashed her a cheeky smile and then lowered his lips brushing them gently against hers. He lingered tenderly and savoured the moment. He then paused and pulled away. Once again, his eyes searched hers, studying her in a seductive, yet thoughtful way. And then he smiled again, the slight gap between his two front white teeth giving him a cute, mischievous appearance.

'You got something on your mind there, Maddie?' Liam's voice broke through her thoughts, just as she felt his fingers brush lightly against her face, making her jump.

'No, not at all,' she lied. 'I was just enjoying the moment.' She moved away from him, but felt his hand grab at her wrist.

'Hey, not so fast. I have something for you,' Liam whispered as he pulled her hand towards him, placing it firmly against his arousal which was more than apparent.

Madeleine took a sharp, inward breath and allowed her gaze to fall upon his mouth, just as he lifted his hand to move a strand of hair away from her face. Their eyes met again as his mouth descended upon hers. She wanted him to be happy, wanted him to stay in a good mood and responded as passionately as she could to the kiss. Her lips parted and she allowed his tongue to delve repeatedly into the recesses of her mouth. His hands tentatively roamed over her breasts and down to her stomach and in one firm and unambiguous movement, he pressed his fingers deep inside her, making Madeleine relax into the lovemaking.

'Are you ready for me, Maddie?' he whispered between kisses. His body moved over hers, but then he eased away momentarily as he tugged roughly at her silk nightdress, pulling it up and over her head, tossing it to the floor, discarded.

Liam's lips grazed her neck, his tongue drew circles on her skin, gently at first but then quickly and ardently his mouth fell upon her breasts, making the blood flow through her veins at speed. She had loved him, had enjoyed making love to him and wondered again if it was possible to return to the relationship they'd once had and for her to get back the Liam that she'd first met.

A soft creak on the staircase made Madeleine freeze. The noise could only mean one thing and her stomach tied in knots, knowing that if Poppy was out of bed, Liam would get angry. Madeleine listened intently for any further evidence that the three-year-old was up and about. For a moment she heard nothing more and started to relax, but then another creak, quickly followed by a timid murmur, which made Madeleine jump up and out of Liam's clutches.

'Mummy,' the young voice beckoned. 'Mummy, I need you. Are you there?'

'Poppy, stay where you are, baby girl. Mummy's coming,' she yelled as she grabbed at her robe, finding herself suddenly eager to cover her naked body from Liam's angry gaze.

'Damn it, Maddie,' he shouted as he leaned out of bed. He rummaged around in search of the boxer shorts that he had discarded the night before and pulled them on. 'I can't remember the last time I got to the end without hearing that stupid, whining little voice behind that bloody door. Can't you control her?'

Madeleine felt her blood boil. 'Control her? She's a child, Liam. Not something you bloody control.' Madeleine glared at him as she got out of bed. He'd taken one too many digs at her daughter and this time she had no intention of letting it pass.

'Why Liam? Why do you do this? Why do you go from being nice Liam one minute, to being a really shitty, nasty Liam the next?' She paused and stared at him, knowing that her daughter was just the other side of the door and no doubt listening to every word. 'I have no idea why the hell I stay.'

She meant every word. When Liam was nice, he could be kind, sensual, generous and even romantic. But then his mood could turn on a sixpence and he'd turn mean without warning, and when he did this to Poppy she hated him with a vengeance. How dare he be cruel to her daughter?

She stared into the green eyes which had now turned cold and piercing, watched the indecision in his gaze and waited for him to challenge her in return. She knew his mood would and could go either way, and then, just as though someone had flicked a switch, he smiled, got off the bed and walked towards her.

'Oh, Maddie, I'm sorry, forgive me.' His arms were suddenly around her, his lips grazed her forehead and once again he was 'nice Liam', gentle and loving. 'It's just that, you know, I was so turned on. I mean, come on, Maddie, what am I supposed to do with this?' He gripped her wrist and pulled her hand towards him. She could feel the erection beneath his boxers, still proud and throbbing. She closed her eyes and thought carefully about her next move.

'Liam, let go of my hand. Now. My daughter needs me.' A shudder ran through her, unsure of what he would do next and she looked back at the closed door, more than aware that Poppy would still be standing on the other side, clutching a teddy bear, waiting.

Liam pushed Madeleine towards the bed. She unbalanced and landed heavily. He then stamped across the room and snatched open the door to reveal a small girl, crouched on the corner of the landing, making a soft whimpering sound and with her teddy bear pulled up in front of her to hide her face.

'Get gone to your Mammy,' he snarled as he stepped past the frightened child, down the landing and into the bathroom. To Madeleine's relief, the shower burst into life.

'Morning, precious girl,' Madeleine whispered as she watched a terrified and timid Poppy creep towards her, dragging her teddy bear behind her with one hand, the thumb of the other firmly clamped in her mouth. 'You want to snuggle?' Madeleine asked as she climbed back into bed, threw back the quilt and watched as a huge smile came over Poppy's face. She squealed with delight and immediately raced over to where her mother lay, jumped under the covers and nestled in, clinging to her like a small and over-enthusiastic chameleon.

'I take it you'll be working from home today?' Liam asked as he straightened his tie and took a swig of his tea. The question was more an order than a question and Madeleine felt her stomach flip with nerves.

'Actually, I've arranged to go shopping with Jess.' Madeleine smiled at the thought of spending the whole day with her sister, lifted the kettle and made herself a coffee. 'That is okay, isn't it?'

'Maddie, it's Monday. You work on a Monday. We agreed.'

'Come on, Liam. Don't do this. It's just a day out with Jess. I haven't seen her for months. Don't spoil it.'

He looked up in the air, thinking. 'Oh, oh, okay. It's okay for Poppy to spoil my fun, is it? But not for me to spoil yours.'

The words were cruel and once again directed at Poppy. Madeleine looked around for her daughter, who, as always when Liam was around, had taken herself off somewhere else in the house to play.

Madeleine looked down at the floor, turned towards him and swallowed hard. 'She's a baby, Liam. Just a baby. Please understand, she needs me.'

He picked up his almost empty mug and drained it. He then threw it at the sink where it shattered against the tiles, making her jump. He turned around at speed, he was so close that Madeleine could feel his breath on her cheek. '*Understand*? Oh, okay, Maddie, I'll understand her, just as soon as you learn that I need a woman in my bed, not a nursemaid to a needy child.' His eyes were cold, fixed. They stared deep into her soul and Madeleine felt herself weaken. 'Besides, it's Monday and you need to work on a Monday. We agreed.'

Madeleine felt tears form behind her eyes. She'd been looking forward to spending the day with Jess and didn't need the extra stress of wondering what mood Liam would be in when she returned home. She tried to choke back the tears, didn't want him to know how much he hurt her and carefully prepared her reply.

'Didn't I tell you? I've finished my latest book. I'm just waiting for Bridget to get back to me with suggestions for the edits.' She thought the mention of a finished project might please him and watched his face as it visibly softened.

He looked thoughtful and almost smiled. 'What's happening with Poppy while you're off gallivanting around town on a shopping trip?' He was late and anxiously glanced at his watch.

'Well, I thought she could look after herself. You know, leave her here. Duct tape her to the staircase till I get back.'

'You're doing what?' his voice challenged her and Madeleine knew that her attempt at a joke had seriously backfired.

'Liam, for goodness' sake. She's going to the childminder. The one you insisted she goes to. As you said, it's Monday.'

'*Insisted*? No, no, no. I didn't insist. We agreed Maddie. Don't you remember, we both agreed, not just me. We both agreed that you needed to work, didn't we?'

'Liam, please let's not argue,' Madeleine whispered. She was sick of the shouting, the arguments and of his constant need to win every conversation, as though it were a battle.

'I'm not arguing, Maddie.' He stroked her cheek and unexpectedly leaned forward to kiss her lightly on the lips. 'You agreed that you'd feel better about living here, in my house, if you paid your way. After all, I can't pay for everything, can I? And it's not as though her father contributes now, is it?'

'Wow, Liam. Even for you, that's a low blow. Michael's dead and you know it. He's hardly in a position to contribute now, is he?' Her mind flashed back to that knock on the door, that policeman's face and the devastation that had followed which had included Poppy being born two months prematurely.

'Hey, don't blame me, Maddie. He wasn't even responsible enough to leave you with an insurance policy, now was he? You know, something for you to live on.'

'Do you know what, Liam? We could barely afford heating or food. So shopping for an insurance policy was hardly on his damn radar, don't you get that?'

It was true. Michael hadn't been insured. When he'd died and Poppy had been born, there had been no money and she'd had no choice but to quit her part-time job and become a 'stay at home mum'. But living on benefits, with no other income, had given her many hours alone. She'd had too much time to think and the endless empty hours had driven her insane. It had been then that she'd begun to write and her stories had become her lifeline, a way of keeping her mind busy, a way of forgetting the reality, and a form of therapy.

With her emotions running high, the stories had developed into strong, powerful manuscripts. Each paragraph written had helped ease her pain and in less than a year she'd written not one, but two whole novels. Both had been drafts and both had had a million and one mistakes. But, one at a time, they'd been rewritten, changed, altered and perfected in turn.

Now, three years later, she had just finished her fourth novel. But, as Poppy had grown and become more mobile, Maddie found the hours in which she could write were reduced. When she'd finally moved in with Liam two months before, and after much persuasion on his part, they'd agreed that she would help contribute to the household bills, and for her to do that, he'd insisted that Poppy go to a childminder, giving her the time to write. Her agent, Bridget, was doing all she could to make Maddie as much money from her work as possible, but six figure publishing advances were a thing of the past and to keep earning, she had to keep writing.

Madeleine looked up into Liam's eyes, placed her arms around his neck, smiled and tried to ease the tension for Poppy's sake. Ultimately it would be her that he took it out on, if and when he came home in a bad mood. 'Look, I'm sorry. I should have mentioned the day out earlier; I won't do it again.'

Liam shrugged her off. Puffed out his chest and looked pleased at the thought that she'd backed down. 'Right then, I'm off.' He headed to the hallway, where Poppy sat quietly playing with something on the rug. Madeleine noticed Poppy quickly move to the bottom of the stairs and her heart lurched as the child almost cowered before him.

Liam knelt down beside Poppy and for once Madeleine thought he'd show her some affection. But then, in one swift action he snatched the keys that Poppy had been playing with out of her hands and growled. 'You see that, Poppy?' He pointed to the penknife that hung alongside the shiny keys, which all hung in size order. 'That is dangerous and you are not to play with them. Do you understand?' He spoke sternly as Poppy's eyes filled with tears.

Madeleine jumped in. 'Come on, baby girl. Come to your mummy.' She ran down the hall, swooped Poppy up and immediately felt her bury her face into the nape of her neck. Damp tears landed on her shoulder and an inconsolable Poppy sobbed.

Liam pulled a handkerchief from his pocket and began polishing each of the keys in turn. 'She had dirty fingers. Tell her she's not to touch my things with her dirty hands, is that clear?' Once satisfied that the keys were clean, he placed them in his pocket and then flicked an imaginary dust particle from his lapel. 'I'll phone you, as normal, at eleven o'clock. Make sure you answer.' He turned and opened the door, then looked back in her direction. 'And, Maddie, don't spend too much.'

Madeleine glared at the back of Liam as he walked away, all suited and booted with a briefcase in his hand. If any of the neighbours were watching they'd think he was a highly respected businessman, a family man, not the bully that he really was.

'Oh, Poppy, come on. Don't cry. It's not your fault. Mummy should have known better.' She pulled the child away for a moment and smiled at the tear-stained face. 'I know, tomorrow morning, you remind Mummy and we'll scrub-a-dub you all over until you sparkle like a princess.' She watched as Poppy began to smile.

'Come on, sweetheart. Let's go and let Buddy in.' Both glanced in the hallway mirror in a well-practiced manoeuvre, flicked their hair back simultaneously and laughed at each other, before running through the old Victorian terraced house, past the two rooms at the front and down the passage that led to the back room and the old kitchen that had long since seen better days.

Madeleine quickly placed Poppy on the floor and opened the back door where an excited Springer Spaniel puppy sat waiting.

Buddy jumped up and down. His tail wagged a hundred miles an hour and as soon as the opening was big enough, he burst in through the back door and straight into the arms of a waiting Poppy, who collapsed on the floor, giggling, as he licked, jumped and wagged his whole body excitedly.

Madeleine smiled. Poppy was so different when Liam wasn't there. She was happier, playful and appeared to blossom in his absence. Whereas when he was home, she tended to sleep, play with teddy bears in her room or disappear to a quiet corner where she'd sit for hours playing with Buddy. It broke Maddie's heart to see her daughter unhappy. But what could she do? She'd known moving in with Liam was a mistake but she'd had no choice. The block of flats that she lived in was being demolished. She'd been dating Liam for eight months and he had seemed the perfect boyfriend, loving to her and kind to Poppy, so when he suggested she move in with him, she'd agreed.

'Look, Poppy, do you think Buddy wants his breakfast?' she asked and Poppy started nodding enthusiastically.

Reaching for Buddy's bowl, Maddie pulled a biscuit from the box, broke it with her fingers and crumbled the pieces into the ceramic dish. She then soaked it in milk before placing the bowl on the floor where Buddy immediately pounced, his nose disappearing deep within the dish as it began to rattle around the floor.

'Would Poppy like some breakfast too?' Madeleine asked hopefully, but knew what the answer would be. The immediate shake of Poppy's head confirmed what she'd already thought. She'd noticed over the past two months that Poppy often refused food or only ate tiny amounts and Madeleine nodded her head in confirmation of what she'd been trying to avoid: the days that Poppy didn't eat always seemed to coincide with Liam being mean to her and Madeleine knew what had to be done. She had no choice but to leave. She needed to take Poppy as far away from this environment as she could.

Madeleine pulled another biscuit from the box and knelt down on the floor. 'Here, Poppy, watch Buddy eat his biscuits.' She held the treat up in her hand and waited for Buddy to sit before her. 'Buddy, speak.' The puppy barked to order and both Poppy and Madeleine began to clap. 'Good boy. See, Poppy, Buddy loves his breakfast. Do you think that you'd eat some lovely breakfast too?' But once again Poppy shook her head, clasped her hand over her mouth and lay down on the kitchen floor.

Madeleine shrugged her shoulders. She had to get her daughter to eat and began searching the cupboards for something that might tempt her, but the cupboards were almost empty and she resigned herself to pushing a slice of bread in the toaster. Maybe she'd find a way to persuade Poppy to eat it.

Madeleine turned around and laughed as she caught sight of Poppy lying flat on her back on the kitchen floor, submerged in what was left of the milky cereal, giggling and squirming as Buddy pinned her to the floor, licking at every remnant he could find. Seeing her daughter returned to the carefree three-year-old that she should be all the time, Maddie knew that her decision was the right one. She really didn't have a choice. She had to leave Liam. And the sooner the better.

Chapter Two

'Hey, Jess, are you okay?' Madeleine asked with concern as she met Jess outside the café. Normally Jess was a happy, bubbly character, but today she had slits for eyes, a red nose and a miserable look all over her face.

'Oh, I'm okay. I've been like this for days. Full of cold, but I think it's getting better now.' Jess's voice could only just be heard over the sound of the traffic and Madeleine quickly ushered her inside the café, sat her down and held the back of her hand to Jess's forehead.

For sisters, Maddie and Jess couldn't have looked more different. Maddie was five feet six inches tall, with fair skin and shoulder length blonde hair, while Jess was short, just five feet tall, deep mocha skin and jet black fuzzy Afro hair that always looked a little wild, but suited Jess perfectly.

'Ignore me, I'm just moaning. My throat's a bit sore, that's all.'

'Oh, honey, why didn't you cancel? You could have called me.'

'Because I wanted to see you, it's been nearly seven months,' Jess said pouting.

'That long? It can't be.' She thought back to the last time she'd seen Jess and realised she was right. It had been for a meal to celebrate her birthday in April – her first birthday since their mother had died and Liam had taken her, Jess and Poppy out for dinner.

'Of course it is. I've only been on dry land for three weeks and I was away for six months.' Jess's job as a ship's purser took her away for months at a time and usually Madeleine would count the days off on a calendar until she returned. So why hadn't she done so this time and why had she waited three whole weeks since Jess had been back before they'd got to see each other?

'I need coffee, lots and lots of coffee,' Jess announced as her eyes travelled across the cake counter. 'Oh, and, Maddie, while you're there, I like the look of that big chocolate cake.' She batted her eyelids, smiled, took her coat off and settled down in the chair.

'Okay, I'll fall for it. Let's get you a cake and a coffee. My treat,' she said as she ordered the drinks, indicated the cakes and pulled her last twenty pound note from her purse.

Carrying the tray, she sat down beside where her sister slouched, placed the coffee and chocolate cake before her and unbuttoned her coat. 'There, get that down you. You really should have lots of fluids, Jess. How long did you say you've felt like this? Mum used to tell us to take paracetamol or ibuprofen? Do you have any of those?' She fired the questions like bullets, one after the other.

'I took meds, Maddie. Honestly. You're not Mum, so stop. How do you think I manage, living all by myself? Now let me drink my coffee and listen to how things are with you and him.'

Madeleine hung her coat on the back of her chair and looked at her sister, not knowing where to start. It was more than obvious that Jess didn't like Liam, but she still had no idea how to tell her that she was right and that moving in with him had probably been the biggest, most stupid thing she'd ever done. What's more, all Madeleine really wanted to do was turn back the clock to a time when Michael was still alive.

She and Michael had been teenage sweethearts. From the day they'd met in secondary school, they'd lived, and loved and breathed for each other. Every moment they'd spent together had been a pleasure and every moment apart had been painful with longing. But no one understood and, much to everyone's disapproval, they'd married at nineteen, rented the cheapest, tiniest second floor flat that they could find and had managed to beg, steal and borrow enough pieces of furniture to make the flat a home. But it hadn't been the material things that had mattered to Maddie; they had a home full of love and even though they had very little, she'd loved every minute.

But then, less than a year after their marriage, her whole life had turned into an obscure, turbulent blur. The police were knocking on the door. Michael was dead and the police had unleashed a whole whirlwind of words, along with possible reasons and assumptions for how his car had ended up in a roadside ravine. She'd sat silently, not believing what she was being told, while at the same time a long shrill internal scream had begun and had refused to stop.

Nine days later Poppy was born, six weeks prematurely.

Her thoughts returned to the café and to Jess who was looking at her with concern.

'So, tell me, when is your next tour, where are you going and, most important, how long will you be away?'

Jess sipped at the coffee. 'Oh, it's ages away. I haven't signed my next contract yet, but it's looking like it won't be until the end of the year and, until they tell me, I have no idea in the world where I'll be going. So, that's all my news. Do you want to tell me what's troubling you?'

Madeleine had always known that Jess was astute. She could read Maddie like a book and knew when something was wrong. She had also never been slow at asking the difficult questions.

'Oh, Jess, I don't know what to do. I've made a terrible mistake and I have no idea how to put it right.'

Jess searched her eyes. 'What do you mean? You've not done anything illegal, have you?' she asked, pushing a large piece of the chocolate cake into her mouth.

Madeleine shook her head and laughed. She'd never done anything illegal in her life and it amused her that her sister thought she might start now.

'Not at all. It's Liam. How the hell did I end up living with him? I barely know him, Jess. What on earth possessed me? I know I was desperate, what with the flat and everything, but—'

'Why didn't you move into mine while I was away?' Jess asked.

'Oh, Jess, I wish I had but Liam was so persuasive and said he'd look after me and Poppy, convinced me how good it would be, the three of us.' She paused and took a deep breath. 'But it's not good. One minute he's fine, the nicest person you could meet and the next he's really horrible. It's like he's Jekyll and Hyde, he turns on a sixpence and I can't cope with it, especially when he's nasty and cruel to Poppy.'

Jess slammed her coffee mug down on the table, making two women on the next table turn around and stare. 'What did he do to Poppy?' Her voice trembled with anger and Madeleine paused for a while before replying.

'Oh, Jess. He used to be so nice to her, you know, before we moved in. Some days he'd call and bring her sweets, other days he'd bring a teddy bear and ... well, as you know one day he got really cross with her and the next time he came to the flat he brought Buddy with him. I mean, come on, Jess, who the hell buys a bloody puppy as an apology?' She paused, and picked at her cake. Madeleine felt her eyes fill with tears. Saying everything aloud made it all seem more real. 'He even shouted at me this morning when Poppy disturbed us, doing ... you know. She'd woken up and needed me and he told me I had to control her, Jess. Who in their right mind would say that? He's a bully.'

Jess took another sip of her coffee, placed the mug down on the table and took Madeleine's hands in hers. Madeleine could feel her sister trembling and was surprised at how calmly she spoke. 'First, you need to leave. Second, you need to do it fast. Because, one, you can't and won't let Poppy live like that, it's cruel and two, if I get my scrawny hands on his neck, he's going to wish he'd never troubled either you or my niece, do you understand that, Maddie? He lays one hand on either of you, I'll be doing time, for murder.' She smiled sweetly, dropped Madeleine's hands and continued to eat her cake.

Madeleine stared into the depths of her coffee cup, blew at the surface and then took a gulp of the fluid. She couldn't respond and a tear dropped down her cheek. Jess was right, again. There was no excuse. Even if she traded all the nice things that Liam had ever done, she couldn't make any excuses for the digs, comments or gestures. She couldn't forgive him, nor could she allow it to go on.

'What are you going to do, Maddie?' Jess rubbed her throat, swallowed hard and then took another sip of her coffee. 'Well?'

'I don't know.' She paused, actually she did know.

'Do you realise how much I hate him right now? I knew he was wrong for you. Didn't I say when I first met him that I thought him a bit odd? I did say that, Maddie. For someone you'd only known a short while, he was really clingy and possessive. It was the first time he'd met me and all he was interested in was what time I might leave. Also, sometimes when I ring from the ship to speak to you Liam tells me that you are not home, even when I'm sure I can hear you and Poppy in the background.'

Madeleine looked thoughtful. 'The wrong numbers. We get so many wrong numbers. Is that what he's been doing?'

'And what's more ...' Jess was on a roll now. '... remember that first time you took me to his house? I asked about all those locked doors and why he was living in his parents' house. Parents who you say never phone or visit. I mean, come on, Maddie, even you have to admit it's a bit strange.' She stopped, took a look at Madeleine's face and then continued. 'Well, don't look so shocked. I did say all this before, didn't I? But you didn't listen.'

'The rooms are locked because they're filled with his

parents' belongings, that's not weird. It is their house; they are entitled to privacy.'

Jess pursed her lips and glared. 'Okay, Maddie. But if his parents have moved back to Ireland, why on earth haven't they taken all their prized possessions with them? Don't forget, these possessions are so valuable they need locking in a room that has three bloody locks on the door. As I said, Maddie, it's weird.'

Jess was right. It was strange. But Madeleine had missed Michael so much that when Liam eventually came along, she'd thought he'd fill the huge void that was her heart. She'd been prepared to overlook some of his odd behaviour, some of the things he'd done, in favour of the intimacy, and the companionship. But instead of cushioning the hole in her heart, he'd torn it back apart.

Madeleine sobbed. 'You're right. I once made Poppy a promise, Jess. Do you remember when she lay in that incubator as a tiny baby? We both sat there, me and you, night after night, and I kept promising that I'd be both mother and father to her, do you remember that? I promised that if she'd only survive, I'd look after her, protect her and keep her safe and I'm not doing that, Jess, am I? I'm letting her down.' The tears now fell unashamedly down her face and she picked up a napkin, drying her eyes.

Jess once again caught hold of her hands. 'You are not letting her down, you're a wonderful mother. But as for him, you need to get rid. He's possessive and cruel. He doesn't love you, Maddie. He wouldn't act like this, not if he really loved you. And as for where you'd go, that's easy, you can come and stay with me. We'd manage, we always do.'

Madeleine shook her head. 'Oh, Jess, that's so sweet of you but you haven't thought this through, have you? Things have changed. We can't just bunk up together like we did as teenagers. I have Poppy to think of now and Buddy to consider. And you, my darling sister, have a one-bedroomed flat, with no garden. It'd be great fun for the first night, but it'd soon become a problem. It just wouldn't be practical.'

Jess turned to the counter and ordered more coffee. 'So what then? You could rent, there's a nice ground floor flat near me. That'd be okay for Buddy, wouldn't it?'

Madeleine shrugged her shoulders. 'I'm not sure they'd want me. I gave up my benefits when I moved in with Liam. All I get now are my royalties and they're sporadic. I never know what money is coming in, nor whether it's enough to actually live on.'

Madeleine listened as Jess came up with every idea she could think of – none of them realistic. There was nothing she could do and nowhere she could go. She was trapped.

'Okay, okay, I know it's a long shot, but you could always ask your dad for help,' Jess said finally. 'He has that big hotel over near Scarborough. Couldn't you stay there? Surely he'd have the room?' Jess held her hands up and shrugged her shoulders. 'Besides, it's about time he did something other than send you jewellery at Christmas and money on your birthdays.'

Madeleine gulped and choked on her coffee. Splatters of the liquid sprayed out of her mouth and into the napkin that she still held in her hand. Coughing wildly, she took in deep breaths in an attempt to control her breathing, as Jess banged her wildly on the back.

'Hell, Maddie, are you okay?'

'Jess, do ... do ... you have any idea what you're suggesting? Mum left him, you know ... when I was five. I didn't see him very often after that and haven't seen him at all since he married Josie.' She looked at Jess apologetically as she said the words. She was going to say that their mum had left him just a few days after Jess had been born and it had become very obvious that Jess was not his.

Jess shrugged. 'So?'

'So, what do you suggest I do, knock on the bloody door and introduce myself?'

'It'd be a start.'

Madeleine shook her head. 'What would I say, "Hi Dad, it's me, Maddie. I know we haven't seen each other for years, but can I, my three-year-old daughter and a puppy who pees like a greyhound come and live with you?"' Madeleine sighed.

She knew her father had cared: they'd seen each other weekly at first and had tea together every Tuesday and a whole afternoon each Sunday. But then her mother had made it difficult for the meetings to continue and her father had eventually re-married. After which, she'd insist that she pick her up from school on a Tuesday and take her out, ensuring they were not home when Madeleine's father had arrived to pick her up. It hadn't occurred to Madeleine what was happening at first. The novelty of outings with her mother after school had been fun. But Sundays had been different, she'd sat for hours waiting for her father to arrive. Then her mother would come into the room, tell her that her father had phoned and that their visit had been cancelled. But none of it was true. Her mother had made the excuses, told him not to come and ensured that after he'd married Josie, Madeleine had no time to get to know her at all.

He'd written for years, sent birthday cards and Christmas gifts. He'd sent money to help support her, paid for her to go to college, her prom dress and had sent her a cheque for a thousand pounds after Poppy had been born. The money had bought a crib, a pram, numerous baby clothes and a whole year's supply of nappies. Yet he hadn't visited. He'd been missing on so many occasions. Occasions that Madeleine had hoped and wished he'd turn up for.

'At least you know where your dad is, Maddie. God only knows where my sperm donor ended up?' Jess was trying to ease the tension, trying to make Madeleine smile, but to say that Jess was bitter about her own father was an understatement. Their mother had once tried to explain that Jess's father had been a one-night stand. He'd been a tall, obviously very dark, smooth, charming, gorgeous Caribbean sailor. They'd spent a few hours chatting, gone for a drink and one thing had led to another. A quick fumble behind the club had led to Jess being born and without a name or phone number to trace him by.

'There has to be another way, Jess.'

Jess laughed. 'Mmmmm let me think. Oh, yeah, what are the options: you could either join a sect in another country, ask your dad for help, or you could come and live with me.'

Madeleine joined in the laughter. 'Me, live in a sect. Oh, Jess, be real, I doubt that I'd conform. Besides, I have to work. I want to work.'

Jess drained the last of her coffee. 'Maddie, you're an author. I would have thought you could work anywhere.'

It was true, as long as she had her laptop, she could work from anywhere in the world. But she really didn't want to move, she liked living in Yorkshire. No, she loved living in Yorkshire and what's more she wanted Poppy to go to school in Yorkshire, just like she had.

Madeleine picked up her coat. 'Come on, you look awful and need your bed and I need to go back to Liam's and start packing.'

Chapter Three

Madeleine drove at speed.

It was just after eleven o'clock and her phone had been ringing repeatedly for the past five minutes. She looked at the screen and once again, Liam's name flashed before her eyes and, for what seemed like the millionth time, she pressed the red button, rejecting the call.

He was so predictable, so controlling and always called at eleven o'clock without fail. What's more she knew he'd be angry that she hadn't answered, but she didn't care. He wouldn't be home for hours. Only then would she have the chance to speak to him properly, look him in the eye and tell him that she was going to leave him.

With her car parked in the garage, Madeleine entered the house by the back door, let Buddy out into the garden and then headed to the front of the house and up the stairs, stepping into the room where she normally wrote. Madeleine looked at the desk and immediately wished she had more light and space. She'd have been happier closer to the window, and had begged Liam time and time again to allow her to move the desk to a position where she could have looked out at the trees and moorland that surrounded the house. But in his normal fashion, Liam had been adamant that she had her desk in a dark corner, tucked away behind the door. He'd insisted that it was the only place it could go, but she didn't like it there and she made herself a promise that once she'd escaped and moved to her own place, she'd have all the light that she could find.

She tripped over the edge of a rolled up carpet. The room was cluttered, another reason for her hating it and another reason why Liam had positioned the desk where he had. The room was filled with Liam's golf clubs, football boots, and an old metal-framed junior bed that stood in one corner, with no mattress. On top of it were numerous cardboard boxes that were piled up high. Each one on top of the other, yet none had any identifying labels to indicate what might be hidden inside. She sighed. Jess had been right. All of this was weird, especially the hideous, old antique vase that had apparently been his ma's pride and joy.

The house still belonged to his parents and most of the boxes had been left behind when they'd moved back to Ireland many years before, yet as Jess had said, in the time that Madeleine had lived there, they'd never been back to visit, never phoned and as far as she knew never contacted Liam in any way, which made Madeleine wonder when they might return and if they ever did, whether they'd take their hideous furniture back with them.

'Okay, let's start.' Madeleine looked up at the loft ladder, pulled it down and went up the steps to retrieve her bags. She knew that packing wouldn't be easy and that since she'd moved in she'd accumulated so much more than she'd brought with her, but her mind was made up. She had to leave and leaving meant packing.

She sat at the desk, looking through her books. They were all important to her and had to be packed. Her eyes glanced at the boxes that stood in the room and she decided that if she emptied some, she could re-use the boxes. Liam had always told her not to touch his parents' things, but he hadn't said that she couldn't tip the contents out and re-use the box, now had he?

She'd packed three bags and six boxes when her concentration was broken.

She looked up at the door. She was sure she'd heard something. Sitting silently, she heard the noise again. It was a key. A key in the front door. Then giggling, followed by loud, high pitched squealing. Then the door opened and slammed shut.

Madeleine held her breath. Someone was in the house. But who?

She was scared. No one should have a key. Creeping on her hands and knees to the top of the stairs, she manoeuvred herself behind a cupboard that stood halfway along the landing. No one knew she was home and her breathing quickened with fear.

'Don't worry, she's out shopping with her so-called sister,' Liam's voice echoed through the hallway as Madeleine peeped out from behind the cupboard. He was leaning towards the wall. Pressed beneath him was a young woman with long blonde hair, in what may have been a very short black skirt – the remnants of which were lifted high above her waist and now resembled a shiny belt. His hand and fingers worked fervently, tearing her underwear in his eagerness to expose her and his lips were kissing her face, neck and mouth so quickly that he barely took breath.

Madeleine gasped, and then closed her eyes.

Every conceivable thought went through her mind, along with all forms of fear and anguish. Pushing her fingers in her ears, her mind spiralled as she tried to decide what to do. The last thing she needed was to see or hear the huffing and puffing that was going on at the bottom of the stairs.

She'd wanted to leave. She was packing her things and was planning to tell him, but hadn't realised that her leaving might have to come so soon. Her mind spun. She felt as though she were on the fastest rollercoaster she'd ever been on, with its stop stations whizzing past and at each stop station she had a choice, to jump or not to jump. But with each choice came a different scenario or outcome and each scenario was just as horrible or life changing as the one before.

She peered down the hall to where her bedroom stood. This had been her home for two months. It was where she lived, where Poppy lived and by confronting him she knew that she'd be rendering them both homeless and penniless.

But what choice did she have?

Taking in a deep breath, fury took over. He might have put a roof over her head, but he had no right do this to her. How dare he betray her by bringing some piece of skirt into their home and shagging her all over the hallway where only that morning, she'd kissed him goodbye?

Madeleine's whole body shook with temper as she stood up, ready to confront him.

'Liam O'Grady, you son of a bitch. I hope she's worth it.' She gulped as a shrill and constant scream came from somewhere deep within her and she wasn't sure if the scream had left her mouth or not.

Liam gasped, jumped backward and then hurriedly dropped the woman in a heap on the hallway floor.

'Angelina, get dressed.' He pulled a coat from the coat hook and threw it over her partially naked body, as he rapidly fought to cover his own dignity. He then looked back up the wide Victorian staircase to where a furious Madeleine stood, still screaming.

'What the hell are you doing home? You … You were going out shopping, you said you'd be gone all day.' The words were pathetic. 'Why the hell didn't you answer the phone to me?' He didn't know what else to say. She'd said she'd be out. She'd lied and he wasn't impressed, but he had no choice, he needed to make things right. He glanced at the clock, wished he could roll it back, but knew he couldn't.

He turned to see Angelina's angry face as she glared at him before opening the front door and stomping away at speed. His boss had gone and with her his job would probably have gone too. For a moment he hesitated, didn't know which way to run. If he ran one way, he'd lose his job. If he ran the other, he'd be in danger of losing Madeleine, forever, and after all he'd gone through to get her, he had to keep her at all costs.

He'd loved her since school. He'd been two years above her

and smiled, hovered in corridors and watched her every day in the hope that she'd speak to him, or give him the slightest smile in return. He remembered holding open doors, ensuring he was in the right place at the right time and whenever she'd been alone in the lunch hall, he'd made his way over to sit at the same table, perching nervously at the end in silence, without eating. He'd lost count of the times his food had gone cold, the times when his stomach had been tied up in so many knots that eating would have physically made him vomit. She'd never spoken to him, didn't seem to know that he was there and then, to add insult to injury, she'd met Michael and he'd had to watch as they'd swooned over each other in the school corridors, watch while they obviously fell in love and then finally, he'd felt his heart break as she blossomed from child to woman in another man's arms.

Liam tried to remember if he'd ever spoken to Michael Frost, but couldn't. He didn't really know him, but had hated him so much, despising him for having what he'd wanted the most and ensured that when the time had been right, when he'd thought that Madeleine was ready, he'd been the one in the right place, on the right day, to claim her.

Liam sighed. He knew that he'd been stupid. He'd thought that by getting close to Angelina, he'd save his job. Already he'd been on the redundancy list twice and Angelina had been part of the decision-making. So, without thinking, he'd embarked on a charm offensive, taking her out and treating her nice and when the opportunity had arisen that morning, when he'd thought that Madeleine would be out all day, he'd allowed his body and libido to rule his head. He'd needed the sex, needed the release and with Poppy in the house, he sure as hell wasn't getting it at home. But he loved Madeleine, he couldn't live without her and was terrified that now she'd want to go, but he couldn't and wouldn't allow her to leave him. She belonged to him. He would never let her go.

He took a step towards the bottom of the stairs. 'Darlin',

listen. You've got to believe me. I can explain. What you saw there, it's not how it looked. It meant nothing, honestly.' He shuffled from one foot to another. 'You know that it's you that I love; you do know that, don't you?' he cried feebly, his arms outstretched. 'It was my job, Maddie. They're making redundancies, I didn't want it to be me and Angelina could have spoken up for me, put in a good word. Besides, with Poppy bursting in all the time, you can't blame me for having needs, can you?'

He knew that Madeleine had stopped listening. She'd disappeared from the top of the stairs and he inched himself onto the first step, stood on his tiptoes and tried to work out where she'd gone. But as soon as his foot touched the step, he saw a torrent of his possessions begin to fly towards him. He cowered pathetically, just as a second huge bundle of clothes hurtled their way over the banister, hangers still attached.

'Don't you dare insult my bloody intelligence, Liam. Don't you bloody well dare.' Madeleine ran back into the spare bedroom, and picked up his golf clubs. She paused momentarily, thinking of the damage they'd do. They were heavy and the last thing she wanted was to damage her home. But then, in an instant, the reality tore through her: this house wasn't her home, and with that thought, she threw them one by one, as Liam hid in the entrance of the front room. She watched as he stood behind the door, cowering and protecting himself from the onslaught, as one by one the clubs were launched towards him. Madeleine stopped throwing them temporarily, ran to his wardrobe and grabbed a box full of shoes; once again she began launching them over the banister, knowing that at the speed and velocity she was throwing them, he'd have no time to gain his composure in between the attacks.

She watched as they all landed randomly in a mess at the bottom of the stairs and laughed. He liked his clothes to be perfectly pressed, his shoes to be polished to a shine and she knew how much he'd hate to see everything strewn all over the floor.

There was a moment of silence as Liam began crawling on his hands and knees in a frantic attempt to pick up his scattered clothes. He began folding them neatly, as another rail of clothes fell next to where he knelt.

'Maddie, you are so out of order,' he screamed. 'You do know that, Maddie, don't you?'

Madeleine saw red. '*Me*, I'm out of order. How the hell can you say that?' She looked around for something new to throw. A large soft suitcase came into view; it had been hidden under the bed frame and she pulled it out before throwing it at where he stood. 'Pack that and get out.' The case hit him square on the back of his head making him squeal.

'Arrrgghhh. You'd better stop throwing things, Maddie. I'm warning you,' he shouted as his football boots flew towards him.

Madeleine glared. 'Oh, you're warning me, are you. Wow, Liam, does that make you feel like a big man, warning me? Well, I'm scared, can you see me shaking?' She didn't care how much she hurt him any more. She was leaving him anyway and could honestly say that she wouldn't care if the whole house collapsed on top of him. She noticed a dint in the front door that had been made by one of the golf clubs and cringed. She'd painted that door, used masking tape to protect the glass and had lovingly finished it one day while Liam had been at work.

'Darlin'', you'd better stop, right now. This house isn't yours, it's mine and it's you that has to leave. It's you that'll lose it all.' He looked smug and Madeleine turned to look at the cupboard, wondering whether or not she could possibly throw that down the stairs too. 'You do know that you'd hurt Poppy, don't you? You have no money, and it's her that would suffer. Now, be sensible, you don't want to make Poppy homeless now, do you? Besides, where would you go? It's not like you have too many options there, Maddie, is it?'

She watched as he fidgeted and stepped from one foot to another, a sure sign that he was panicking, trying to think quickly and looking for ways to make her change her mind. But Madeleine had become wise to his tricks, learned his mannerisms and knew when he'd become indecisive.

'Don't you dare bring my daughter into this. What do you care about Poppy? You're horrible to her every chance that you get.' Madeleine leaned against the banister. He was right. This was his house and it was true, Poppy would be homeless, but things had gone too far and his bringing another woman back to the house for sex was the final straw. There was no going back now and no matter what happened next, no matter what he said or how many times he apologised, she couldn't forgive him.

'I ... I do care about Poppy. I bought her Buddy, didn't I?' Liam protested.

'You are a lying, nasty piece of work, Liam O'Grady,' Madeleine screamed. She turned around, her eyes darting around the room and she picked up his mother's favourite ornate vase. It was ugly, she'd never liked it and without giving it another thought, she threw it over the banister, making him jump with fear as it shattered by his feet.

'You just wait, Maddie. I'm gonna make you regret you did that.' Liam jumped to his feet and launched himself towards the stairs, just as a pounding noise began on the door behind him.

'What the hell is going on?' Jess screamed as she thrust open the door which had not shut properly after Angelina's swift exit. She took one look at the carnage and immediately picked up one of the golf clubs and swung it viciously towards where Liam stood. 'You'd better not have hurt her or so help me, I'll kill you.'

Madeleine began to hyperventilate at the thought of what had been about to happen and of what Liam might have done next. She sucked in her breath, her legs were shaky and she felt a sudden wave of nausea pass through her. She was okay. It was over. Jess was here and everything would be okay.

'What are you doing here, Jess? I thought you'd gone home to bed?' she shouted down the stairs to where her sister stood.

Liam squared up to Jess. 'Yeah, Jess. What are you doing here?' He walked over to where she stood and with his nose almost touching her, he glared into her eyes.

'Get away from me.' Jess took a step back and once again waved the golf club menacingly at him.

'And you're big enough to use that, are you, little girl?' His words were a challenge, but Jess didn't falter. She stood her ground, stared deep into his eyes and held the club in the air.

'You'd better believe it,' Jess threatened, once again swinging the club in Liam's direction. 'Maddie, call nine nine nine, unless your man here is sensible enough to pack some stuff and get out?'

Liam was furious and glared between Madeleine and her sister. He took deep breaths and thought about his options. He couldn't win, not today, not after what had happened and knew that if he stayed he might well do something that he would regret forever. He had to leave, had to let Madeleine calm down and then win her over. He knew how to do that. He'd done it before and would do so again but for now he'd take Jess's advice, pack a few bits and leave. But this wasn't over. This was far from over and he was determined that he wouldn't lose Madeleine, not after all he'd gone through to get her in the first place.

'No need for the police,' he said calmly to Jess, hands up and backing away from her. 'I'll go, but this is my house, Maddie. Remember what's mine is mine, including you.'

Chapter Four

'Okay, Liam, calm down. I'm packing as fast as I can, but I have nowhere to go,' Madeleine growled before pulling the phone away from her ear, as the constant and relentless torrent of insults and pleading flooded at her down the handset. She was almost sure that if she placed the handset on the sideboard and walked away for twenty minutes, not only would she still be able to hear his words, but he'd probably still be ranting on when she returned.

'Have you thought about ringing that agent of yours? Surely she'd have some advice, some way of interfering, or isn't she around any more?'

'Yes, Liam, I know, I have tried to phone Bridget, many times. All I've been getting for the past week is her answerphone. Wait a minute, how do you know she isn't around?'

He didn't answer her question but replied, 'Why don't you move in with Jess? She seemed to be the one who wanted to come in and save the day.'

'Don't be stupid. How the hell can I move in with Jess? You know she only has one bedroom. It's hardly an ideal place for me, my daughter and a puppy to live, is it?'

'Well, you don't have to leave, do you? You could stop being so pig-headed and we could get back together. No one would have to live anywhere else. I could come home. We could sort things out. We could start again?' Liam paused and Madeleine knew he was waiting for an answer that didn't come. 'How about it, Maddie, darlin'? You and me, what do you say? I love you.'

Madeleine laughed.

'Come on, Maddie, don't laugh. It could be special. All of us, me and you, and Poppy, we could be a real family.'

He paused. 'I know, let's book a holiday, let's go abroad, somewhere warm.' Madeleine had heard everything now. He'd tried so hard to get her back. He'd promised so many times that things would be different. That he'd be nice to Poppy, that they'd all have a home, together. But Madeleine didn't believe a word that he said, didn't trust his promises and even if he got on his knees and begged, she'd never, ever allow him near Poppy again.

'Oh, Liam. Only in your wildest dreams would that happen. What part of "I will never ever trust you again" don't you understand? Besides, I would never take Poppy abroad. She's far too young.'

'Maddie, darlin', come on. You have no money. You can't get hold of Bridget. Think of it as a greater force telling you that we should be together.'

Madeleine pondered his words and felt a sudden moment of panic. Moving the phone from one ear to the other, she stared at the chaos around her. There was an ever growing pile of packing boxes and bubble wrap which formed expanding mini mountains at the edges of the rear lounge. Right in the middle of the chaos sat the rather lively Buddy who looked up at her, eager for her to put the phone down and play. Picking up one of Poppy's discarded socks, he shook it and then held it in his mouth, while his chocolate brown tail wafted from side to side in hope and anticipation that Madeleine might join in the game.

Then, in direct contrast, at the opposite end of the room was a less than energetic Poppy, who seemed to have crawled into an empty box and promptly curled up with her teddy bear and blanket for an impromptu mid-afternoon sleep.

Looking at the chaos that was her life, her temper boiled. 'You're a real nasty piece of work, Liam O'Grady. Do you know that? I can't wait to get as far away from you as possible. Oh, and while we're at it, don't you dare call me darlin'. You lost your right to call me that when I caught you shagging your scrawny arsed boss in the hallway of what used to be our home.'

She took in deep breaths in an attempt to control her temper.

'You want to get away from me, do you? Fine, but you'll come running. It'll be you that begs me to take you back. You'll see. You can't even support yourself without me. What are you going to do, get movie rights on one of your books, write a best-seller, maybe? You keep saying you can, but we still need to see some proof, don't we, Maddie, darlin'.'

The words 'Maddie, darlin"' grated and Liam's crude Irish accent had turned into a loud and deep continuous buzz like the hum of a dentist drill whirring away somewhere in the background of her mind. Madeleine tried to close out the noise, make the whirring go away and preferably push the drill while it was still spinning as far down Liam's throat as she possibly could. The merciless image in the back of her mind made her snort as a sadistic smile crossed her face.

'Do you know what, Liam? I might just write a best-seller, with or without movie rights, and when I do, don't you dare come looking for bloody handouts because there won't be any.' She paused and took a breath. 'Did you get that you Irish asshole?' Madeleine bellowed as she slammed the phone down, and then stamped over to where her daughter had peacefully slept through the entire onslaught.

Madeleine closed her eyes, wondering what she'd ever done to deserve Liam. He was supposed to have been a new start in her life. He'd promised her a lovely new beginning. Not a nightmare.

Had any of it been real? Had he cared about her at all? Had it been her fault that he'd needed to have sex with another woman?

It had been just before last Christmas when she'd literally bumped into Liam outside her flat. She'd stepped out of the gate and had suddenly found herself colliding with him, both landing flat on their backs in the snow. They'd both fallen with the grace of baby orangutans, all arms and legs flying in every direction. His trousers were soaked and she'd invited him in. They'd spent the next two hours with him sitting in her dressing gown while his trousers hung over an old wooden clothes horse in front of an equally old and dilapidated gas fire.

The days that followed saw Liam visiting daily. He'd pop in for coffee, then coffee would turn into coffee and lunch and then within a very short space of time, he was there for most of the day making Madeleine question if he had a job. He'd been wonderful when her mother died, caring and comforting and helping her with the arrangements.

He'd entered her life like a tornado that hadn't seemed to leave.

Tears of frustration rolled down her face. She'd been so determined that he wouldn't upset her. But the situation was impossible: she had no money and needed somewhere to live and somehow she had to find a way to make that happen fast.

'Poppy, come on, baby girl.' Madeleine carefully lifted the child's warm body from the floor where she was sleeping. 'Let's get you up to your little bed.'

Poppy stirred. A soft gurgle followed by a snort and then nothing but soft, gentle, repetitive snores. Smiling down at her, Maddie carried her daughter through the hallway and up the stairs, to where the staircase split; she turned right and went up to where the first of the three bedrooms stood.

She watched as Poppy snuggled into her pillow. Her soft blonde curls fell roughly around her face, her sweetheart lips pursed and her tiny fingers curled to unconsciously grab handfuls of Madeleine's shoulder length hair, which Maddie carefully managed to release before kissing her daughter's forehead and leaving her to sleep.

Madeleine walked back down the stairs. Tutting, she picked up the tea towels that Buddy had amazingly pulled down from the kitchen worktop and had now decided to chew. She flicked them towards the fun filled puppy before throwing them at the laundry basket, where they now belonged.

'Ohhhhhhh, Buddy, like I haven't got enough to do.' She wanted to chastise the puppy, but instead knelt down. 'You'd play all day, wouldn't you, little man?' Buddy bounced around, his chocolate brown ears flapping up and down as his whole body sprang around in excitement.

A knock at the front door made Madeleine jump backwards. She landed amongst the bubble wrap, which popped and cracked as she fell heavily onto her bottom, making Buddy even more excitable than he already was. He bounded up and down the hallway, wagging and yapping in anticipation of the unexpected visitor.

The hallway sounded empty and hollow. It hadn't helped taking the curtains she'd bought down from the doorway. She'd paid for them and she didn't see any reason why she shouldn't take them with her. Liam's old curtains were in a box somewhere and she was adamant that if he wanted them re-hanging, he could do it himself. Repeated knocking on the front door echoed like a cymbal as Madeleine anxiously tried to catch Buddy who still ran around at speed. She placed him in his day cage before making her way through the maze of boxes that now filled the hallway to the front door.

'Okay, okay, one minute,' she tried to shout. She had to be just loud enough so that the visitor would hear, but quiet enough not to wake Poppy whose room was at the front of the house.

She wasn't expecting visitors and was puzzled. Fluffing up her hair, Madeleine automatically stared at the empty cream wall where her gilt framed mirror used to hang, fully expecting to see her reflection looking back at her before turning the three different keys that Liam had fitted to the front door.

'Jess, oh my goodness, what a surprise.' Her voice hit a

high-pitched squeal as she opened the door and pulled her sister into her hold.

'Thought I'd drop by and give you a hand,' Jess replied as she marched past Maddie, waving a bag in the air. 'I brought Poppy's favourite muffins. Where is she?'

Madeleine closed the door. 'You mean you brought your favourite muffins and Poppy is fast asleep, so shush.'

Maddie turned and followed Jess who had already set off at a fast and determined pace towards the kitchen. 'I hope the kettle hasn't been packed, I need coffee,' she announced as she navigated her way between the boxes.

'No, the kettle is not packed. It belongs to Liam, like most things in this house.'

The phone rang and Madeleine stopped to answer it.

'Hello, yes, this is Madeleine Frost.' She paused. 'Of course not, ask away.' Again she paused. 'No, I haven't seen her. I've been trying to call her for over a week.' Her voice began to shake. 'Yes, of course. Anything you need.' Madeleine finished the call and looked up to see Jess's worried face.

'What's wrong?' She grabbed hold of Madeleine's arm and ushered her towards the kitchen and a chair.

'That … that was the police. It's Bridget, my agent. She's gone missing. Jess, I've been cursing her. I … I thought she'd gone on holiday without telling me. Do you think she's okay?'

Jess shrugged her shoulders. 'I don't know, Maddie. Why were the police calling you?'

'Well, they said she'd been reported missing and they'd got my number from her answerphone. I've been ringing her repeatedly.'

Jess put her arm around her sister. 'I'm sure she's okay and they'll find her. Now, we have to sort you out, but first, you look like you need coffee.' Jess turned and switched on the kettle.

'What am I going to do, Jess? I don't want to stay, but simply can't afford to leave.'

'You must go and see your dad. In fact, that's why I came. I'm going to stay here tonight with Poppy and you, you are going to see your father. If he turns you away, then we'll go back to plan A and you, Poppy and Buddy will just have to come and live with me. We'd manage somehow.'

Madeleine shook her head. She knew she couldn't go to Jess's but her dad? Could she just turn up on his doorstep and ask him to put a roof over her head?

With coffee and muffins, she and Jess spent the next hour trying to work out what Maddie would say to her father, where Bridget might have gone, and then finishing packing up all the things that actually belonged to Madeleine.

Chapter Five

Madeleine drove through the stone gated entrance, past the gatehouse and up the long and extensive driveway towards the huge gothic building that was Wrea Head Hall. She'd looked the property up on the Internet, but still the sight of it took her breath away as she rounded the corner. It was like an exquisite piece of Victorian history that had been left behind for the twenty-first century to appreciate and admire.

Parking a little way down the lane, Madeleine walked up the final stretch of the drive and even though the trees had begun to shed their leaves, she used them as camouflage, wanting to take in the full beauty of the house for just a few private moments before walking through the doors.

Tawny lamplight twinkled through the many panes of glass that created the huge Victorian windows. An arched stone church-like doorway stood in the centre of the windows, with its impressive solid oak door. She looked up to where turrets lined the roof and from where carved stone gargoyles could be spotted as they peered down to where she stood.

Madeleine began to shake. The thought of meeting her father made her mouth dry and her apprehension began to build as a slight and irritating feeling of nausea took over. He was somewhere in that house. The man whose knee she had sat on as a child, played games with and cuddled up to. But then it occurred to her that he might not be home at all. What if he'd taken a holiday, a trip abroad or, even worse, what if he'd sold the hotel and moved on?

Just for a split second she couldn't decide which would make her more nervous: him being home, or the fact that he might not be home at all.

Her eyes were once again drawn to the huge gothic multi-paned windows. There was a glow which seemed to come from within. Madeleine stood on her tiptoes and watched the people who were congregated inside. Women beautifully dressed in evening wear, men all in black formal dinner jackets, bow ties and crisp white shirts. All held champagne glasses and selected hors d'oeuvres from the vast silver platters that were carried around by waiters. Everyone was smiling, laughing and chatting. A bay bush blocked her view and she struggled to see. It was times like this that she wished she'd been just a few inches taller. A cast iron planter stood to the left of the window and she used it to balance on, as her eyes became drawn to a stone built inglenook fireplace that stood impressively within an oak panelled wall. A disorderly pile of logs lay beside it on the tiled hearth.

A man reached forward, chose a piece of wood and threw it onto the already roaring fire. Looking quite at home, a woman stared into the flames and tucked her feet up on a dark blue Chesterfield settee, just as a man passed her a drink, kissed her on the cheek and smiled lovingly towards her. It was a scene of tranquillity. Everyone looked so very happy. All radiated a glow of warmth, joy and contentment.

Then, from a room to the back of the hall, there was a scream. A scream so shrill and loud, it sounded like the final note of an operatic soprano. People moved away from the glow of the fire and almost ran towards the room beyond.

'He's dead, he's dead, murdered,' a rotund woman shouted as she ran through the crowd towards the window, her hands waving frantically in the air, shaking them above her head, followed by a second scream.

Madeleine panicked, jumped down from her perch and ducked behind the bay tree. Again, her stomach churned and she began to shake. The tree she cowered behind was hardly the hiding place of the year, its thin willowy trunk and small cast iron tub barely hid her at all. But fear overcame her and she did not dare move. She had to think rationally, had to decide what to do. Something wasn't right. The guests hadn't seemed overly alarmed, nor had the waiters and it occurred to her that one or two had actually laughed.

Holding her breath, she began to move slowly around the outskirts of the house. She should have phoned her father first, arriving like this was probably not the best of ideas, after all it was suddenly obvious that the hotel was in the middle of a party and the last thing he needed was her turning up like the proverbial bad penny.

She needed to get to her car without being seen and began creeping from one bush to another, one eye on the house, the other on her car which now seemed to be much further up the lane than she'd originally thought.

'What the hell?' a man's voice bellowed as she felt herself being grabbed from behind and thrown to the ground. Her arms and legs lashed out, kicking and punching as best she could. She managed to land one definite punch before she landed flat on her back; her arms were pushed upward and she was pinned to the damp tarmac, as a man's body straddled her from above, making it difficult to breathe.

'HEEEEELLLLLPPPPPP ... I can't ... I can't ... breathe. GET ... OFF ... ME. Ouuuuuuuuchhhhhhhhhhh ...'

'Be quiet for goodness' sake, you'll disturb the guests.' He manoeuvred his weight, allowing her to regain her breath. 'What the hell are you doing creeping around? Staking the place out?'

Albeit terrified, logic took over and Madeleine began to calm down. Her attacker was asking questions, not the normal actions of a man who was trying to murder or hurt someone.

The daylight had quickly turned to dusk and Madeleine squinted to take in the stranger's appearance. His hair looked a little unkempt. His chin seemed to be covered in thin, trimmed stubble, but his smile showed a set of perfectly straight teeth. His breath smelled of fresh mint and he was dressed in army combat clothes.

'I want to see my father,' she suddenly managed to blurt out as once again her fighting spirit returned and she began flailing her legs in a desperate attempt to kick her attacker.

His gaze suddenly changed from stern and angry to amused and just for a moment their breathing fell into unison as they stared at one another in silence.

'Feisty little madam, aren't we?' he said and as quickly as he'd pinned her to the floor he had jumped up and his hand was held out towards her. 'You getting up, or staying down there?' His voice was deep, with a distinct Yorkshire accent.

'I wasn't planning on being down here in the first place, you asshole. Do you often go around attacking people and throwing them to the floor in the middle of winter?' Madeleine growled as she stared up at him.

'Firstly, it was still autumn the last time I checked and second, I only attack people who look like they're about to rob the place.' He picked up her handbag and passed it to her.

'Semantics,' Madeleine tried to baffle him with words as she nervously looked over her shoulder. 'I came to see my father and then I changed my mind. The hotel looked busy. I was heading back to my car and trying to be discreet. Until you knocked me flying.'

He began laughing and couldn't stop. 'Ma'am, it's a hotel. Of course it's busy, what did you expect? We're having a murder mystery weekend.'

'Ma'am? Ma'am?' Madeleine questioned. 'Who the hell do you think I am, my mother?' She glared at him and nervously began brushing the dirt from her trousers.

There was a momentary silence as Madeleine slowly digested what he'd said and looked over her shoulder. She caught his eye and a smile crossed her lips but she quickly tried to disguise it. 'Fine, so that explains it, a murder mystery weekend.' She blushed and kicked at the gravel.

She looked down at her trousers and once again began to rub the grime from them.

He bowed his head and held out a hand. 'The name's Bandit.'

Madeleine shook his hand. 'Bandit? Is that your name, really? Didn't your mother like you?'

He laughed. 'It's a nickname, given to me when I was in the marines. It kind of stuck, but if it offends you, the real name is Christopher, Christopher Lawless. Now, you say your father lives here? Shall I call the boss or do you want to go and creep around in the trees some more?'

'Providing the boss is still Morris Pocklington, go ahead. I'm sure my father will be pleased to see how you welcomed his daughter to—' Madeleine stopped in mid-flow as she looked up to see her cross-armed father standing before her on the doorstep of Wrea Head Hall.

Chapter Six

Madeleine watched as her father paced nervously around the room before settling himself in a green leather captain's chair that was situated behind the Victorian double-sided mahogany desk. He rested his elbows on the arms of his chair, his hands tightly clasped together, and looked at her.

'I wouldn't ask, but I have to get away from Liam and I'm desperate, I literally have nowhere else to go.' Madeleine twisted her hands together as though wringing out wet cloths and studied her father for the first time in years. He looked distinguished, his hair and beard were both mottled with grey, but the expensive cut gave him an eminent look. She knew she'd shocked him by turning up at the hotel, yet he appeared to be calm, patient, and looked thoughtful before speaking.

'Why come now, Madeleine? Why would you want to come and live here now? Couldn't you stay with your mother? After all she did a good job of dominating you as a child.' Her father spoke quietly, yet sternly and watched for her reaction. 'I mean it's not like she ever really allowed us to keep in touch now, is it?'

Madeleine gulped and her stomach fell, making her close her eyes, while she waited for the room to stop spinning. 'Mother ... she died. Just before Christmas. I thought you knew.'

'Oh my God, I'm so sorry. No one told me. I had no idea.'

Madeleine sat back in her chair. She didn't understand why her father looked so shocked. Liam said he'd phoned him. But if her father hadn't known, it did explain why he hadn't been in touch.

'Are you sorry she's dead, or sorry that you didn't know?' She knew she sounded abrupt, but felt as though she needed an answer to the question.

'Both. What happened?'

Madeleine watched his reactions. He genuinely looked shocked and after the way Liam had acted of late, she had no reason not to believe her father. 'She had an anaphylactic shock, as you know she was allergic to nuts. We still don't understand it; she was normally so careful.' Madeleine felt herself begin to tremble. The day of her mother's death was still vivid in her mind. She remembered walking into her mother's house to find her curled up in a tight ball, her eyes wide open; her face was the palest ashen grey, yet her lips the brightest red, all contorted and swollen. Her Epi-pen lay beside her, empty, as though it had been discharged, but hadn't worked.

Madeleine stood up to hide the tears that threatened to flow. She allowed her finger to run along the dark wood panelling that surrounded the room. It generated a feeling of texture and warmth. 'I realise it's a big ask, you know, coming to live here. But as I said, when I had to give my flat up, I moved in with Liam and now ... now I have nowhere else to go. I've made the biggest mistake of my life and I don't know what to do. I just don't trust him. He's changed, one minute he's the most loving person you could meet and the next he's cruel. I have to think of Poppy.' She pulled a tissue from her pocket and blew her nose before she could continue. 'I don't expect to come here rent free. I'm happy to work, earn my keep so to speak and what's more I wouldn't be here for long. I promise. As soon as my royalty cheques come through, I'll find somewhere else to go.'

Morris closed his eyes. He'd waited years for the day that his daughter might want to spend time with him, wished that one day she might walk in through the door, meet him for dinner or allow him to be a part of her family. Now here she was, asking if she, her daughter and her Spaniel puppy might all move into the hall.

So why didn't that make him happy?

'I tried to see you, so many times,' he whispered. He thought of the day he'd called at her flat. He'd felt so alone, so in need of support. His wife, Josie, had died and even though Madeleine had never met her, he felt it only right that she should hear of her stepmother's death from him. But Madeleine hadn't been home and Liam had sent him away, insisting that Madeleine wouldn't want to see him and adamant that he should leave before she returned.

'Really, I … I didn't know. Mother always said you couldn't make it, couldn't see me and that you had better things to do.' It was apparent to him that Madeleine was thinking of her childhood and it hadn't occurred to her that he'd been to visit her more recently.

'It was never like that, Maddie. I always wanted to see you. Your mother wouldn't allow it, especially after I married Josie …' He paused. '… Margaret didn't want me, but she didn't want anyone else to have me either.'

'I didn't know.'

Her father nodded and once again defensively crossed his arms. 'How did you know where to find me?'

He saw her smile. 'I saw a picture of you in the *Yorkshire Post*. You were standing in front of the hotel after some charity event that you'd been involved in last year. Looked like you'd raised loads of money. I was so very proud of you.'

He gasped. The last thing he'd ever expected was for Madeleine to ever say she'd been proud of him. He hadn't even realised that she'd known where he was.

'So, how long have you owned the hotel?' she asked, hoping to change the subject. Her eyes searched the room in a desperate attempt not to cry for the years that she'd lost.

'Around nine years. I bought the place with Josie.' His arm swept upwards. 'We wanted to make it the most romantic hotel in the north. All Josie, of course, she was the romantic one.'

'Well, for what it's worth, I think you both succeeded. It's beautiful.'

Madeleine once again studied the wood panels. She thought of Josie, of the stepmother that she'd never met and she wondered what she was like. How they lived and what kind of life she and her father had had together. There were so many questions that she wanted the answers to, but knew she'd never dare ask. Jealousy seared through her as she silently thought of the life he'd had without her.

'It was all Josie, she used to make the hall sing with happiness. Its beauty and romance was all down to her.'

Madeleine's eyes opened wide. Her father spoke in the past tense. Did he mean that Josie had left, or died?

She had no idea which it was, but immediately wished that she could run and hold her father as she saw the pain flash across his face.

'I did try to see you, after Josie died.' He had watched the shock cross Madeleine's face and was sure she hadn't known that Josie was dead. 'I came to your flat. Spoke to him.'

'Really, did you, when?' She genuinely looked shocked and it became immediately apparent to him that she appeared to know nothing about his visit, about how rude Liam had been and how he'd been sent away, full of grief.

He'd waited for days in the hope that Liam had told her of his visit, but she hadn't called. Instead of a sympathy card she'd sent a letter. The letter had broken his heart; it had told him to stay away. To keep out of her life, that she was more than happy without him and not to contact her again. He'd been distraught and had read it over and over again until finally, he'd believed it and his dreams of rekindling his family had ended. And on a day when he'd needed Madeleine the most, he'd stood alone by Josie's grave, surrounded by staff and strangers, but no family member to call his own.

'Maddie, you know I wouldn't turn you away. I've wanted

you here for years. You're more than welcome to stay for as long as you want.' He spoke the words, but glanced down at the desk drawer where the letter had been locked. The gold key held his attention and he thought for a moment before looking back up. If Madeleine hadn't been aware of his visit, then who had sent him the letter?

Was it possible that Madeleine would have written a letter in that way and then turn up, asking if she could move in and expect it not to matter?

'Well, we could sure use an extra pair of hands around here. Your contribution to the hotel would help.' He wanted her to come, wanted her to know that she was welcome, but didn't know how to show her his feelings.

'Here, write your address down. I'll organise a van for you.' He passed her a pad, rummaged in the drawer and pulled out a pen, tossing it across the desk.

Morris wanted her to write, he wanted to see the words on the page, see her handwriting, the style and the fluidity that she wrote in, and what's more he wanted her to do it without realising what he was up to. If she didn't know about the letter, which he suspected she didn't, it was the only way he'd know for sure if she'd written it or not.

He knew he was being distant, withdrawn and probably a lot more unwelcoming than his daughter might have expected and maybe he was being unfair. Madeleine had become a beautiful young woman. She was sitting before him and for the first time in her life, she was asking for his help.

'I know of a good removals firm. I'll get one over to you tomorrow.' He stood up and walked over to a unit. Pulling a directory from its shelf he began thumbing through the pages.

Madeleine closed her eyes, realising for just a moment how little she knew her own father. They'd spent most of their lives apart, even though none of it had been his fault. It was true what he'd previously said; her mother had dominated her life. She'd given birth to Jess, and her dark olive skin and jet black hair had made it immediately obvious that Morris was not the father and that Jess had been the result of her mother's infidelity. She'd left him just a few days later, feeling that she didn't have a choice. But by doing that, she'd taken Madeleine away from her father, thus robbing them of each other.

Everyone had said that her father would re-marry. He'd always been a family man and loved family life. However, she couldn't help but feel just a little sad that he'd spent so many years living in another house, with all those Christmases, birthdays, holidays and bedtime stories that she'd missed out on. How different her life could have been with him in it.

She looked up.

'Dad.' She paused and grabbed at her breath. 'Is ... is it okay to call you that?' For some reason Madeleine found it hard to continue. She immediately looked back down at her mud-covered shoes and searched for the right words. 'It's been so long.'

Morris Pocklington gulped. He was shocked at the question. He knew he'd been distant towards her, but didn't know how else to be. Had he really been such a bad father?

He looked at the young woman that sat before him. It was the same young woman that he'd held moments after her birth, the same baby that he'd spoon-fed and the same child who had sat on his knee. He'd read her books, over and over again, taught her how to ride a bike and now, she was all grown up. She was beautiful and appeared to be intelligent. He closed his eyes, wishing he'd been there to watch her grow. There had been so many times in the past when he'd wanted to be there for her. Yet, never once had he imagined a day when she'd turn up at his home, and ask if she were still allowed to call him 'Dad'.

'Have I really been such a bad father that you'd have to

ask?' The words were simple yet anxious and his eyes filled with emotion and tears.

He held out his arms to where his daughter sat. He desperately wanted to hold her and knew that it was time to at least try and put the past where it belonged. He knew it would be difficult, knew the past would haunt them both, but knew he had to try.

'I'd really like to hug my daughter, if that's okay?'

He watched as Madeleine stood up and walked towards him. Slow and tentative, yet somewhere deep inside, she was still his little Maddie. His fingers rested on her shoulders as the tears continued to well up in his eyes. His emotions twisted one way and then the other.

He glanced across to where she'd placed the notepad down on his desk. There was no doubt in his mind: the writing on the letter and the writing on the pad were very different. He'd read the letter so many times that the words and its handwriting were imprinted on his mind. He gritted his teeth in anger, now sure that Liam O'Grady had been behind it all along.

He finally pulled Madeleine towards him. He shook from head to toe, nervous of his own flesh and blood. But for the first time in years he held onto his daughter as though his life depended on it.

Chapter Seven

'I guess this is it.' Madeleine turned to Jess and hugged her. The van containing all of her possessions pulled away, as she and Jess stood awkwardly outside Liam's house. 'You wouldn't believe how relieved I am to do this,' she suddenly announced as she posted the keys through the letterbox. Another chapter of her life was over. She'd never see Liam again.

Jess stepped from foot to foot. 'Actually, Maddie, I'm not sure how to tell you this, but I'm relieved too. Something really isn't right about that house and last night, while I was lying on Poppy's bed with her, reading her a story, I heard a noise. I think Liam came back.' She paused and Madeleine dropped her bag on the floor, beside the car.

'Go on,' she urged, knowing that whatever Jess was about to say, she wasn't going to like it.

'Well, actually, I know he did. I guess when he didn't see your car out front he thought the house was empty. I froze and hid with Poppy in her bedroom, if I'm honest.'

'What was he doing?'

'I don't know. He wasn't here long and then I heard the front door slam and knew that he was gone. I went to see what he'd been up to and when I went into your bedroom, I found this, your locket, it was just lying there on the bed. All broken.'

Madeleine looked at the necklace that now lay in two separate pieces in Jess's hand. It was a locket that her father had bought her some years before and that she'd worn at every important event in her life, a locket that everyone knew that she cherished. 'Who, I mean, why? It was him, right? I'll kill him.'

Jess nodded. 'It had to be him, I mean, who else would it have been? They had a key,' she said as she closed her hand over the locket and placed it back in her bag. 'I'll take it into town, get it mended for you,' she said as once again she pulled her sister into a hold.

Madeleine choked back the tears. 'I love you so much, Jess. I can't believe I'm going to be so far away from you.'

Jess sniggered. 'Oh, Maddie, it's just thirty miles from my flat to Scarborough. Thirty miles is nothing nowadays, I could be there in forty minutes, faster if I had to. I don't have to be back on the cruise ships for a couple of months and in that time, we'll see each other loads. You'll see.'

Madeleine wasn't so sure. She'd agreed to work for her keep. The hotel was busy all year round and at this point she had no idea what her workload would be. She presumed she'd have to work set days at the hotel and on top of that, she had to find time to write and look after both Poppy and Buddy. And, with all that had happened in the past, she would have to tread carefully before inviting Jess to visit the hall.

'It's just temporary, Jess. It's not ideal, but I have to think of Poppy. At least she'll be safe at Wrea Head Hall, even though I'll most probably have to find her a minder on the days that I work. She'll finally get the chance to get to know her granddad. He's so excited to meet her.'

'But you said he was a little distant with you. Are you sure you really want to live there?'

'He did seem distant at first. But then, he seemed okay. I think it'll be fine. And no one can be distant with Poppy, can they?' Madeleine smiled as she looked in the back of the red Mazda where Poppy slept. Her sleepover with Jess and the sudden upheaval today had left her totally exhausted. A small cage rested beside her on the backseat where Buddy sat inside, looking sad, forlorn and completely unimpressed. He hated being restricted and hated the small car cage, even more than he hated the bigger day cage, and welcomed Jess's hand as she reached in to stroke him goodbye.

* * *

The journey was uneventful. Especially seeing as Madeleine had driven slowly, and had ignored Buddy's whining which began the moment they set off and didn't stop unless they slowed down at junctions, where he thought the car might stop and he'd escape from his prison.

Thirty miles felt more like fifty, but her excitement rose as the sight of Wrea Head Hall once again loomed up before her on the distant hill.

It was beautiful, impressive and already she loved it.

Pulling up outside the hall, she carefully parked her car and when she unstrapped her daughter from her car seat an animated Poppy jumped out of the car.

'Mummy, it's this big.' She tried to demonstrate as her arms spread wide. 'And this tall. Wow. Is this really my house? Do I have a bedroom? Where will Buddy sleep? Where's my new granddad?' She looked around, eager to see him as soon as she could. 'Mummy, you promised. Where is he?'

'He's right here.' Her father emerged from a small wooden doorway that was sunk into a brick wall, beyond the car park. His voice was deep, distinct and much more cheerful than it had been the day before. Poppy suddenly turned shy. She jumped back in the car, pulled her blanket over her legs and began an animated, meaningless conversation with Buddy.

'Hi, Dad. How are you?' Madeleine smiled, immediately walking to him, holding out her arms for a hug. It was all still new, slightly awkward and a little uncomfortable, yet she yearned for the years she'd lost. Of course, she knew she'd never retrieve that time, but from now on, she'd do her best to make up for every lost moment.

After a brief hug with her father she walked back to the car. 'Come on, Poppy, say hello.' She pulled the blanket from the child's legs and watched as Poppy crept nervously out of the car. Her eyes opened wide. She looked upward and studied her grandfather, who immediately dropped to his knees, making himself more her height. He smiled and pushed his hand deep into his pocket, pulling out a bag of chocolate buttons, which made Poppy's eyes sparkle with excitement.

'Mummy, do you think my beautiful granddaughter would like these?' He waved them in front of Poppy, who smiled and with a nod of Madeleine's head, she reached forward and with the uncertainty that she now seemed to have around men, she took the sweets and whispered a thank you.

Morris stood up and held out his hand to Poppy. 'Shall we get you settled in?'

Morris walked towards the back door of the hall, with Poppy skipping beside him, holding tightly onto his hand. The sight gave Madeleine a warm glow; it was one she'd wanted to see since Poppy had been born and something she'd never thought would happen.

'We have a kennel block out here. I know Buddy isn't used to them, but hopefully he'll settle in. I've bought a new bed and fresh blankets for him.' He looked apologetically towards Poppy as he opened a kennel door and turned the heat lamps on for Buddy's use. 'I didn't want Buddy to be cold. So, I had these fitted last night to keep him warm.' He pointed to the heat lamp.

Poppy stared into the concrete kennel with horrified eyes. 'But Buddy sleeps with me. He likes it in my bed.' She nodded and tried to use her big eyes to convince her grandfather that she was telling the truth.

'Oh, no, Buddy does not,' Madeleine jumped in as she led Buddy into the kennel and closed the metal mesh door behind the pup. 'He slept in the kitchen at our old house. This is a hotel, Poppy. Doggies can't sleep in the kitchen here. Granddad would get into all sorts of trouble if he allowed it and you wouldn't want that, would you? Besides, look the kennel has a tiled floor just like our old kitchen, a lovely bed and a warm blanket and Granddad installed this heater specially to keep him warm.'

Poppy didn't look convinced. She peered through the

kennel door and pushed out her bottom lip. Madeleine knew that the whole move to such a huge house might just take her daughter some getting used to and this was just the first barrier that they needed to jump.

'Oh, I know, Poppy. Do you think Buddy will want a biscuit?' Maddie asked as she dug in her pocket. 'I think I have one in here somewhere. Now where is it?' She wriggled and pretended that her pocket was deeper than it was, making Poppy laugh and nod at the same time. They opened the kennel door and Poppy knelt down on the floor.

'Okay, what do we say to Buddy?'

Madeleine watched Poppy look up at her granddad. 'Watch Granddad, it's a trick.' She held the biscuit up in her hand and waited until the puppy sat down before her. 'Speak, Buddy,' she shouted just as she'd been taught and waited for the pup to bark back at her before throwing him the biscuit. 'See, Granddad, he speaks.' She giggled, grabbed hold of her grandfather's hand and allowed him to walk her to the house.

Madeleine's father then directed her and Poppy inside and showed them upstairs to the rooms that would be their temporary new home.

Madeleine looked around her new room. The whole of it was wood panelled halfway up the walls and both the panels and the walls were painted in a beautiful soft sage-green. A huge dark wood four-poster bed stood centrally. A door opened to its side showing a smaller room, which contained a Poppy-sized sleigh bed. It stood in one corner with a white, mirrored dressing table to its side. Pink curtains had been hung in Poppy's honour and a huge pink teddy bear sat at the foot of the bed.

'Look, Poppy, Granddad did this for you.' Madeleine pushed the door open as far as it would go as Poppy ran into the room to inspect it, immediately launching herself up and onto the bed, bouncing up and down with glee.

'Mummy, it's bouncy and I'm right next door to you.'

Both father and daughter struggled for something to say and a silence fell between them; only Poppy managed to chat aimlessly. 'Thank you, Granddad. I love my room. It's pink.' She walked around the room, stroking everything that was pink as though the colour was the most important thing in the world.

'Err … I … I didn't fill the rooms with too much furniture on purpose,' Morris finally said. 'I know your desk is following. I thought you'd like your own things around you. Let me know if there's anything else you need. I'm sure we'd have a spare of almost anything, somewhere in the hotel.'

'Dad. I'm so relieved to have got away from Liam. You have no idea how much this means to me.' Madeleine walked over to the window, taking in the view. It looked over rolling green lawns, an old Victorian garden and in the distance trees stood, all partially bare as their leaves had already dropped in the October winds. To the left of the house stood an old broken greenhouse. It had originally been made of wood and glass but in its current state some of the wood looked to have decayed, and, at one end, pieces of glass seemed to have been missing for quite some years. The weeds and undergrowth had slowly taken over and had entwined themselves around the structure, making it look as though the garden had made an attempt to grow up and over the top of it, burying it from view. Next to the greenhouse was a vegetable garden. Only half of it was used. Vegetables and herbs appeared to grow within low brick walled structures, which was no doubt a good supply for the hotel's kitchen. The other half of the area was also covered with the low brick walls, but these walls were full of overgrown summer weeds, which had now turned brown with the onset of autumn.

Her father joined her at the window and looked out at the garden. 'Sorry about the view. The greenhouse is about to be refurbished. It was one of the last jobs on the list and we kind of ran out of money. Besides, not many of the guest bedrooms overlook it, so I had to prioritise and the house, kitchen and guest rooms had to come first.'

A movement in the distant woods made her squint to take a closer look. Bandit came into view between the trees. He walked effortlessly, even though he carried a huge bag on one shoulder and a brace of pheasants in his hand.

'That man over there,' she said, pointing. 'Who is he to the hotel?'

Her father stared into the distance. 'Ah, he's called Christopher, but everyone knows him as Bandit. He works here. He's the gamekeeper, but he also does a bit of gardening, chops the wood for the log fires and, as you saw last night, he does a bit of light security. He lives in the gatehouse at the bottom of the estate; it belongs to his father. He's worked for me since he left the marines and we tend to eat what he hunts. Why?'

Madeleine thought for a moment. She remembered the gatehouse. It was run-down, stone built and had stood by the gates. It had a rusty white four bar metal fence with a rickety metal gate. There had been a white front door, along with white wooden windows, all of which had looked in need of repainting. In fact, the whole place had looked in need of renovation, albeit, it occurred to her, that the grass lawn and gardens had all been well tended.

'No reason. As you saw, I ran into him last night. Well, actually, he ran into me like a damn bulldozer, knocked me over.' A flush of colour began rising through her cheeks and she made a mental note to cautiously find out what times he was normally around. After their encounter the night before, she decided that avoiding him for a day or two might just be a good idea.

'I take it you don't like him?'

She watched as Bandit strode out of the woodland and began walking towards the house. He looked strong, muscle-bound and had a certain something about him that infuriated her. Not only had he unceremoniously thrown her to the floor, he hadn't apologised either. His hair was overgrown; he needed a shave and possessed a stupid nickname.

What was there to like?

'I don't know him.' She decided not to share her thoughts.

'He'll have meant no harm. Trust me. He's one of the good guys. Besides, you might have to get used to him, he's around here a lot.'

'Great. He's annoying. He reminds me of an over-excited baboon.'

Her father laughed. 'Honey, seriously, he's harmless, just protective. Avoid him if you like, he drops in early for breakfast each morning and Nomsa normally sends him away with a home cooked pie for his tea. She just loves to feed him and he seems to enjoy her food. It's a good arrangement, it makes us all happy.'

'Are they a couple?' Madeleine questioned as she turned to the bed where Poppy had made herself comfortable with the new and oversized pink teddy bear lying by her side.

Her father once again laughed. 'Bandit and Nomsa? God, no, they're not a couple. Wait till you meet Nomsa, she'd actually find that really funny. She's probably old enough to be his mum.'

For the remainder of the afternoon Madeleine stayed in her room. She busied herself, unpacking the boxes that the removal men had dropped off, while Poppy slept peacefully in her new bed. Her desk, laptop and box files full of research were all placed in the corner of her room, along with her numerous boxes of books. She wondered if she should ask about a bookcase but decided to keep the boxes where they were. The last thing she wanted to do was to impose for too long. She'd made herself a promise that as soon as she could afford it, she'd rent a small cottage, somewhere of her own, with a garden where Poppy could play.

Poppy woke with renewed enthusiasm as she realised that her toys had arrived while she'd slept and had been carried into her new bedroom along with her piles of teddies, special pillow and baskets full of clothes. By the time she'd finished placing them exactly where she wanted them, her bed looked like an overgrown teddy bear mountain, in which she sat centrally, a huge smile plastered across her face.

'Mummy, look at me. They're all around me.'

'Poppy, are you really going to sleep with all the teddies on your bed, all at once?' Madeleine watched as her daughter ran out of the room and jumped up on the four-poster bed.

'Nope, I'm gonna sleep in this big bed with you.' She laughed.

Madeleine shook her head. 'Oh, no, you are not. This big bed is for your mummy. It's not for little girls with a bounce like Tigger.'

She began to tickle her daughter who squealed with delight and then ran back into her own room, disappearing beneath the teddy mountain like a hedgehog hibernating beneath a pile of autumn leaves.

Madeleine smiled, knowing that although she could still quite clearly see Poppy's legs, her daughter actually believed that she was now invisible beneath the bears. She waited for a few moments, knowing that within seconds, she'd begin giggling and peeping out.

'Ah well, Poppy seems to have disappeared. I might just have to take Buddy for a walk all by myself,' she announced as she stood up and began to leave the room.

Walking out of the door, she looked over her shoulder and counted to three and just as she'd thought, Poppy ran towards her.

'Mummy, wait, don't go without me. He's my Buddy too.'

Chapter Eight

Liam slipped a key into each of the front door locks, knowing that once he entered the house, Madeleine would be gone and his pain would begin. Nevertheless, he stepped through the door with purpose and carefully surveyed his home.

He dropped a large heavy suitcase and a shopping bag down in the entrance, walked down the corridor and stood in the doorway of each room in turn. He wanted to see what she'd taken with her, but, more importantly, he wanted to be sure of what she'd left behind.

Taking deep, deliberate breaths, he walked into the dining room and allowed his hand to travel across the keys of the piano, the noise reminding him of the days his mother would play and sing. Even then, the piano had been as out of tune as his mother and, though it had been in the room for as long as he remembered, he'd never once thought to learn how to play it himself, or to have it tuned.

His eyes glanced down at the pedals. A small piece of blue Lego was trapped beneath and he knelt down to retrieve it, banging his head as he did. He cursed and picked it up, held it tightly in his hand and looked around the room for the box that it belonged in. The Lego had been his, a toy he'd loved as a child and he'd repeatedly told Madeleine that Poppy shouldn't play with it, but like everything else, she'd gone behind his back and permitted Poppy to do whatever she wanted, in his house, in his absence.

He felt the tension build up inside him, the tightening of his stomach and the acceleration of his heartbeat. He threw the small piece of plastic as hard as he could and screamed as it bounced off the wall and onto the dining table, where it landed, with an unimpressive tap.

He couldn't find the box and stamped out of the room and

down to the kitchen, where he began opening cupboards. They were practically empty, but what remained was untidy and he began moving what was left into the tidy straight lines that he preferred. Everything had been moved, nothing was how it had been and he kicked at a door with a foot, while his arm swept the entire content of the worktop onto the floor. Warm, almost hot water spilled from the kettle and splashed up onto his sock, making him realise that it hadn't been long since Madeleine had left.

He stared into space. 'She has to come back. I will make her come back,' he shouted at the carnage that now littered the floor. He shook his head. 'But what if she doesn't? What if you've lost her forever?' He slapped himself on the face. 'It's your own fault. You're a fool, you should have held onto her. You should have made her stay.'

He picked up the phone, dialled Madeleine's number and waited as the call went to voicemail. 'You won't ignore me,' he shouted as he hit the off button. He stared at the phone, at its dialling options and knew that wherever Madeleine had gone, she'd have used the phone to arrange it. He clicked his way through the redial numbers, looking for any he didn't recognise and then called them one by one.

'Good afternoon, Wrea Head Hall, how may I direct your call?' the receptionist cheerfully asked, but Liam was furious and slammed the phone back into its cradle.

'We've run to Daddy, have we?' His voice became high-pitched, his mind spun around and he could feel himself getting hotter and hotter. His chest ached and he could feel the palpitations begin, fluttering away like a fast moving engine.

He'd thought he'd taken care of her father the day he'd turned up at Madeleine's flat. Thought he'd made it clear that Madeleine didn't want him in her life and afterwards he'd taken steps to make sure her father was out of the picture for good.

He paced up and down the hall, backwards and forwards. He knew he had to think, knew he had to work out what to do, but the more he paced, the angrier he became. He forced himself to stop and tried everything he could to get the thought of Madeleine and her father out of his mind. Besides, he couldn't think about that now, he had other things to take care of, things that couldn't wait and his first job was to get the suitcase safely up the stairs before anyone came, empty it of its contents and then and only then would he have time to think about dealing with both Madeleine and her father.

Chapter Nine

'Damn woman,' Bandit cursed as he glanced up at the hotel and saw Madeleine watching him from the window. Raising the axe high above his head, he brought it down with a satisfying thud, making the log split in two and fall to the ground. He scooped up the logs that he'd previously cut and threw them into the wheelbarrow that stood by his side. It was still early autumn and without the glow of embers in the open fires, the house could easily turn cool at night. Besides, the reception rooms always looked much nicer with the logs alight, the guests preferred it and it was his job to ensure that there was enough dry wood to keep each of the three fires going right through the winter. But he knew he had to be ahead of his game, this wood would need to be stacked and dried out for at least six months before it would be ready to burn.

He saw the back door open and watched as Morris Pocklington emerged.

'Look, I'm really sorry about last night. I didn't know that Madeleine was your daughter,' Bandit said, pre-empting the conversation that he guessed was about to happen.

'She's pretty pissed at you,' Morris replied with a laugh. 'I'm not sure I'd want to get on the wrong side of her.'

'Shouldn't be going round pretending to be a burglar then, should she?' Bandit fired back as he picked up another log and brought the axe down to split it. There was no way he could have known who she was. He hadn't even known that the boss had a daughter, so he couldn't be blamed for not knowing who she was when he'd seen her creeping around like a hunting tiger, looking for its next meal. But tigress she was not. He'd seen the way she'd looked up at him like a frightened doe in the darkness. Her eyes wide open with fear.

She'd appeared vulnerable yet powerful, and timid yet fiery, all at once. She was so similar to the type of women he'd encountered in the marines. Women who could cut you down with words at ten paces, or shoot you from a distance and, to be honest, he wasn't sure he wanted to encounter women like that again. Not after Karen.

'You don't like her?' Morris asked as he stepped up on the log to perch on the fence and pushed his hands deep in his pockets.

Bandit bit his lip. 'I barely know her.'

He thought of the deep musky perfume that she'd been wearing; its scent had annoyingly stayed with him through the night. She'd had a feisty personality, a spark about her that could have lit a campfire from a distance, yet he couldn't work out what annoyed him the most; her high spirits, her feisty personality or the vulnerability that shone from within. None of them could possibly be a good thing.

'Afghanistan, it changed you, Bandit.'

It was true. Afghanistan had changed him. Karen had changed him. 'I know.'

'Do you want to talk about it yet?'

'No, I don't.' The words were sharp, harsh and meant to stop the conversation. The very last thing he ever wanted to talk about was Afghanistan. Just the thought made his palms begin to sweat and he rubbed them down his jeans as he felt his whole body begin to tremble. He wanted to close his eyes, but couldn't. On some nights there was no sleep at all, some nights he'd sleep for an hour or two, but then the nightmares would begin. Every sudden noise reminded him of the explosion, every beach reminded him of the desert and every woman reminded him of Karen. Everything that had happened played on his mind. One minute he'd been part of an elite group, the next he was flying home: inadequate, alone and uncertain of his future.

The only thing that he had ever been certain of in his life

had been his father and his home, the gatehouse at Wrea Head Hall. The whole estate had drawn him in, surrounded him with the safety blanket that he liked and needed. He looked up at the hall and the grounds that surrounded it. It was beautiful.

He walked away from where Morris was perched. He walked over to the fence and made his way beyond the stables, sitting down on the grass and out of view. He allowed himself to glance back at the hall again, to the window where Madeleine had been standing, but she was no longer there.

He stared into the distance and took long, deep breaths. It was the only way he could rest, the only way the flashbacks would stay away.

A noise in the grounds attracted his attention and he looked across to see Madeleine as she walked towards the trees. With her was a young girl and a spaniel, who ran back and forth at a hundred miles an hour.

Ignoring them, he looked back at the gatehouse. It was his home, where his father had lived before him. A place so precious to him that he had to keep it at all costs, because one day, when he was well enough, he'd bring his father back here to live.

Bandit thought of how his father's eyes would light up each time the gatehouse was mentioned and how he could recall the past, the history and the gatehouse's connection with Wrea Head Hall.

Bandit smiled as he thought of what his father had said during his last visit. 'I liked the lady. I'd go through the tunnels each Sunday for tea.'

He shook his head. His father certainly had a good imagination, or did he? Could the tunnels that he spoke of really exist? Could he have really gone through them to visit the hall? And if he had, why would he have gone every Sunday for tea? The thought of a secret tunnel had intrigued him for years, but he'd never found any evidence of them existing. It was as though every time the name of the house was mentioned it sparked a memory, and his father would repeat the same things over and over. The words were always about the gatehouse, about a lady, the tunnels and about the hall. Bandit knew that somewhere deep within his father's mind were many memories that were locked away and the truth may be lost forever, but the house was still there and so was its history. All he had to do was help his father unlock the memories that were trapped within his mind and hopefully, by doing so, bring his father back to the present.

Chapter Ten

'Buddy, come back!' Madeleine shouted for what seemed like the hundredth time that afternoon as she ambled her way through the acres of woodland that circled the house. Poppy ran ahead with the over energetic puppy, who continually doubled back to where she stood.

Madeleine stopped for a moment to look up at the beauty of the trees. Sunlight cascaded down between the bare branches like Christmas tree lights, twinkling between its many shades of ochre and gold. Not one tree was the same shade and each one took on its own identity as it blew in the breeze. Each had a life and personality of its own that appeared to be fading with the end of the year. Her hand reached out to touch a tree that stood all alone.

'Poppy, come look at this tree,' she shouted as she stroked the old craggy tree that stood in a small clearing of the woods. Its trunk and branches twisted and turned in every direction. Its search for sunlight apparent as it reached high up into the sky. 'We could bring paper and wax crayons. Do bark rubbings,' she suggested as Poppy's eyes opened up like saucers making Madeleine spin around on the spot.

'Can I help with the bark rubbings?' Bandit questioned. He was leaning against a tree behind them and she noticed that his eyes seemed to dance with amusement at the knowledge that he'd startled her.

'Come here, little guy,' Bandit said as Buddy ran up to him, yapping, barking and wagging his tail. His whole body bent in two as his tail whipped from side to side before he rolled onto his back, waiting to be fussed. Coming down to his level, Bandit knelt on the floor and began rubbing the pup's belly until his back leg appeared to scratch frantically in mid-air. 'Aren't you just beautiful?'

'Where the hell did you come from?' Maddie snapped at Bandit as Poppy ran towards her, leaping into her arms.

'Sorry, I thought you knew that I work here.'

Madeleine shook her head in annoyance. She watched as Buddy lovingly curled up by Bandit's feet. 'You, young man, are supposed to be a guard dog. Not a friend to all.'

She didn't know why she was so aggravated by Bandit's surprise appearance; she just knew that she was. She began to look him up and down. Her eyes started at his feet and slowly worked their way up to his arms, until she finally stared at his unwashed and unshaven face.

'Poppy, say hello to Mr Bandit,' she told the child who was still clinging onto her for life itself, her head buried in the crook of Madeleine's neck. 'Hey, don't be rude. Say hello.' Eventually, after much prodding, Poppy turned her head and sheepishly stared.

'Mummy,' she tentatively whispered and slowly pointed to where Bandit stood. Maddie held her breath in anticipation of what Poppy might say. 'That man ... Mummy ... that Mr Bang'it man has a brush, right there, right under his nose.'

Bandit smiled and put Buddy down. 'I guess I do need a shave,' he said as he lifted his fingers to his face, rubbing his beard with his hand.

Madeleine was embarrassed and nervously began to laugh. 'Oh my goodness. I'm so sorry, you never know what they'll come out with next,' she tried to apologise, but knew that Poppy was right. He did have a brush under his nose and Madeleine couldn't help but wonder what a good-looking man he'd be, if he'd only have a shave.

She put Poppy down on the ground and watched as she immediately set off with Buddy running through the trees, showing no embarrassment or interest in the man she'd just insulted. Madeleine watched as Poppy picked up newly fallen autumn leaves that covered the ground and threw them up in the air, while a frantic Buddy jumped up and down trying to catch them in his mouth. A shallow stream came into view and Poppy scampered towards it, mischievously stepping in and out as the water trickled past.

'Poppy, stay away from the water!' Madeleine shouted just a little too late as Poppy sat down in the shallow stream. The shock of the cold water made her scream. 'Poppy, get up. Silly girl, now you're all wet and it's cold. Come on, we'd better get you home before the sharks jump out of the water and get you.'

Poppy looked inquisitively back towards the shallow water and then straight at Bandit. 'What's a shark, Mr Bang'it man?'

Bandit shrugged his shoulders. 'It's like a big fish,' he replied as he picked up a stick and threw it for Buddy to chase.

'Bandit … is that really your name? I'm sorry, you did tell me your real name last night. Did you say you were called Christopher?' Madeleine questioned. 'Which do you prefer, what do I call you?'

'Bandit's fine.' He glanced up to where she now leaned against a tree, a wet Poppy now held tightly in her arms.

'What sort of a name is that?' she asked, genuinely curious.

'I was a marine; it was a nickname.' He pulled up the arm of his shirt and pointed to a tattoo of a crowned lion clearly imprinted on his right shoulder. 'My surname's Lawless, a lawless man is a bandit. Do you get it?'

Madeleine understood. 'Okay. So, it's just a play on words, is it, Mr Lawless?'

'It's Bandit. The only person still called Mr Lawless is my father.'

She felt awkward and placed Poppy back down on the floor. 'We'd best get back to the house.'

Bandit looked up at the sky. 'Must be around four o'clock. Nomsa should have cake and tea ready in the kitchen by now. I'm sure that knowing you've arrived she'd have made extra.' The words were directed at Poppy, whose ears immediately pricked up at the mention of cake.

Poppy smiled. 'Cake, Mr Bang'it. I like cake,' she shouted as once again she ran through the trees with Buddy. 'Come on, Mr Bang'it man. Do you know how to play hide and seek?'

Madeleine watched as Poppy suddenly weaved from side to side and ran back down the path, through the trees and towards the house with Buddy close behind her as she began looking for a suitable hiding place.

Bandit looked at Madeleine for approval and only when she nodded did he begin to look around the trees where Poppy had headed. 'Is Poppy up this tree?' he shouted as he looked up the tallest tree. 'Or maybe, Mummy, maybe Poppy is under this leaf?' He picked up a small leaf and turned it over to show Madeleine beneath, whilst a hiding Poppy giggled loudly in the distance. 'Oh, I know,' he announced. 'I bet she's in the greenhouse.'

'Noooooo, she's not in there,' shouted Poppy from where she hid.

'Oh, okay, she must be under the bridge.'

'Noooooo, she isn't under the bridge,' Poppy's voice echoed and then a moment's silence was quickly followed by, 'Mr Bang'it man. What's a greenhouse?'

The house came into view, the game of hide and seek quickly forgotten. What was also gone was the frightened child that Poppy had become whenever Liam had been near, the child who'd refused to play games, who'd hidden and stayed quiet, and it occurred to Madeleine just how terrified Poppy really must have been.

'Look, Poppy, that's a greenhouse,' Madeleine pointed to the rickety old building that she'd noticed earlier that day.

'But it's not green,' she shouted, making both Madeleine and Bandit laugh.

'No, Poppy. The greenhouse isn't green. It's a little house where green plants and green bushes go to grow. Do you know the people who lived here long ago were called the

Victorians; they used to call it a glasshouse. Kind of makes more sense to me. As you say, it's not green, is it?' Bandit tried to explain but gave up as he caught Madeleine's eye.

'Look, Mummy, it's where the plants come to live.'

'I don't think many plants have lived there for quite a while,' Madeleine said as Poppy suddenly rushed in through the door.

'Nooooo!' Bandit shouted and, without a thought for himself, ran into the greenhouse behind Poppy. His hand shot out, caught a piece of glass that suddenly fell from the roof and scooped Poppy up by the waist. There was a crash, a bang and a flash of light and for just a moment, he was back in Afghanistan, moving quickly, desperately trying to save lives. Crimson blood immediately covered his hand, but he didn't care. Poppy was safe.

'I've got you.' He pulled his shirt over his head and wrapped it around his wounded hand and began to inhale deeply. 'Oh, Poppy. You should stay where your mummy is sweetheart. The dangers ... there are so many dangers.'

His whole body began to shake uncontrollably. Sweat poured from his temple and lights flashed behind his eyes.

'Here, Poppy, go to your mummy,' he whispered gently as he tried to push the child away from him and towards Madeleine. But Poppy didn't want to go.

'Noooooo, Mummy, I want Mr Bang'it man!' Poppy screamed as she scrambled back to where Bandit sat, wound her arms tightly around his neck and snuggled her face into his chest.

Bandit looked apologetically at Madeleine. 'I'm sorry. Is ... this ... is this okay?' he mouthed towards Madeleine as he held his hands away from the child until Madeleine nodded.

'You're safe now. I won't ever let the greenhouse hurt you again, I promise. Bandit's going to get rid of the nasty greenhouse for you,' he whispered with gentle, comforting words as he rocked and cradled the crying child in his arms. He inched his way to a sitting position on the grass beside where Madeleine had collapsed to the floor and was crying, a shocked and frightened Poppy still wrapped tightly around him.

He closed his eyes. Afghanistan had been back. The visions that he'd tried so hard to keep away had fired around in his mind, like fireworks on Bonfire Night. He'd immediately begun seeing the explosions and the carnage. There had been men, women and children killed; his friends, his colleagues, Karen.

He shook his head, first gently, then more vigorously to rid himself of the images that flashed continually through his mind.

He opened his eyes wide and gulped in the fresh air. This was not Afghanistan and the realisation hit him, but the dangers here were just as real. He'd watched one too many people get hurt in the past and he fully intended to keep his promise to Poppy that she would not be the next.

Chapter Eleven

'I swear, Jess. He just ran in, caught the glass as it dropped, slashed his hand in the process and dragged Poppy out. I couldn't believe it,' Madeleine whispered holding her hand around the phone as she stood to one side of the hotel reception and smiled at guests as they walked past the open stone and wood window frame, which looked out into the hallway. It was through this frame that the guests would collect their keys, pay their bills and request extras for their rooms. It was an extension to the original coach house where a butler's window could still be seen, indicating the place where the original house had ended and the new wing had begun.

Two guests walked out from a door next to reception and Madeleine watched as the lady tapped away, texting on her phone.

'Good evening, Mr and Mrs Woolass. Thank you,' she said as she lowered the phone from her mouth, took their room key and hung it on the rack. 'Enjoy your meal.'

She waited for just a moment, ensuring the guests had left before returning to the call. 'Jess. Are you still there?'

'Yeah, I'm here. I'm eating Hobnobs and thinking about your Rambo man.'

Madeleine giggled at Jess's statement as another middle-aged couple walked in through the front door, waved and took a left towards the bar. Madeleine had offered to look after reception for an hour between the day staff leaving and the night staff coming in. Her father would normally work then but had set off early that morning on a mission to look at a reproduction bed that he wanted to buy as soon as he'd heard about the sale. Beds of that quality didn't stay on the market long, he'd told her, and he'd known the moment he saw it on the Internet that it would be a perfect fit for one of the newly refurbished rooms. Each room had been decorated in the style of Victorian gothic revival and beautifully recreated wallpapers and bathrooms had been used in them all.

At this time of the evening, the hotel was normally quiet. Some guests sat in the bar, or by the fire. But most would be still in their rooms, watching TV, napping, changing and getting ready for their evening ahead.

Poppy had already taken a shine to Nomsa and had happily trotted behind her to the kitchen for tea.

'He's not Rambo. He's rough, ready and just a little bit bloody annoying, if you know what I mean.'

'Mmmmm, that makes him sound even more intriguing.'

Madeleine stared up into the air. She wanted to describe Bandit. Wanted to explain to Jess how he was, and what he looked like, but couldn't find the words.

'Ohhhhhh, how can I describe him? Err.' She tipped her head from side to side. 'He needs a bit of a tidy up, I guess, bit of a haircut, a shave and all that. He looks a bit like Brad Pitt in that movie we watched last New Year's Eve, what was it called?'

'God, Maddie. I don't know. Which one was Brad Pitt?'

'You know, the one where they live in the wilderness. The one with that *Silence of the Lambs* man in it ... Oh ... Oh ... I know, *Legends of the Fall*.'

Jess went quiet.

'Do you remember who I mean?'

'Give me a minute, I'm googling him.' Madeleine could hear a tapping sound at the end of the phone followed by, 'Ohhhhhh, if that's how he looks, I'm definitely coming over.'

Madeleine sat down at the desk and began to panic as she watched three new emails drop into the inbox. 'Jess, I have enquiries on the email. Do you think I have to deal with them, or do you think Ann will sort them all out when she arrives?'

'So, you like him then?' Jess asked, totally ignoring her question and bringing her thoughts back to Bandit.

'No, yes, oh I don't know. He's really annoying.'

'Wow. Annoying or not, if you don't like him, I could always take him for a turn.'

'*Jess*,' Madeleine squealed. 'Didn't I bring you up with any etiquette at all? You don't take men for a turn.'

She smiled; she had missed Jess. They had always been close, but the whole incident with Liam had brought them even closer and she was determined that they wouldn't leave it months before they saw each other again.

'Oh, Jess, I'd love to see you,' she said, knowing that Jess visiting Wrea Head Hall might not go down well with her father.

Madeleine watched as a female guest excitedly ran down the stairs, crashing straight into a young waiter walking through the hall. The contents of his silver tray almost flew out of his hands, making him stop abruptly in his tracks.

'For God's sake, watch where you are going,' the woman rudely bellowed as she threw back her shoulders and glanced back at her boyfriend, smirking in his direction.

'I'm so sorry, Miss Woods.' The collision hadn't been his fault, but the young man who Madeleine's father had introduced to her as Jack apologised politely. He waited for them to pass, before continuing on his way to deliver the drinks. It was obvious to Madeleine that he'd been trained in hospitality. He knew how to smile in all the right places and had handled the situation perfectly. He hadn't deserved to be spoken to like that, yet Madeleine knew there was nothing she could do.

She returned to her phone call with Jess. 'Are you still there?'

'What on earth was that?'

'Oh, Jess, it was nothing. The customer is always right and all that. Look, I'd better go.' She looked towards the kitchen where Poppy was most probably refusing to eat. They'd only been here a few days and already Poppy had bent Nomsa around her little finger, getting her to make her exactly what food she required. Which, in Poppy's world, meant chocolate spread on bread or chocolate spread on just about anything else.

Madeleine loved speaking to Jess, but was also aware that she couldn't expect Nomsa to babysit Poppy for much longer, even though her father had made it very clear that Poppy should be allowed to enjoy the hotel. Nomsa had her own job to do and at this time of night, she really should be assisting chef with preparations for the evening meal.

'Okay, honey, take care. I'll speak to you soon. Love you.'

'Love you too, Jess.'

She hung up the phone and turned as Jack walked back into reception. The telephone immediately sprang back into life and without thought, he answered it, took a booking and then made his way back to the dining room where he began to seat couples for dinner. He seemed to be everywhere, all at once. There didn't seem to be a job that he didn't do and Madeleine watched as he chatted easily to the guests who were waiting to be served. It was the way that she'd need to be with guests too and she hoped that in time she could do it just as well as Jack did.

When Ann arrived, Madeleine excused herself, walked through the back corridor and into the kitchen, where Poppy sat quite happily eating a bowl of strawberries and ice cream at the kitchen table. Nomsa sat at one side of her and Bandit sat on the other.

Madeleine stopped in her tracks, watching her daughter who appeared not only to be happily feeding herself the strawberries, but also sharing them. She offered her new friend, Bandit, the spoon. He laughed, shook his head and pushed the bowl back to her.

'Let's see how many you can eat. Your mummy's going to be really amazed if you eat them all up,' Madeleine heard him say as Nomsa placed a second bowl of strawberries on the table before him.

'There you go, Bandit, some strawberries for you too. Let's see which one of you eats them all up first,' Nomsa sang out as Madeleine watched both Poppy and Bandit tuck into the strawberries, both giggling and dribbling ice cream down their chins, yet neither seemed to mind.

Bandit had been right. Madeleine was amazed. Not only was she amazed, she was completely astonished to see the child eating at all. Not just eating, she was actually having fun while she was doing it.

'Ohhhhhh, look at you two. Can I have some?' Madeleine asked as she sat down beside Bandit.

'Nope,' Poppy said with a giggle. 'You have to eat all your dinner first. Nomsa said.'

Madeleine poked her daughter and then began fidgeting with the salt and pepper pot which stood central to the table. She was acutely aware of the kitchen staff who were busy chopping fresh food ready for the evening service and felt as though they were intruding on a normally well run kitchen.

'Here you go, my lady, there's your dinner,' Nomsa's rhythmic Caribbean voice sang as she placed a plate on the table before Madeleine. She looked between her and Bandit, raised her eyebrows, tapped her temple with a finger and then nodded with a knowing look.

Madeleine smiled, she liked Nomsa already. She was short, rotund and wore a permanent smile. She seemed to embrace life, enjoying everything she was doing and what's more she had a way about her that made you listen when she spoke. Poppy had loved her the moment she'd set eyes on her and for a child who barely ate, she'd already eaten more in the last few days than she would normally have done in a week.

Nomsa was a darker version of Jess, yet almost old enough to be their mother, and Madeleine guessed that she'd be somewhere around forty years old.

'Thanks, Nomsa.' Madeleine smiled as she happily tucked into the perfectly presented steak.

'Mummy, Mister Bang'it said he'll show us the ha-ha,' Poppy proudly announced as her new friend shrugged his shoulders in a silent apology. His eyes caught Maddie's and held them for just a moment too long, making her nervously glance back down at the steak.

'I would have asked,' he sheepishly explained. 'It's only on the front lawn. I thought you might like to see it too.'

Madeleine was hungry and pushed another piece of the steak in her mouth.

'I'll tell you what, young Madeleine, if it's okay with you I'll go with them, just while you finish your dinner?' Nomsa said as she picked Poppy up from the bench and headed for the back door. 'It is just on the front lawn. You can easily see us from the house.'

Maddie nodded and continued to eat her dinner as the others went outside. She felt comfortable that Nomsa was with Poppy and after she'd finished eating, she used the opportunity to walk around and study the hotel. The wood panelled dining room was beginning to fill up with couples; some chatted happily, and others sat silently. The main courses were just starting to go out. Each meal was perfectly plated, individually created. The head chef, Bernie, had worked wonders with the pheasant, duck and rabbit, all of which Bandit had brought back for him fresh from the hunt that morning.

'Each dish is based on the food that would have been eaten here in the late eighteen hundreds,' Nomsa had explained earlier. 'It was the time when the house was first built. The family had lived in London for most of the week, only travelling to Wrea Head on weekends and holidays.'

'Some weekend retreat,' Madeleine had thought as she looked everywhere for pictures that might show her who the family had been. She was amazed that the whole house had retained all of its original character. Its history screamed from every wall and she felt sure that someone would have saved photographs from the past. Surely the guests would be interested in its history too, of seeing the family, of how they'd looked and lived. She made her way to stand by the window in the grand hall. She recognised it as the dark wood panelled room where, just a few nights before, she'd spied guests drinking champagne through the windowpanes. Its huge inglenook fireplace stood to her left, its fire already lit and where the logs already crackled and spat as flames shot up the chimney, warm and welcoming, with a luminosity that lit the whole room.

Beyond the grand hall was a bar. It was painted grey and had a bright white frieze around the top of the room. This was where most of the guests seemed to congregate. Madeleine walked towards the door and then changed her mind and headed instead to the library next door, where she found a room surrounded with old mahogany bookcases and a second open fire. There were two huge dark blue Chesterfield settees, which stood opposite each other and gave a warmth to the room.

'Can I get you a drink, Mrs Frost?' Jack's voice made her jump as she looked towards the adjoining door that stood between the library and the bar.

'Thank you, Jack. Do you think Father would mind if I had a small glass of wine?'

'I'm sure he wouldn't mind at all. I'll see to it immediately. Would you like red, or white?'

'Oh, red if that's okay?'

She walked along the bookshelves, digging through the old, dusty books that lined the shelves. There was every classic that she could think of. Everything from *Gulliver's Travels* through to *Pride and Prejudice*. All were beautifully leather bound and perfectly preserved and Madeleine couldn't resist pulling one after the other off the shelf. Opening each one in turn, she flicked through the pages breathing in their scent.

'Mummy,' Poppy's voice shouted from outside. 'Mummy, come look at the ha-ha. I can see the sheep.'

Madeleine replaced the book back on its shelf and walked outside to where an excited three-year-old ran towards her. She grabbed hold of Madeleine's hand and dragged her across the lawn to where the grass suddenly dropped off and down to the meadow below. A four-foot dry stone wall supported the upper lawn, creating an optical illusion that made it look as though the sheep could easily trot right up to the house. Of course, the wall stopped them and Poppy thought it very clever that she could lie on her belly, overhanging the wall and watch the sheep so closely, without them being able to chase her.

Nomsa excused herself and went back to the kitchen, just as Jack appeared behind her. He'd walked down the lawn without being heard and had waited patiently for her to turn around and accept one of the three drinks that were on his tray.

'For Mrs Frost, a red wine,' he politely said as he passed her the drink. 'For the little lady, milk and a chocolate cookie that Nomsa baked for her earlier.' Jack knelt down and allowed Poppy to help herself to the cookie and Madeleine watched as Poppy threw her arms around Jack's neck and gave him a huge thank you hug.

'Thank you, Jack.' Madeleine turned to where Poppy now sat on the grass, happily munching. 'Wow, Poppy. Did Nomsa make you a lovely biscuit?' she asked as Poppy pushed the last piece into her mouth.

'It's all gone, Mummy. Look!' Poppy had cheeks that looked like a hamster, but held out her empty hands to prove a point.

'Your usual, Mr Lawless, sir.' Jack held the tray out to Bandit. A glass of iced water remained and Bandit gladly took it from the tray and drank it down in one.

Chapter Twelve

Poppy was fast asleep, surrounded by piles of teddy bears, along with her large V-shape pillow which went everywhere with her. Her thumb was firmly in her mouth and her soft blonde curls lay around her face. She was so beautiful, so perfect and Maddie felt so guilty for having disrupted her life once again, albeit Poppy seemed to have settled in at Wrea Head Hall far more quickly than she had herself. Even Buddy seemed quite happy in his new surroundings and didn't seem to mind his kennel at all.

Picking up a portable baby monitor, Madeleine took one last look at Poppy before walking out of the room and down a narrow, oak staircase that led down to the back of the hotel. She thought of the servants' staircase that had been in Liam's house. She'd never been allowed to see it and wondered if it had looked anything like this one, with its bare floorboards and unpainted walls. Liam had kept the door to the staircase locked. He'd said that the stairs had woodworm, that they were dangerous and that he'd been worried that she or Poppy would have an accident on them.

Her hand now stroked the wooden banister that was separated into three lengths, each piece made from different wood, yet it looked uncannily new compared to the rest of the decor, making her wonder if it had been a health and safety addition after the house had been turned into a hotel. Surely if it had been there when the house had been built it would have been made of the same wood and rubbed smooth with the constant use of the servants as they'd run up and down to look after the family, who, of course, would have only used the grand staircase that led down into the lounge. There was a long, upholstered window seat halfway up the grand staircase on the landing and Madeleine could imagine that it would have been the perfect place for the women of the house to sit, sew and admire the grounds.

'You okay, dear?' her father asked as she reached the bottom of the stairs and entered the office. Madeleine nodded, yet continued to stare up the staircase as though waiting for the ghosts of the past to follow her down. Turning her attention back to her father, she closed the door and leaned forward to kiss him on the cheek.

'How was the shopping trip? Did you find a new bed?'

'Yes, yes, I did. It arrives a week on Friday.' He smiled. 'Reproduction Victorian beds are so difficult to come by. The one I've found is beautiful and very, very rare. I can't wait for you to see it.'

'Sounds amazing. Do you have any pictures?'

He looked pleased and enthusiastic with his purchase. He picked his phone up and began to flick through the photos showing Madeleine what he'd bought.

'It's beautiful. Look at the carvings. You're going to love it. I thought it would go in room four when it's finished. That room is huge and I'm led to believe that it used to be the room that Mr Ennis slept in. So, it's only fitting that we should give it the best bed that I could find.'

'Mr Ennis? Who's he? Is he the man who built the house?'

'No, the house was built in 1881. Mr Ennis bought it from the original owners who sold in 1928. The elderly daughter of the house inherited it after his death. I'm led to believe that she was a spinster and quite a recluse. Josie and I bought it from her in 2007, just after we were married.'

Madeleine noticed that he'd gone thoughtful and quiet. He was staring into space and she wondered if he was thinking of Josie, of the day they bought the house, or of the day they'd stayed here for the very first time.

'The new bed will look wonderful. I can't wait to see it.'

He didn't reply. Just continued to stare at nothing.

'Dad, what happened to Josie?' Maddie asked eventually.

Even though she hadn't known her, she really wanted to know what had happened and wished she'd asked the question on the first night she'd been here.

He looked down and away before answering.

'Cancer.' His eyes filled with tears. 'I loved her so much, Maddie. We'd been together for nine years, nine very happy years. I honestly thought that we'd spend the rest of our lives together, but then without warning she died.'

'Oh, how sad. It must have been awful for you,' she said and then thought of Poppy. What would happen to Poppy if it had been her? She shuddered and looked away.

'It was so sudden. She was diagnosed last Christmas and within just three weeks of diagnosis, she was gone.'

There was a knock on the door. 'Sorry to bother you, Mr Pocklington, sir, but Mr and Mrs Thompson would like to speak with you,' Jack said, bowing his head as he stood waiting for a response.

'I'll be right there.' Morris Pocklington looked apologetically at his daughter. 'I have to go.'

'Don't worry. I know you have a job to do.' Madeleine stood up just as the baby monitor that she held in her hand made a soft noise and she lifted it to her ear and listened. 'Look, I'd better get back anyhow.' She held the monitor up for him to see. 'I've left Poppy. She's fast asleep, but it's all still a bit new to her.'

She was sorry to cut the conversation short. The past year had obviously been hard on her father and she wished there were something she could do to help him get over the torment that he'd obviously gone through after Josie's death. What's more, she needed to understand him and that meant understanding all the parts of his life that she'd missed.

She kissed him gently on the cheek, and then ran back up the stairs to her room.

Chapter Thirteen

Madeleine pushed her feet into the soft white slippers as she simultaneously slipped into her over-washed white dressing gown. She headed for the bathroom, where she ran her finger across the numerous bottles of bubble bath, and carefully selected a tall bottle of aqua-green liquid. She poured an ample amount into the already steaming water and swished it around with her fingers allowing the bubbles to form and the smell of aloe to fill the room.

Walking back into the bedroom, she spied the outline of her daughter snuggled beneath both a pile of teddy bears and a pink Peppa Pig quilt. She pulled the door closed as the soft, gentle snores filled her room and gave Madeleine the reassurance that Poppy would sleep for hours.

Collecting a towel from the cupboard, she returned to the bathroom and slipped into the water, allowing her body to sink deep beneath the bubbles where the warmth enveloped her as she submerged both her hair and her body. Only her eyes, nose and mouth remained above the water. And for the first time since she'd arrived at the hall she realised that she felt totally settled and content.

A flash lit up the room and then a sudden noise vibrated through the air. It was so loud it made her sit up, wondering what the noise was and where it had come from. She jumped from the water to go to Poppy and ran into her room, where she immediately realised that her baby hadn't moved. Poppy's tiny body remained curled up in a ball and she'd slept soundly through the noise.

Madeleine stood for a moment, listening. Then somewhere in the distance, a pipe clanked and Madeleine grabbed a towel, suddenly realising that she was standing in the middle of the room naked and dripping bubbles and water all over the carpet.

Another flash lit up the room and she realised that it was lightning, followed by a clap of thunder; it was this that had disturbed her bath and she relaxed slightly as she pulled at the towel and quickly began to dry herself.

Madeleine switched off the light and opened the curtains in order to watch the storm. It was something she'd always done and something her mother had done before her. The rain came down in torrents, fast and furious, with water bouncing up from the ground. Flashes of lightning brightened the sky like floodlights at a football match and every part of the garden was lit up, only to fall into darkness just a few seconds later.

Madeleine's eyes darted to the greenhouse. Something had attracted her attention. She saw a movement and waited for the sky to once again explode with light before she could look again. Something or someone was out there, but she couldn't quite make out what it had been as the darkness once again blanketed the garden.

She stared intently into the night.

'Come on, come on, one more flash,' she whispered.

Bandit stared up at the greenhouse, wiped his hair from his face and forcibly pushed at a stubborn piece of wood which had previously refused to move. He took a deep breath as the wind and rain made it difficult for him to see. He needed more light but it had faded fast and the storm hadn't helped as deep, dark clouds hovered above him. Pulling his hood up and over his head he carried on tearing one sheet of glass after the other out of the greenhouse frame. He struggled with his gloves: they were old and torn and made it difficult for him to grip. The glass slipped in his hold and fell from his fingers. It crashed to the floor, making him curse before pulling the gloves off and dropping them on the wall. His damaged hand was loosely bandaged, painful and, due to the constant movement, still oozing blood. He felt around in his pocket and pulled out an old piece of tissue, which he pushed beneath the loose, dirty bandage in an attempt to stem the bleed.

He began counting the sections of the wooden structure. Only the four sections closest to him needed replacing. The rest of the greenhouse was dry; all other panels intact and sound. They could easily be repaired in situ and had been protected by the brick wall that stood behind it.

'For heaven's sake, Bandit. What the hell do you think you are doing?' Madeleine screamed through the noise of the storm, making him jump.

Their eyes locked. The weather was ferocious and dangerous to be out in, but for some reason he was pleased to see her. He stood for a moment thinking of what to say and stared at the big doe eyes that looked back at him. There was something about her that made him want to spend time with her, want to find out more about her, but tonight in this weather should not be the night.

'Go back to the house. You'll catch your death of cold,' he shouted half-heartedly, hoping that she'd refuse and want to stay. Not many women would want to be out in this weather and neither would most men, but tonight he was on a mission. Tonight, he was determined to keep his promise to Poppy and to make the greenhouse safe.

'I will not. I saw you from the window,' she shouted as another crash of thunder echoed through the sky. She ducked and threw her arms above her head as though waiting for something to hit her. 'What the hell are you doing, working in the middle of a storm? Surely my father doesn't pay you enough to do this?'

'I don't do this for the money. I do this because it's not safe. I promised Poppy that it'd never hurt her again, and it won't,' he shouted back, barely able to hear the sound of his own voice. 'Please. Go back inside, you're soaked.'

He averted his eyes. Madeleine's shoulder length blonde hair was already drenched, rivulets of water ran down her face and her nylon top was fast clinging to her body, the shape of her figure becoming more and more apparent.

'Can't this wait till morning? You know, we could do this tomorrow, together?' She held up her arms and pointed to the sky wondering if he'd noticed the torrential weather, or had his training in the marines stopped him from feeling the wet and the cold? She noticed the cheeky grin he gave her and looked down, suddenly realising that her T-shirt was now completely soaked from the rain. It was now totally see through and she turned her back to him, to quickly zip up her coat and hide her breasts.

Bandit frowned. 'Where's Poppy? You haven't left her on her own, have you?'

'No, of course I haven't. I had two choices, lock her in a cupboard or bring her out to play in a thunderstorm.'

Bandit stared at her. 'Seriously, why would you do that?'

'Hey, do you really think I would do that? I gave Nomsa the baby monitor. She's promised to listen out for her between jobs, not that Poppy will wake up. Once she's asleep, waking her is like waking the dead.' Madeleine laughed as she stood back, stepped on an uneven slab and wobbled precariously on the spot.

Bandit's hand grabbed hold of her arm. 'Steady. Are you okay?'

She nodded, stepped backwards and turned away, looking back at the house.

The windows shone light towards her, creating small spot lit areas around the garden. But one by one, the lights were slowly being turned off as guests retired for the night, totally unaware of what was happening in the garden outside their windows.

Madeleine turned her attention to the job in hand. 'Do you have night vision or something?' she asked in an attempt to break the tension. She squinted in the darkness. ''Cos, if you haven't noticed, it happens to be dark and, what's more, there's a storm raging above your head.'

She could tell by his mannerisms that he was determined to carry on; he'd already turned and had begun pulling at the panes of glass and she knew that he was strong-minded and the work would get done, storm or no storm. Looking for cover, she marched to the rear of the greenhouse, just as the rain began to ease.

'Okay. Tell me the plan. What are we doing and where do I start?' Madeleine watched his reaction as she spoke. His whole body had come to a complete stop. He simply stood and stared at her for what seemed an eternity. The rain now fell in gentle drizzles from the sky. It was a moment of reflection, a moment of tranquillity amongst the carnage and a moment when Bandit seemed at peace with the task.

Walking around the greenhouse had become difficult and, after her previous wobble, Madeleine found herself balancing on an old discarded piece of wood to avoid the mud beneath her feet, which was now a quagmire of sludge along with years of weeds that had grown up and in between the slabs.

After what seemed an age Bandit moved towards her, nervously tugging at the blood soaked bandage that hung from the hand that he held out to where she stood.

'It's falling off, could you?' He moved nervously from one foot to the other.

'Of course, here, let me look at that for you,' she said as she pulled him to the rear of the greenhouse and tenderly turned his hand over, trying to see what she was dealing with. They stood, sheltered from the rain amongst the mud, weeds and concrete slabs. Beside them bags of stored wood and wooden crates full of flowerpots were pushed under an old rotting shelf, along with old tins of paint, empty jars and plastic trays.

She pulled the bandage off his hand. There was just enough light from the house to show her the wound beneath. She gasped; the cut looked sore, open and raw. 'You need to get this looked at. Let me get Jack to take you to the hospital.'

'No chance. It's fine. I have to work. I made a promise.' He shrugged her off and began walking back to the door.

'Oh, no, you don't. At least let me dress that for you.' Madeleine pulled a clean handkerchief from her pocket and used it to press against the wound whilst struggling to re-wind the bandage in the darkness.

'Are you always this bossy?' He grinned. 'And who the hell carries a handkerchief in their pocket these days?' He pulled a face as he kept his hand held out towards her.

'A mother, that's who. Mothers always carry handkerchiefs, baby wipes and pockets full of everything else a child tends to need. I probably have a dummy in here somewhere,' she threw back in retort as she patted her pocket and placed the bandage on her knee. 'Do you have kids?' She had no idea why she'd asked, but the question had sprung into her mind and somehow dropped out of her mouth.

'No, no kids. I guess I never met the right woman.' He looked anxiously up at the sky and once again the rain began to drum softly on what was left of the greenhouse roof. 'But, saying that, my father was forty-four when I was born, so you never know, God willing, maybe there's time.'

'Do you know what, I'm so sorry, I shouldn't have asked you that, should I? It was none of my business and I really didn't mean to intrude.'

'It's fine. I do want kids. So, you never know, maybe one day.' He tried to smile and put her back at ease as she struggled to rearrange the bandage in the dark.

'I do wish I had a new dressing. This one's a bit dirty and the wound looks nasty,' she whispered as the last of the bandage was reapplied over the handkerchief and secured at the wrist.

'Here.' He picked up the gloves and passed them to her. 'If you're staying, you're going to need these.' He smiled as he picked up a torch and along with the gloves, threw them both in her direction. 'That is, if you still want to help?'

Madeleine looked at the pair of dirty gloves, pulled them on and tried not to think about what may or may not be lurking inside.

'As I pass the glass to you, carefully take it and put it in the wheelbarrow,' Bandit instructed as she saw the first pane of glass being lowered down to her. 'Prop the torch near the barrow, it'll help light up the area for you.'

She balanced the torch on the windowsill and pointed it directly towards where they worked. Carefully taking the first piece of glass from him, she lowered it into the wheelbarrow and then turned to Bandit. She watched and waited as he pulled the next piece from the structure and placed it in her hands. Some pieces were whole, but most were not and each one looked sharp and dangerous. Madeleine dreaded to think what would have happened to Poppy if Bandit hadn't reacted so quickly.

Bandit climbed up a ladder and began pulling at the remainder of the glass. As each piece was pulled from its wooden frame, Madeleine gasped and waited for it to crash to the ground, but when it didn't, she felt a breath of relief leave her body as she mentally counted the ones that remained. The four panels had almost been taken apart as the last light from the house windows went out. Now only the torchlight showed them where to place the glass, whilst perfectly silhouetting Bandit's body as he reached up in the moonlight.

Suddenly, and without warning, the rain once again began to pour. Another flash of lightning lit up the sky, making Madeleine jump and she screamed and slipped all at once. Her feet were there one minute and gone the next and she felt herself falling.

'Throw it,' Bandit screamed as a look of fear and anguish crossed his face.

In a split second, her hands threw the glass and she heard it drop into the wheelbarrow, shattering loudly: just as she fell heavily in the mud. Pain seared through her arms and buttocks, which had cushioned her fall, both now hurt and were stippled with gravel.

Bandit jumped down from the ladder and grabbed her by the shoulders. 'Are you okay? Don't move, let me check you out.'

She saw the words leave his lips as he looked deep into her eyes, searching for her pain. 'Where does it hurt?' he asked as she felt his hands move quickly and expertly over her limbs, checking and searching for signs of trauma, whilst his eyes stayed firmly on hers.

'Just my pride and my backside,' Madeleine replied, 'and I really don't think you want to check that out, do you?'

She pulled herself out of his grip, sat up and grabbed the torch. 'I'm just going to sit over there for a while. Is that okay?' she said as she pointed to a crate at the back of the greenhouse where she would be shielded from the rain.

He helped her to her feet and she walked further into the greenhouse, turned the crate over, sat down and turned her body away from Bandit's gaze, closing her eyes as she did so. Her whole body began to shake as tears cascaded down her face. He couldn't see her cry. She wouldn't allow him to see her cry.

The fall had wounded her pride. Not to mention the throbbing she now felt in her hands, backside and lower back. The glass shattering had frightened her, but Bandit's reaction had frightened her more. The look in his eyes had been deep and cavernous, yet once again she'd noticed the mixture of terror and vulnerability in his eyes that she'd seen there when he'd comforted Poppy.

Bandit seemed so dependable, so very protective, yet it was more than obvious that there was something he feared. What had happened to him to make him terrified of both the past and of the future? She watched him work; he must have a story and, as a writer, it intrigued her.

Madeleine began pulling at boxes and crates that lay under the disused shelves. She needed something to do, to concentrate on to stop her from crying. Her torch flashed in-between the crates and followed a huge spider that ran out from its hiding space, making her throw one of the gloves towards where it ran in the hope that it would change its route and head in the opposite direction. She smirked as she remembered how terrified Liam had been of spiders. Even small ones had made him squeal like a child and he'd jumped on a chair the last time he'd spotted one, leaving her to catch it and throw it outside. She watched the area where the spider had run, ensuring it had gone before pulling out more and more boxes and checking their contents before discarding them and moving onto the next. Most were filled with old gardening equipment, plant pots and chopped up wood. All were covered in years of dirt. Each box moved revealed different contents, all with the same covering of grime.

Most of the pots and trays could probably be thrown away. But some could be used again and Madeleine wondered if she could start a vegetable garden with Poppy.

There was another crash of thunder, making her jump up and she carefully made her way back to where Bandit stood.

'Come on, let's get out of here,' he shouted above the noise of the storm and picked up the wheelbarrow handles, quickly running out of the greenhouse and towards a door.

'Where to? The house?'

'No. Let's shelter in here for a while, it's closer and that storm's coming in worse.'

Bandit opened a door that was buried in the wall behind the greenhouse and pushed Madeleine inside. 'Wait here. I'm going to get rid of the glass.'

Madeleine immediately fumbled with the torch and shone it in through the door. The shelter was a brick room, around fifteen feet square with what looked like an old steam train engine standing in the corner, with a bench to its side. It was surprisingly clean and polished and looked as though it had recently been lit.

'What is this place?' she asked as Bandit returned.

'It's the old boiler room. The engine is a heater for the greenhouse. The original owner used to grow grapes and the boiler kept the grapes warm. He was a part of the rail industry, which meant that he had access to steam trains.' He pointed to the engine. 'I know it's not, but it looks like new. I bet we could get it going if I had some dry wood.'

Madeleine flashed her torch around the shelter. No wood jumped out but the intense and direct light of her torch did catch sight of something under the engine. 'What's that?'

She pointed the torch at what she'd seen and Bandit got down on all fours and then onto his side to look underneath.

'I'm not sure. It looks like a metal box,' he answered. 'It must have been under there for years. It looks as though it's purposely been pushed underneath. I'm surprised it's not scorched.'

'Can you pull it out?' Madeleine asked eagerly as she watched Bandit struggle to move the box. He looked around for a tool and used an old metal bar to manoeuvre the box out.

'It's probably just full of seeds,' he said as he placed it on the floor before her.

'Can you open it?' Madeleine whispered.

He opened the lid easily and then pulled away tissue paper that lay within to reveal a small book. Madeleine held the torch closer and noticed the words 'Emily Ennis' clearly written on the front.

'Oh, my word,' she whispered as she carefully lifted the perfectly intact book from out of the metal tin.

'I think you've just found one of Emily Ennis's diaries,' Bandit said as his fingers carefully turned the paper-thin page to reveal a beautiful script-like handwriting. 'Here, take a look.'

Chapter Fourteen

January 18th, 1942

The house is cold and the weather here in Yorkshire is relentless. The snow is falling and Father has finally agreed to light the huge fire in the parlour, but we need other ways of keeping warm and walk around the house wearing several layers of clothing.

Mary and I both cuddle up in our rooms and sleep together most of the time. It's much warmer this way and even though our mother often tells us that at eighteen we are much too old to sleep together, we treat it like a game and wait until she's asleep before sneaking from one room to the other. One night is spent in my room, the next in Mary's. We've tried to explain the twin thing, but no one understands it but us. Besides, we like to chat to one another and make up ghost stories, just as soon as the lights go out.

I'm worried about Jimmy; he's sixteen now and seems to have reached an age where he's taking an unhealthy interest in the chambermaids. Our father has been heard reprimanding him so many times. But then, I'm not sure that it's all Jimmy's fault. I've seen how the maids linger in the family rooms whenever he is home, especially Molly. Her family are poor and live in the village, whereas Jimmy is a young man with an inheritance who would be a coup for Molly to entrap, especially seeing as he is so young and so easily swayed. Molly seems quite the temptress and just a little too bold and forthright for her own good. I've tried to warn him of the dangers, that the gold-diggers are out there, but he's young and bored and I doubt that he cares, so long as he's getting what he wants. After all, he is a man. I worry where it will all end and some days I pray for the holidays to be over and for Father to send him back to school.

Mary has taken a liking to Benjamin, the new valet. He's much older than her, but rather handsome. He does smile at her sweetly and she seems to enjoy his attentions. I saw her with him in the garden today. He lifted his hand and stroked her cheek and I'm sure that they're in love, but as yet she still hasn't said.

It's now late, yet still Mary hasn't come to my room as we'd planned earlier today, so I fear she's gone to meet him after dark, which upsets me a little. But, if she has gone to meet him, I hope that she is being sensible and isn't taking any risks. Our mother would internally combust if Mary ever announced that she were pregnant.

I walked past Eddie today. My whole heart lifted when he whistled at me and winked. It was his normal sign to meet him at teatime, and even though I know that I shouldn't and that I worry about the others being involved with the staff, Eddie is different and I go to meet him whenever I can, without Father's permission. There would be no point in even trying to get Father to allow it. I've never met anyone quite as mean and I just know that he would never understand that two people from such different backgrounds could actually be friends and if he found out he'd probably go mad.

Eddie and I meet on the staircase, the one that's hidden within the house and leads to a single room beneath the bell tower. Not even the servants know that it's there. Only the immediate family know how to find it and I've taken a risk showing Eddie. It was the only place I could think of where we could meet undisturbed and where Father wouldn't stumble upon us during his evening walk around the house.

I let Eddie in and we both went one by one up the staircase and, after letting ourselves through the panel, we sat on the wooden steps and held hands for at least an hour. We spoke to each other non-stop, until the hourly chiming of the bell tower indicated that it was time for tea. It also got so loud that we ended up running down the stairs laughing, with our hands over our ears, and had to hold our breath at the bottom so that no one heard us giggle. I know it's wrong for us to act like this and if we were found out it would bring disgrace upon me and upon my family, but I wonder if it would be so wrong to take Eddie up to the room beyond the staircase. It'd be much warmer than sitting on the steps, but there's a bed up there and that's what makes me nervous. I'm a little worried that he'd get the wrong idea, even though I doubt that he'd ever take advantage, but I'd be terrified that our being up there in the first place would be seen as an invitation.

Father expects me to marry well. He expects me to marry a solicitor or a doctor or someone of consequence and within the year will be introducing me to every eligible bachelor that he can think of. They'll be invited to dinner at first and if we get along, there would be a reason why he and his parents would come to stay at the house and pretend to be fascinated in what I do. Of course, I'll do my best to be boring and feign an interest in needlepoint, knitting or reading. I wouldn't talk much and I may even pretend to be sick or not to like boys at all. One by one, I expect they'll ask me to marry them. Their parents would expect them to ask, whether they like me or not, and would probably be sat with Father in the library waiting for news.

The thought of being paraded before so many men terrifies me to the core and, if I'm honest, I feel as though I'm trapped in Victorian England, not in 1942. Our whole family acts with such propriety, but then again Father is an important man and I dare not argue. Father wouldn't expect me to question him. Instead, one by one, I'll just have to refuse and find some petty reason for doing so.

However, with Mary and I being twins, it will be a race to see which one of us they can marry off first. I'm sure we'll both be expected to marry before we're twenty-one, just like our mother did and though I'm sure that Mother loves our father now, the last thing I want is a marriage with no room *for sentiment. I just hope and pray that the times change and, if nothing else, I would rather be single than marry someone I don't love.*

I'm sure Eddie would ask me to marry him if he thought that Father would allow it, but he knows not to ask for fear of losing his job. The gatehouse, in which Eddie and his mother live, is tied to the hall and if Eddie didn't work here, he and his mother might lose their home, which means that we wouldn't get to see one another at all.

Madeleine's fingers turned the wafer thin pages of the diary as she sat shivering beside Bandit. They looked at each other in amazement as the diary began to reveal its secrets.

'I can't believe she talks like this in 1942. She sounds as though she were born in eighteen hundred and something,' Bandit said as Madeleine turned to the next page. 'Don't you think?'

Madeleine shook her head. 'I think it's really sad. It must have been awful for her to know that her parents were going to introduce her to all of those men and, what's more, she'd be expected to marry one of them. I mean, what if she didn't like them? She loved Eddie.' Madeleine pouted and flicked over the page, hoping to read some more words that Emily had written, but the words had stopped and in their place were the most beautiful pencil drawings she'd ever seen.

'Wow, Emily must have been quite an accomplished artist, look at these,' she said as the five or six very small pictures came to life before them. Each picture sat alone with a smudged blend of pencil between each to bring them together on the page.

But, it was the drawing central to the page that caught Madeleine's eye. It was of a man dressed in old, torn clothing. His trousers were far too short for his legs, yet he wore a shirt and a waistcoat. He was leaning on a spade that was propped up firmly in the ground, as though taking a break from doing the gardening. His right hand was just about to touch his cap, making Madeleine think that maybe he was about to take it off. It was a natural pose, his eyes looked kind and he smiled towards the place where Emily must have sat drawing him. Maybe she'd asked him to pose that way, or maybe she'd caught an image of Eddie in her memory, a snapshot of his day as he'd stood there working her father's land.

'Do you think that's Eddie?' Madeleine looked up and into Bandit's face, which in the lamplight had softened and she noticed how he gazed in a dream-like fashion at the picture.

Bandit shook his head. 'Who knows.'

Madeleine held the torch up and slightly away from the picture. It looked ghostlike in the shadows and even though the man was smiling, he looked sad.

'At least people are allowed to love who they like nowadays,' Maddie whispered as her finger lightly brushed the image.

Of all the marriages she knew, and of all her married friends, not one of them would have followed the rules of times gone by. Most wouldn't have even been allowed to marry in those days. Yet here they were not so many years later and most were happy, most were completely untraditional and Madeleine couldn't help but think that she was pleased that times had changed.

She stared at the picture and then back at Bandit. There was a resemblance there and it occurred to her that, if it hadn't been drawn over seventy years ago, it could almost have been a picture of him; the eyes were the same shape, the mouth tipped up at one corner in a similar way and the jawline was square and symmetrical. She shook her head and smiled to herself. She hadn't realised until now that she'd taken quite so much notice of Bandit's appearance.

Chapter Fifteen

Madeleine was still damp from the rain and now shivered with the cold after sitting outside in the boiler room for over two hours. She and Bandit had read the first few pages of the diary with interest, looked at the pictures and had talked about how life must have been for Emily and it was only when the torchlight had begun to flicker that they'd closed the pages and made their way back to the house.

She walked through the office and climbed up the back staircase to her bedroom. But as soon as she entered her room she knew that something was different. There was a smell that she couldn't place, a perfume or aftershave, and as she looked around she noticed that the huge pink teddy bear that her father had given Poppy was sitting in the middle of her four-poster bed. She immediately went to check on Poppy through the open bedroom door but then stopped in her tracks, as she distinctly remembered closing Poppy's door before going out to help Bandit. So why was it now open? A look into Poppy's room showed her that her daughter was still fast asleep, tucked up in the middle of her teddy bear mountain and looked as though she hadn't moved. So, who had opened the door and how had the bear got on to her bed?

Madeleine moved to the bed and picked up the bear. It had a blindfold over its eyes made from Madeleine's favourite long satin nightdress. A perfect bow was tied and the bear had been balanced carefully in position. She looked towards the room where her daughter slept. Could Poppy have tied such a perfect bow? Madeleine shook her head, it couldn't be Poppy, could it? She couldn't even tie a knot. But if it hadn't been Poppy, then who?

Tired and disturbed by the night's events, Maddie placed the teddy bear back in Poppy's room and double checked the locks on the door, vowing that in the future, she'd ensure it was locked at all times.

Morris Pocklington poured a glass of whisky, then walked into the lounge and sat down in the blue winged captain's chair, toasting his feet before the wood burning fire and staring into its depths.

'Never waste a log, Jack,' he said as Jack walked out of the bar and through the grand hall towards the kitchen.

'I agree, Mr Pocklington. It would be a shame to do so, wouldn't it? Can I get you anything, sir?' Jack asked in his normal polite manner.

Morris nodded. 'Another whisky, if you will. It's been quite a night.' He finished the dregs of the whisky already in his glass and passed it to Jack.

Jack had worked at the hall almost since the first day that Morris had bought it. He was young, still in his twenties, but had a head on his shoulders of someone much older and so much more mature. Morris liked him and quite early on, due to his hard work and enthusiasm, he'd been earmarked for promotion. When Josie had died, Morris had offered him the post of junior manager, a position he'd been proud to accept and thrived upon. He was the perfect host, good at his job and, more often than not, worked extra hours, going far beyond his duties to ensure that the running of Wrea Head was done to the best of his ability. What's more, he often sat with Morris on a night when the older man felt lonely. Often stayed an extra hour and was always the one that Morris turned to.

'Would you join me, Jack?' Morris asked as he indicated the inglenook seat that stood by the fire. 'Please, pour yourself a drink. It's time to relax a little. Nothing more needs doing.'

Jack paused for a moment, then disappeared into the bar, returning with two glasses of whisky, one considerably larger than the other, which he passed to Morris. He sat on the settee opposite his boss. Both sat in silence, both thoughtful, both enjoying the glow of the fire that created a sense of peace and tranquillity within the grand hall, now empty of guests. It was something to be savoured and they both sipped at their drinks companionably while staring into the fire, watching it until the last of the logs had burnt down and just the embers remained.

Morris finally spoke. 'My life's a mess, Jack. There are so many unanswered questions.'

'Are you thinking of Mrs Pocklington, sir?'

'Every single day, Jack. I miss her so much, but it's not only that.'

Jack looked awkwardly down to the floor, then took a sip of his whisky and nodded. 'I'm sure everything happens for a reason, Mr Pocklington, and at least you have your daughter here now. It must be good to have Mrs Frost back in the fold?'

Morris thought for a moment and nodded in affirmation. He'd often mentioned Madeleine to Jack and had told him how disappointed he'd been when she hadn't attended Josie's funeral. He still felt an overwhelming sadness at how he'd stood alone by the graveside, with no one to call his own family. But that was in the past now, he had to look forward and it was good to have Madeleine here; in fact he couldn't wish for anything better. There were so many parts of his life that he'd got wrong, so many things he should have done differently. But being Madeleine's father wasn't one of them. He'd been delighted when she'd turned up at Wrea Head Hall. It had been a day he'd dreamed of and meeting her again, seeing how she'd turned into such an intelligent and beautiful young woman, had made his heart swell. Even though he berated himself for having had no real influence in her upbringing.

He hated the fact that Margaret had taken her away from him. He'd hated the times that he couldn't see her, couldn't tuck her up in bed and couldn't nurse her when he'd known she'd been ill. But her mother had dominated Maddie's life, had controlled his access and it was only now that he felt a huge sense of guilt for not having been stronger and for not having insisted that he had a right to see his own child. He'd have been willing to care for Jess too; he'd have even brought her up as his own, if only Margaret had allowed it.

Morris took a deep breath as it occurred to him just how much of Madeleine's life he'd missed and how much he could never get back. He couldn't alter any of that now. He couldn't turn back time, but what he could do was put things right. He had already made her sole beneficiary in his will – had done so after Josie died, even though he was so hurt by her letter. But now he had the chance to finally get to know her – and his beautiful granddaughter, who reminded him so much of Maddie at that age – he knew that he had made the right decision.

He sipped the whisky in his glass. 'If only Josie was here. She was so astute, she'd know exactly what to do.'

Jack smiled. 'She was a wonderful lady. I do, however, remember being a little afraid of her at first. I'd never met a woman that was quite so sure of herself before, sir.'

Morris chuckled. 'You're right there, Jack. I was often a little afraid of her myself. Do you know, I used to feel her presence?'

'Really?'

'Yes. I used to sit here late at night, stare into the flames and swear that I could feel her walk past. I could smell her perfume. Oh, I know it was just my imagination, but I swear, I used to breathe in deeply and it was as though she really was there, sitting beside me.' He sipped the amber whisky that he swirled round the glass. 'For a while, I thought I was going mad. In fact, I probably was going mad; after all I'd been there when she passed away. But it was so clear. The smell was so distinct and I felt as though I wanted to run around the grand hall and find her. But it hasn't happened for a while now.'

'I'm so very sorry, sir,' Jack apologised, bowing his head.

Morris laughed. 'What would you be sorry for, Jack?'

He looked thoughtful in his reply and hesitated before he spoke. 'I'm just sorry that you're so sad, sir. It pains me to see you that way.'

Morris patted him on the knee in a gesture of thanks. 'Don't worry, Jack. I'm okay now. What I have to take care of is the future, not the ghosts of the past.' He patted his pocket where he'd placed the letter that had long resided in his desk drawer. He knew who had written it. What he didn't understand was why, but he intended to find out.

Chapter Sixteen

Madeleine tapped away at her keyboard. It was just after eight in the morning; the sun had risen and a soft hue had drifted across the lawn and towards the woods. Her work in progress wasn't coming along as she wished. Her characters were attempting to do their own thing and she found herself in turmoil as she attempted to correct her plot. The first draft of a book was always the hardest. Things happened that threw her in directions that she never imagined, but she knew that the only way to complete it was to battle to the end. It had to be written. The rewrite would help it shine, and the second rewrite would add the magic, then it would go to her editor. By the time the manuscript was finished, it would have been changed at least a dozen times or more.

Her eyes fell upon the diary. It had intrigued her and she picked it up and flicked through the pages. It had mentioned a secret staircase, a secret room and a bell tower, none of which she'd seen since she had been at the hotel. She walked along the corridor, wondering where the entrance to it might be. It obviously had to be hidden in some way, otherwise it wouldn't have been a secret at all and all the servants would have easily known of its existence. The diary had said that it led to a room. She knew the house was big, but she thought that to hide a whole room within a house like this would have taken an engineering genius.

Emily's diary had said that they let themselves in through the back door and had mentioned a panel. Her eyes searched the line of the wall, as her hand pressed on the wood as she went. She'd often seen it on television where people would tap, knock and kick panels to see which sounded hollow, but at eight in the morning, some of the guests would still be sleeping and a knocking in the corridor would not make them happy. Besides, surely if there was a loose panel, there would be some way of noticing it, something slightly or even remotely visual, especially if you were looking for it. Maybe the paintwork or the carpet in that area would look different, a little more worn, chipped, or scuffed.

A noise behind her broke her thoughts and she turned to see her father appear in the corridor. Even though it was early, he was formally dressed in a suit and tie. She smiled. It was so good to see him and her face immediately lit up as he approached.

'Morning, Dad.'

'Morning, Maddie,' he said as he held out his arms for a hug. 'Do you know what? I don't think I'll ever get sick of saying that. I love having you and Poppy here.'

'And we love being here. You've made us so welcome and it's so good to be able to spend time with you at last,' she whispered as she hugged him back.

'Well, now you're here, we've got plenty of time to spend together. I can't wait to show you the summer house, take you on a proper father daughter date or just simply show you off to all my friends.'

Madeleine blushed. 'That would be amazing. I always wanted things like that and I really wished you'd come to my wedding, given me away and we'd have had the father of the bride dance. We missed out on so much. You'd have loved Michael; he was so special.'

'Oh, Maddie. We've now got all the time in the world to dance.' He pulled her back into a hold and began waltzing her up and down the corridor as they both suppressed laughter, still fully aware that people slept beyond the bedroom doors. 'We don't need an excuse to dance, my darling, we just need to make time in the day.'

'I feel as though a part of my life went missing,' she said as she stared up into his gentle, loving eyes.

'It did and I'm so very sorry, but I promise I'll make it up to you,' he replied. 'I really do wish I'd have met Michael. I'm sure he was a good and decent man. I was so sorry to hear about what happened.'

They both stopped dancing and stood awkwardly for a moment. Madeleine held back the tears that were threatening to flow and grabbed hold of the balustrade for support.

'My world ended. I loved him so much. It was so unfair; he was taken away from me at a time when I needed him the most. Just like you. I really needed you as a child, but Mum took us away and then suddenly, you weren't there at all.' She felt guilty for saying this, but he needed to know how it had been for her.

Again he hugged her. 'I'm so sorry. But, do you know what? I'm never going to leave you again. Not till we're both old and grey.'

'I know.' Her mind flashed back to the teddy bear. Someone had been in her room while Poppy slept. She didn't like it and knew that the whole teddy bear incident had been planned to scare her, which meant that someone didn't want them there and she knew she wouldn't settle properly until she found out who.

'Do you?' he questioned as he once again began to dance. 'How about we start right away, let's go out for the day tomorrow, all of us, my treat?'

Madeleine beamed. The thought of a family day out appealed. 'That would be wonderful. Where are we going?' she asked excitedly.

Morris looked thoughtful for a moment. 'Leave that one to me. I know just the place.' He paused and then looked directly at her. 'I'll tell you what, why don't you phone Jess? Ask her to come along too?'

Madeleine gasped. 'Are you sure?'

He laughed. 'Of course I'm sure. None of what happened was Jess's fault and it's about time we put the past where it belongs and leave it there.'

Madeleine sighed as the tears that had threatened now trickled down her face. 'Oh, Dad. You have no idea how happy that makes me.'

He held her for just a moment longer and then turned to walk back towards the staircase. 'I intend to make you happy. I have a lot of making up to do, a lot of things that I need to put right.' He stopped and turned back to her. 'What were you up to when I came along?'

'Oh, nothing really. I found an old book. It's an old diary of Emily Ennis. She mentions a secret staircase. It's got me quite fascinated and, to be honest, I was being nosey and looking for it.'

Her father looked amused. 'Really? Who'd have known that this old place had a missing diary and a secret staircase? That's excellent.' He laughed. 'Could you spread the rumours around? You know, so the guests hear about it? In fact, let the papers know. Mystery gives a place like this intrigue; people will travel from miles to search for secret staircases, so if you find it, don't tell anyone where it is.' His laugh filled the corridor.

'Do you really think people would come from miles around?'

'I know so,' he said with a chuckle. 'A bit of mystery and intrigue didn't do the Orient Express any harm, now did it?' He walked down the corridor and towards the back staircase.

Madeleine headed in the direction of her room, all the while carrying on her search as she went, checking each inner and outer wall that she passed. She even checked the space that was under existing staircases, but found nothing. The only loose panels belonged to the doors of the linen cupboards, which were all full to the brim of clean bedding, pillows and toiletries. Perhaps the secret staircase had been uncovered years before and could now be serving as one of the guest staircases which led up and down to each of the wings.

Madeleine made a mental note to try and find the original architect's plans of the house. She knew that Emily had mentioned the bell tower but wondered if the diary would give any more clues that would make its whereabouts a little more apparent.

Madeleine headed back to her room where her daughter was wriggling around in the centre of Madeleine's bed.

Madeleine smiled at the sight of her daughter, who sparkled with happiness. Slipping off her slippers, she crawled back into bed with her and wrapped herself as tightly as she could around her daughter.

'Hey, baby girl. What you doing in my bed?' She watched as Poppy closed her eyes and pretended to sleep. 'You awake, Princess?' she asked as she poked her in the ribs.

'Nope.'

'Don't you fib? Yes, you are,' Madeleine said as she began to tickle Poppy, who squirmed beneath her touch.

'Arrrghhhhhh, Muuummmmmy ... Stop, Mummy, stop.'

'Not till you tell Mummy the truth.' Madeleine laughed as she continued to tickle. 'Are you awake?'

'Arrrghhhhh, stop.'

'Stop or what?'

'Or, or, or, I'll tell Mister Bang'it on you, he'll get you,' Poppy squealed as she jumped down from the bed and ran into her own room where she immediately dived into the centre of the teddy bear mountain.

'Oh, will you now?'

Her daughter obviously believed that her new friend 'Mister Bang'it' would protect her from everything and everyone. Madeleine laughed as she thought of the muscle bound Bandit who'd sat the night before staring and stroking the pages of the diary with tenderness. She'd watched his face as he'd turned the pages in awe and was sure his eyes had been glistening, but she had no idea why.

'Come on, get dressed,' Madeleine said as she saw Poppy peer around the doorway of her room. 'Mummy's hungry. Is Poppy hungry?'

Madeleine thought of the breakfast that Nomsa had promised her. She'd watched plates of eggs Benedict on top of muffins, with crispy bacon going out to the guests the day before and had been assured that a plate full would be waiting for her the moment she got up.

But it wasn't just the food that she looked forward to. She loved everything about the hall. She loved having the chance to get to know her father and wished that she could find a way to stay forever. But she knew the probability of that was slim and ultimately she knew that living in a hotel was hardly practical for a small child and she really did need to find her and Poppy a place to live. And even though it was nice that staff did everything for you, she needed a home where she cooked her own breakfast, cleaned her own windows and made her own beds, especially if someone did resent them being there.

Her mouth salivated though at the thought of the food that was prepared downstairs. It all smelt amazing, but if she kept eating it at the rate that Nomsa wanted to feed it to her, she'd end up the size of a house by Christmas. Especially when normally she spent most of her day sitting on her bottom in front of her keyboard.

'Goodbye waistline,' she whispered as she changed into a comfy pair of old jogging bottoms. She winced as she lifted her leg; her bottom and lower back still hurt from the tumble she'd had in the mud the night before and she made a mental note to try and take it a little easier for a day or two, but with a three-year-old and a puppy, taking it easy would be more difficult than it sounded.

She looked down at the jogging bottoms and then at Poppy.

'Come on, Poppy, let's find your welly boots. I think we'll go for a bit of a walk in the garden before breakfast. Do you think Buddy would like to go and run in the woods?'

Chapter Seventeen

Bandit walked back through the trees and towards the hall. He loved his early starts to the day, the time before the rest of the world woke up and before the sun had fully risen. It was a time when he was all alone, at one with his thoughts and with nature.

Soft droplets of rain spat down making the grass glisten with diamond shaped beads. The ground underfoot was still soft and muddy following the thunderstorm the previous night, but the air was clean, fresh, and crisp and smelt of the fast approaching frosts that would soon be upon them.

A noise came from behind the hall. It was a squeal, followed by a bark and then the contagious sound of a child's laughter, which could only mean one thing. Hiding in the trees he watched as they emerged, Madeleine and Poppy walking hand in hand while Buddy ran on ahead with his ball clearly in his mouth. Dropping it on the floor, he spun around impatiently waiting for it to be thrown and Bandit noticed Madeleine rub her back as she bent to pick it up.

He couldn't remember the last time he'd heard laughter as he did right now. Josie's sudden illness and death had brought a dignified but very obvious silence to the hall.

Morris and Josie had arrived as the new owners one Christmas, bringing a fresh new ambience to the hall. Christmas trees twenty-five feet high had been erected in the parlour, the dining room and the bar. All were decorated with the most beautiful ornaments, and gifts were laid out for each and every member of staff. They'd built an atmosphere of love, which had surrounded the rooms, yet a constant air of professionalism was maintained. The refurbishment of the rooms began, each one decorated to the highest standard, the fires were once again lit and the whole hall had been brought back to life.

Bandit remembered the first Christmas that he'd been here after he'd left the marines. The family and staff had all sat together later that evening for a huge Christmas dinner. He'd had the feeling of once again belonging to a community of people who all worked towards the same aims, all providing a first-class service to those who came to stay at the hall. It had overwhelmed him to begin with, but both Nomsa and Bernie had welcomed him with open arms, put him at ease and included him in their day to day work at the hall.

Then, without warning, the Christmas before, Josie had gone and for months it had been like someone had deflated a balloon. All the air had been sucked out of the house and everyone had worked on professional autopilot. Everything had changed and everyone quickly realised that nothing would ever be the same.

Bandit walked back towards the house, hiding the three pheasants, six ducks and a rabbit in the greenhouse. He'd taken to putting them in a sack since Poppy had arrived. The last thing he wanted was to scare her by carrying the dead animals past her in the grounds. He headed to the back door.

'There you are, my boy. I bet you smelt my tea brewing?' Nomsa smiled as Bandit walked in. He took off his boots and washed his hands in the utility room before sitting down at the kitchen table. This table was his favourite place at Wrea Head Hall. Everyone sat around it every day of every week. It was like having a huge family gathering on a daily basis. However, he dreaded to think how many gallons of tea he alone would have drunk here. Not to mention the cake, breakfasts and afternoon teas. He rubbed his stomach with contentment.

'I certainly did. I kind of thought I could smell scones too, but I could be mistaken,' he said cheekily and winked at Nomsa as she poured the tea.

'If I didn't know better, I'd think you were some kind of a mind reader,' she replied with a giggle and her deep Caribbean laugh began to fill the room. Walking over to the range, she picked up two freshly baked cherry and coconut scones from the cooling tray.

'Nomsa, I don't need to be a mind reader. It's Friday. The Women's Institute come for afternoon tea on a Friday, and you always bake cherry scones. It's like a tradition.'

'Ahhhh, get on with you. I should have known better,' she said as she buttered the scones. 'What you going to be doing today?'

'Well, it's the last day of the month so I'll be going into town to visit my father.'

'I bet your daddy will be pleased to see you.'

'He probably won't even notice I'm there.' Bandit shook his head and took a bite of the scone.

Again, Nomsa thought before she spoke. 'You'd be surprised what your daddy would notice. He probably knows a lot more than you think.'

Bandit shook his head. 'I hope you're right. The only thing he ever talks about nowadays is this old place.'

'Well, that's because this place holds memories of his happy times. You have to remember, he was a strong, independent man before the accident.'

Bandit took a second bite of the scone and chewed.

'Nomsa, we both know it wasn't an accident. The driver that hit him was drunk and now a part of Dad's brain is dead and will never be repaired.' It was true. What was left of him now was a seventy-three-year-old man who'd been reduced to having the mind of a child. It was an existence where nothing made sense.

Nomsa turned to the kettle, picked it up and filled the china teapot that stood on the table. 'Does he remember the gatehouse?'

Bandit nodded. 'All he does all day is talk about the gatehouse, about the hall and about the past. He seems to believe that there are secret tunnels that lead between one and the other. Everyone around him thinks he's a bit mad. But do you know what? I think some of what he says could be a real memory. I just have to work out which parts are real and which parts are not.'

He looked out through the window. Madeleine was walking back to the house. She kept stopping to rub her back and to wait for Poppy who kept sitting down on wet grass at every opportunity she got, while Buddy ran circles around her, dropping his ball and tugging at the sleeve of her jumper with his teeth.

'Time I was gone. I have to get to York.'

Standing up, he headed out of the back door and briskly walked down the lane that led to the gatehouse.

Chapter Eighteen

February 5th, 1942

Today the sky was grey. It rained for most of the morning and this afternoon while I was sitting with Eddie on the staircase, he suddenly went very quiet and seemed moody. I actually thought that he was preparing to tell me something really bad. But then, out of the blue, he turned towards me, lifted his hand and stroked my cheek with a tenderness that I've never previously known. And then, without warning, he kissed me softly on the lips. Not just once, but a dozen times. I can still feel a tingling upon my lips and I'm floating on a cloud of air. Even though he hasn't said the words, I'm sure that he loves me and I know that I love him. Is it possible that we can love each other so very much, at our age?

I hope that Eddie asks me to marry him soon. I fear that I shall die with anticipation until he does. But Father will never agree and I know the anguish that will be caused when Eddie goes to him and asks for my hand. However, Father will have to allow us to marry, especially if he finds out that we have already kissed. What's more, I'm sure that if the tower bells hadn't rung, we'd have still been sitting on the stairs and Eddie would still have been kissing me and, if I'm honest, I really wouldn't have minded.

Father has gone back to work in London. He will probably stay at the city house for the whole of February and wanted us to go with him but Mother had other plans, so Mary and I have been left behind to stay with her. We spend many hours just sitting in the parlour pretending to sew and do jigsaws or we escape to the kitchen and help cook with the chores. The kitchen has warmth that comes from the range and it's a relief some days to help with the chopping of vegetables for dinner.

From the kitchen window, I can see Eddie doing his work in the garden. I'm sure that he knows we are there and chooses his workload accordingly so that he can wave to me when he passes the window and knows that cook isn't looking. I'm sure that cook would prefer her kitchen to herself but the weather is so cold at the moment we have to find something to do, because Mother wouldn't allow us to venture outside. Taking a walk would give her a panic attack. She is sure we'll catch pneumonia or slip over in the frost and turn an ankle or two. Which means my time with Eddie is limited to our secret meetings on the staircase at a time when the rest of the house sleeps.

However, I can't help but feel that I've done wrong, but last night it was so cold, we made our way into the secret room. We cuddled up on the bed under a blanket which I've stolen from my bedroom. I know this is wrong and I know that both Mother and Father would be furious if they found out, but I also know that Eddie loves me and I know in my heart that I am quite safe and he would not take advantage of the situation.

The war is upon us and food is now rationed. We are so lucky to have the vegetable gardens that Eddie tends so lovingly and, of course, we have our own chickens, pheasants and sheep on the land. Father has built pens in the woods where the animals are kept and hidden; these have been kept for our personal use, just in case the war effort demands that our animals are turned over, which Father really does believe will happen at some point. He also fears that they will take the house. Many houses have been commandeered already to use as nursing homes for the wounded or offices for the military. If that should happen we would all have to move back to London and my time with Eddie will end until the war is over. I'm terrified. How would I live a single day without him now?

The whole family have been invited to a masked Valentine

ball at one of the houses in Scarborough, which would be quite a treat in wartime. It means that Father would come home for the night. I'm not sure where they will find all the food, but it's been promised that it will be a grand affair, everyone will be there and our best dresses will be worn. Mary and I are lucky that we made new dresses just before the war, but I've heard that some of the other girls will make their new dresses from old material such as disused curtains and bedding.

Eddie has asked me not to go. I could see in his eyes that he's scared. He's frightened that I might meet someone else. Maybe one of the men that Mother wants me to marry, or someone from our own circle, but I've assured him that no man would ever compare to him. And it's true, I would never look, but he's frightfully upset at the thought of my going out dancing and having fun; yet I have to admit that the thought of a party fills my heart with joy and I can't bear to miss out, especially after such a bleak, cold and harsh winter.

Madeleine turned over the page but the words had stopped abruptly. It looked as though halfway through writing, Emily had been disturbed because the next entry she'd written was in March and made no mention of the ball, making Madeleine wonder if she'd actually gone at all or whether her love for Eddie had made the decision for her and she'd stayed at home.

Disappointed, she closed the book and phoned Jess.

Chapter Nineteen

'Seriously, Dad, I can't ice skate.' Madeleine protested as her father opened the car door. 'I really can't, ask anyone. Ask Jess.'

'Of course you can. Everyone can skate, it just takes practise, doesn't it, Jess?' He held out his hand and both Jess and Poppy jumped out of the car giggling.

Madeleine was amazed at how quickly he and Jess had got along. They'd greeted each other with hugs at the hotel and had chatted about anything and everything during the drive to Whitby, while Madeleine had happily allowed herself to be demoted to the back seat of the Range Rover to keep an eye on Poppy.

'Mummy, come on. It'll be fun,' Poppy screamed as she dragged her grandfather towards the door. 'Granddad says we can have chocolate ice cream. Two scoops.' She held her two fingers up in the air in a gesture that made everyone giggle.

Madeleine grabbed her hand and shook her head at how easily bought her daughter was with promises of ice cream and followed them into the building to line up for skates.

'Jess, I can't do it. Seriously, I'm like Bambi on ice, both of my legs want to go in different directions at the same time.' Madeleine pulled on the boots that had been offered and watched as her father helped Poppy with hers.

Jess supressed a giggle. 'Maddie, don't be a spoilsport, you'll be fine. Just hold onto the wall until you feel more confident, or hold onto my hand. I'll show you.' She stood up and stamped her feet. 'I skate all the time on the cruise ships as most of the liners have a rink,' Jess said as she stood back and waited as Madeleine reluctantly finished pulling on the boots.

'Hold my hand, don't leave me,' Madeleine squealed as she

stood up for the first time, wobbled precariously and followed Jess towards the ice. 'I can't believe I let my father talk me into this,' she said with a frown. 'He said something about the fact that we should have done it years ago and that it'd be a great bonding day; well, let me tell you this, if my backside bonds with the ice just once, especially after falling on it the other night, I'm out of here.'

'Come on, Mummy, you're so slow,' came Poppy's shrill shriek, but Madeleine couldn't see her and almost ran to the edge of the ice. 'Mummy, look at me, Mummy, I'm here,' she shouted as she raced around the ice holding onto her granddad's hand. 'Go on, Granddad, spin me again.'

Madeleine watched as her father repeatedly spun Poppy around on the spot, he turned effortlessly and made each move look easy and she began to wonder where and when he'd learnt.

'You coming?' he asked as he passed Poppy to Jess. 'Come on, I'll help you.' Her father held out a reassuring hand and Madeleine took it and stepped onto the ice. 'One foot, then the other, just slide them, you don't need to pick them up, not at first.'

Madeleine could feel her nerves as the concentration overtook her mind and she slowly moved one foot and then allowed her father to pull her until she dared to move the other, while all the time, he travelled backwards. Her legs began to wobble and suddenly she felt her father's hand steady her. 'I just can't do it, Dad. Maybe I'm too old to learn. Maybe, just maybe, someone with two left feet should stay on dry land, or maybe I should go buy the coffees and ice cream. Didn't you promise Poppy ice cream?' She looked into his eyes in the hope that he'd give her a reprieve and allow her to get off the ice, but instead she saw a deep, disturbing sadness cross his face.

'I really thought that by bringing you here, you'd remember.' He held her with one arm around her waist as though dancing a waltz, pursed his lips and sighed. 'You could skate, Maddie, don't you remember?' He looked up and tears filled his eyes. 'I used to take you all the time when you were Poppy's age. We'd go every week. I used to spin you around, you even had a pair of your own boots that I bought for you. You loved being on the ice.'

Madeleine looked at her surroundings and tried to think back. She racked her mind as she felt herself moving over the ice and then looked back at her father's hopeful face. It was then that she remembered. He'd looked the same then as he did now, fresh and relaxed on the ice, travelling backwards and smiling as she'd wobbled precariously as a child. 'Daddy, don't let go. Daddy, look at me, watch what I can do. Daddy, spin me round and round. Daddy, Daddy, am I an ice princess?' The words went over and over in her mind. She remembered constantly shouting to him, wanting his approval and then she remembered skating alone, travelling around the edge of the rink, with him skating beside her. She looked down at her feet, they'd relaxed and so had her body and suddenly, without thought, she was skating unaided.

'That's my girl, you're doing it, you're remembering.'

Madeleine nodded her head and once again took his hands, her feet began moving faster and faster. She began to laugh and looked around to where Poppy now stood, watching her in amazement. She then looked back at her father, who took her in his arms and spun her around and around as though dancing a quick step.

'Do you remember, Maddie? Do you remember us dancing on the ice?'

Maddie smiled and in that moment felt at peace with both her past and her future. She had her father, and Poppy and Jess. She loved them totally and was loved in return and at that moment she felt completely happy for perhaps the first time since Michael had died.

Chapter Twenty

March 9th, 1942

The war is getting worse. The Germans have been killing the Jews and for no apparent reason other than their race. It seems so unfair and Father says that all the available men will soon have been called up to go to war.

What if Eddie has to go? I don't know how I would cope without him, he's so young and naive and from what I hear, he'd be fighting against grown men, Germans who'd be trying their best to kill him.

Even though he never says it, I know that he fears this too. Every day I see the frown lines on his face grow deeper and I've tried asking Father about ways of keeping men away from the war. He was very vague, but explained that only certain careers or medical conditions could really save them.

I watched Eddie working. He digs the ground much faster these days and seems to be in a hurry to get everything done, just in case he gets the letter and doesn't have time to complete his work. He's begun to build a glasshouse. Only the frame at the moment as glass is difficult to come by. He says that the glasshouse is perfectly positioned to grow grapes in the summer and has even installed piping that goes under the ground and is attached to an old railway engine that Father acquired from his job. This will be lit and stoked to create the warmth needed to keep the grapes warm at night. He's housed it in a brick room to keep the weather away and he even made the bricks himself by squeezing clay into a wooden mould and baking them one by one in the old back to back oven that still remains in the cellar.

Mary has stopped watching Benjamin. She saw him walking out with a girl from the village and as far as I'm

aware, they haven't spoken since. Mary now expects me to
spend more time with her and the time I manage to escape
and be with Eddie is now very limited because I'm afraid that
Mary will be jealous and if that happens she could tell Father
what I've been doing. So now, I normally wait for her to be
asleep and then Eddie and I meet on the back staircase, but
most days it's only for a few moments at a time.

Madeleine put the diary down and allowed her mind to think
back over the day before. She'd been ice skating, she'd danced
with her father to the music, remembered how he'd taught
her as a child and had imagined how it would and should
have been like to have a father and daughter dance with him
on her wedding day.

Poppy just loved her granddad so much. He'd been
amazing with both her and Jess. He'd not only opened his
house, but also his arms, giving Jess the biggest hug, when
she'd arrived at the hall. They'd become immediate friends
and they'd all had such a lovely day, first the ice skating and
a boat ride on the sea and then into the warmth where they'd
all eaten fish and chips, followed by the promised ice cream at
Poppy's insistence. Madeleine grinned and remembered how
sick she'd felt from over eating, but how happy that they'd all
been together, enjoying their day and today, today had been a
much quieter day, a day of walking, reading and remembering
all the times that she had spent with her father, rather than
concentrating on the times they'd lost.

But now, it was night. Poppy was fast asleep in her own
bed and Madeleine picked up the glass of wine she'd taken up
with her, took a sip and then relaxed against the pillows. Her
eyes had grown heavy and she allowed herself to surrender to
sleep and for just a moment she felt totally relaxed.

'Mrs Frost, quickly Mrs Frost,' the sound of Hannah's
voice screamed out on the landing.

There was a sudden thumping and banging on Madeleine's

door. Madeleine had heard her shouts long before she'd been close enough to bang on the door and had already jumped from her bed, knowing that for Hannah to shout like that must mean that something was terribly wrong and Madeleine felt an immediate sense of dread take over her body.

She fumbled with the door. 'Shhh, you're going to wake Poppy. What on earth's the matter?'

Hannah stood before her obviously out of breath, with the colour fast dissipating from her cheeks as she spoke. 'Miss, there are two policemen. They're downstairs, saying awful things. You need to come down.'

'Stay with Poppy,' Madeleine instructed as she grabbed at her tracksuit bottoms and jumper that she'd taken off earlier. Dressing as fast as she could, she ran into the bathroom, quickly checked her appearance and then headed for the staircase. She took two steps at a time and ran straight into the hallway where the two uniformed men stood.

'Mrs Frost?' one of the policemen questioned as she approached.

'Yes, I'm Madeleine Frost. What's happened?'

'It's your father, miss. I'm very sorry. I'm afraid there's been an accident.'

Madeleine gasped for air as she struggled to breathe. The room began to spin as though it rotated around her and the floor suddenly took on a soft and doughy texture beneath her feet.

'Please God, no.' Her words were barely a whisper as she held onto the staircase for support as she fought back the memory of Michael's death, the two policemen who'd stood before her back then and the dread of what they'd said next. She'd heard it before, the exact words, yet nothing could have prepared her to hear them again. The policeman indicated for her to sit, but her legs were rigid and refused to move. She stepped forward and gripped the back of a settee in the hope that it would hold her weight. Her knees threatened to give way and her breathing became laboured and shallow. A strangled scream left her throat, the room once again began to spin and her body began shaking with a persistence that took over and wouldn't stop.

'What ... what happened? Where is he?' she managed to say.

'He fell, miss, from the cliff in Whitby. We're not sure what happened at this stage, Mrs Frost, but I'm sorry to inform you that it may have been suicide. He's been taken to the mortuary. There will have to be a post mortem, it will take place in the morning.' The words sank in slowly as Madeleine noticed his bottom lip begin to quiver. Her heart immediately went out to him and for no reason she began to wonder how many times he'd had to deliver this same speech before. The only thing more difficult than having to give bad news is to hear it and to know that life from that point forward would never be the same.

'His personal effects, miss,' the policeman said as he held out a brown paper bag.

Madeleine stared at the bag and began to open it but the room was suddenly full, there were people all around. Staff members began to congregate, a few guests came out of the bar; all stood in earshot, all were inquisitive, questioning and concerned.

Madeleine tried to think what to do. What would her father do? She knew that he'd always relied upon his team. 'Bernie, please phone Jack, Nomsa and Bandit. Ask them to come.' Her thoughts were immediately of the guests and she placed the bag down on the table as she ushered the policemen out of sight and into the library. The guests needed to be settled, tea would need to be made.

They shouldn't see this. No, they couldn't see this. What's more, she had to ensure that they didn't. This was their time, their holiday and their memories. Father would have been mortified if he'd thought anyone's stay had been ruined by his untimely death. She felt a sob come from somewhere deep within her. How could this happen? They'd had such a lovely few days, they'd danced on the ice and he'd stood before her and promised that they had plenty of time, that he wouldn't ever leave her again. Why would he say all of that if he was going to do this? She just couldn't believe that he might have been contemplating suicide.

She needed to think. She needed to be strong. She needed Jess to come back to the hall. Her eyes squeezed tight; her father had invited Jess to stay here. Madeleine thought it ironic that just the day after he'd put the past where it had belonged had been the day that he died.

'Please, everyone, please, go back to what you were doing. Everything's fine.' Her voice seemed to come through a mist that surrounded her. But nothing was fine and her voice felt like a delusional hallucination that reverberated around the room. To her, it didn't even sound like her voice. 'I'll ask Nomsa to make some tea, please, there's nothing to see here.' The words automatically fell from her mouth.

Jack appeared from nowhere and Bernie quickly told him the news. He went pale, clutched for a chair and slumped down. His head immediately dropped into his hands. He struggled to compose himself and stared at the floor before searching the room and then finally he slowly stood up, took in a deep breath, and then walked over to where Madeleine stood holding onto the library door.

'Sorry, Mrs Frost,' she heard Jack say. 'Forgive me, I'm so sorry for your loss.'

Madeleine shook her head. 'I'm sorry for your loss too, Jack. I know that you and my father were close.'

Her heart went out to him. Morris Pocklington may have been her father, but Jack had probably known him better than she had. They'd worked together, relied on each other and worked side by side for years. Her father had spoken highly of him and no one could have ever doubted Jack's loyalty.

'Jack, when Nomsa arrives, could you ask her to make some tea for the guests?' She paused. 'Yes, I think we should make tea, isn't that what we should do?'

'Yes, Mrs Frost. Leave it with me,' he said.

Turning away, Madeleine went to walk back into the library where the two policemen still waited.

Bandit ran towards the hall, past the horses, the sheep and the pigs. He breathed naturally, running had always been a big part of his life and although the lane was long he sprinted up it without thought. He could see the police cars at the front of the house and immediately headed to the back.

He'd heard the news, knew what had happened and knew that the night would be long, full of tears, memories and devastation. He had no idea what he would do once he got into the house. No idea what his job would be, except that he knew he had to be there, be part of the team, do what was needed and help with whatever he was told.

He burst through the door, just moments after Nomsa, who immediately collapsed into his arms.

'It's okay. It'll be okay, we all have each other.' He held her as tightly as he could. Her sobs racked through her entire body and she fell to her knees. He'd never seen her so distraught, even when Josie died she'd refused to cry, refused to fall apart.

'Poor Mr Pocklington, he was still so young, so young,' she wailed, 'and what about those girls, poor Madeleine and that poor child, Poppy. They have only just found him. Oh, Bandit, it's so unfair, so very wrong and they're saying he did this himself. He couldn't have done, could he? That wasn't his way.'

Both Jack and Bernie joined in the hug and for a moment all four of them stood together in the middle of the kitchen, conjoined.

'Hey there, come on,' Bandit said eventually, trying to ease the tension. 'We have to be strong. It's what Mr Pocklington would have wanted.' He pulled away and one by one he looked them all squarely in the face. 'Madeleine and the guests, they all need us right now. It's our turn to step up and help them, just like they've always helped us.'

Pulling a huge white handkerchief from her apron, Nomsa blew her nose loudly and then wiped her eyes before returning the handkerchief to her pocket. She then turned towards the kettle, pulled a selection of teapots down from the shelf, along with assorted china teacups, and laid them out on a mixture of trays. All were presented just as they should be with small milk jugs and bowls containing lumps of both brown and white sugar.

Bandit watched with admiration. It was the one thing that made him love this house so much. Even at a time of distress, the staff of Wrea Head Hall always did things properly.

Bernie helped by filling one teapot after the other. Each tray was perfectly presented and he nodded at both Jack and Bandit who dutifully picked up the trays and carried them through the hall.

Bandit felt that even the air had a different texture as he carefully knocked on the library door and walked in.

Madeleine wiped her eyes and looked up just as he entered.

'Madeleine, gentlemen, Nomsa has sent tea for you,' he said as he placed the tray on the coffee table that stood between the two settees.

'Thank you,' she managed to say as she looked directly into his glistening, volcanic eyes. They held hers for a moment too long; he didn't have to say the words to her. She knew how sorry he felt, just by the look in his eyes.

Chapter Twenty-One

'Do I look okay?' Madeleine asked as she studied her appearance in the free-standing mirror that stood in the corner of her room, beside the window.

'You look great, honestly,' Jess said as she sat on the floor. She was leaning back against the wooden four-poster footboard, where Poppy had insisted she sat while they played.

Jess had been there for the past six days, taking care of Poppy, and being a constant sounding block for Madeleine, who'd cried, shouted and screamed at every opportunity about the unfairness of losing her father. Her distress had turned to rage and she now felt nothing but anger towards him. How could he have done this? She had no idea how to run a hotel, nor did she know about antiques, laundry orders or Victorian shaped taps.

The house had been full of people for the past two days. Hannah had sent emails out cancelling all guest bookings for the week, in the hope that the pressure of not being around people would help. But then, one by one, members of Josie's family had arrived. There were aunts, cousins and a sister that Madeleine had never met. Most had travelled from the south and, even though they hadn't been invited to stay, they'd seen it as their right and moved into the rooms, making full and free use of the hotel.

Looking back in the mirror, Madeleine turned to look herself up and down from each angle, just to be sure she looked okay. Her father had died and she looked every part the grieving daughter, but she barely knew him, and felt such a fraud.

Even though she'd spent just a few days in his company, rather than the years that she should have had, she really had loved him. Yet she still felt as though she was the ringmaster at the circus. The centre of a show that was to be put on for all the people expected to attend and, as his daughter, his next of kin, she was expected to lead the procession.

'Are you sure you don't mind staying with Poppy?' she asked Jess who now lay on the floor playing doll's house with her niece.

'Of course I don't. I barely knew him, I only really met him the once, so I'm hardly a mourner, am I?' she said as Poppy dropped her doll down the chimney of the doll's house and began laughing hysterically as it crashed into the kitchen below. 'Besides, it's no place for Poppy. I'll take her out with Buddy. We'll go for a walk in the grounds and before you say it, I know, we won't go near the greenhouse.'

Madeleine smiled. If nothing else, Jess was always protective of Poppy and she was right, a funeral was no place for a three-year-old. Even if she had been his granddaughter.

'Right, I'll be off then,' she said, taking one last look in the mirror.

Jess jumped up and hugged her before Madeleine headed down the main staircase.

The day was all about grandeur, but even though she was putting on the show that was expected, she became overwhelmed by the crowds of people who fell silent as she walked down the stairs. Lilies and white roses were displayed along the hallway, their scent infiltrating the room with a powerful aroma that caused her to pull a tissue from her pocket in case she might sneeze. They were the biggest lilies she'd ever seen and they stood alongside the biggest church candles ever. Everyone was dressed in black, drank gold liquid from crystal glasses and, for some reason, reminded her of that very first night she'd looked in through the window, watching guests congregate for the murder mystery weekend.

Her eyes drifted across the room. She looked towards the library door. Her eyes became fixed on one man.

Bandit.

He stood tall and proud, wearing his military uniform. His green beret carefully tilted, the badge of a crowned lion sitting on a crown above a crest pinned to it, clearly displayed above his left eye. Everything about him looked different. It was not only his clothes that had changed, his hair was shorter, he was clean shaven and for the first time Madeleine could see the pure chiselled symmetry of his jawline. He was a striking and handsome man, making her wonder why he'd been hiding beneath the overgrown look that she'd fast become accustomed to.

He walked towards her, held out a hand. 'May I?'

She took his hand and felt him tremble as he escorted her through the crowd to the black limousine. The hearse stood in front, her father's solid oak coffin within, covered in so many flowers that it could barely be seen.

'Thank you,' Madeleine whispered to Bandit, grateful for his gesture. She climbed into the car and looked back to where he stood, head bowed waiting for the car to depart before he moved. Her eyes were captivated by his new look and she stared at him long after the limousine door was closed.

Madeleine watched as the hearse made its way into the village. The streets were lined with people, all bowing their heads. Some removed their caps, held their hands to their heart or drew imaginary crosses in front of their faces, making a sob catch in her throat.

They eventually pulled up outside the church and she stepped out of the limousine and straight into the arms of Liam O'Grady.

Chapter Twenty-Two

'Not a chance, Liam. We're not getting back together and no you are not coming to live here,' Madeleine bellowed for what seemed like the twentieth time since the funeral had been over. She made a mental note to lower her voice; albeit most of the family members had gone home, some still remained and as far as she was aware, they had now gone back up to their rooms for the night. 'What on earth would make you think that that would happen?'

Liam slouched in the chair as he pointed aimlessly around the room. He was obviously worse for wear on the free drink, which had flowed continuously during the afternoon. He sat with his arm above his head, looking very much at home in the library.

'Maddie, darlin', you know it makes sense. I kind of thought we'd start again, you know, a fresh start. We were good together, you know that. What could be better than me and you being here, together? I mean look at this place.'

Madeleine turned her back to him and stared out through the library's huge Victorian window. Darkness had descended hours before and the beauty of the garden was now hidden from view. She could see his reflection in the glass and cringed. It was only now that she truly wondered what on earth she'd seen in him in the first place.

'Come on, Maddie. We could be happy here.'

'In which brain cell do you honestly believe that we would ever be happy?'

He really did think that they could pick up where they'd left off, pretend nothing had happened and live happily ever after. She felt furious at the thought that he could actually believe that she would fall back into his arms. Which she wouldn't. It would be impossible for her to ever trust him again and only with trust could there ever be love.

'No, Liam. What you mean is you'd be happy here. I'd never believe anything you ever did or said again.'

'Darlin', I know it would take time, but we could start slow.'

'Slow?' she said with a laugh. 'I don't want you near me. You repulse me. Don't you understand that?'

He shook his head. It was more than obvious that he didn't understand and chose to ignore every word that she was saying.

'I think you should consider it. This place will take some running. Everyone loves my charm, Maddie. I could work front of house, meet and greet the guests. Maybe sit with them for a drink, chat and tell them the history of the house.'

Madeleine glared at Liam. He looked so confident, so utterly at home and so irritatingly sure of himself. 'Wow. You've got it all worked out, haven't you? You really can see yourself as lord of the manor, can't you?' She reached out and held onto the mantle for support. 'Have you already ordered your suit, Liam? I mean, lords always wear suits, don't they, waistcoats maybe?'

He smiled, sipped his whisky and slouched further down in the chair. 'You know it makes sense, Maddie. Of course, I'd have to look the part. Guests expect a certain amount of pomp and ceremony in hotels like this. Besides you need a man around here, you need someone to protect you.'

'I can look after myself, so if you don't mind, I think it's time you left.'

Liam laughed. 'Don't be silly now. I've had far too much to drink to go anywhere tonight. Besides you have a huge four-poster bed up there in your room. You could show it to me, wouldn't be the first time we've shared now, would it?' He stood up and staggered over to where she stood, moved a strand of hair from in front of her face and leaned forward, lips pursed. 'I promise to take it slow, darlin'.'

'Touch me and I'll stab you,' she growled through gritted

teeth as she picked up a toasting fork from beside the hearth. 'Today was my father's funeral and I'm really not in the mood to listen to your pathetic drivel, Liam. You got that?'

'Come on, darlin', put that thing down, you don't mean it.' He wobbled, puckered and then fell backwards onto the settee that stood behind him. His legs flew up into the air as he landed heavily on his bottom. He began to laugh and made an attempt to clamber back to his feet. 'You know we're good together, we could make this work.'

'I'll get you a taxi.'

'Don't be stupid, Maddie. There's your bedroom right up the stairs.' He pointed towards the back staircase, making Madeleine's mind do somersaults.

'Liam O'Grady, how the hell do you know, one, where my bedroom is and two, that it has a four-poster in it? Now, get out or I'll call the police,' she shouted as she moved to the door, opening it in the hope that he'd manage to stand up and walk right through.

'Maddie, come on.' He walked right up to where she stood, his hand dropped heavily onto her shoulder dragging her to him.

'Okay, I've heard enough. Touch her once more and you'll have me to deal with,' Bandit growled menacingly as he burst into the room with the energy and propulsion of a tornado. He grabbed Liam's shoulder and launched him to the other side of the room.

'You okay?' he asked Madeleine as a protective arm went around her shoulders. She nodded, grateful that he had intervened and for once she felt assured by his over protective nature.

'You ... You ... can't do that. Me and Maddie, we were talking,' Liam tried to explain as he stood up and wobbled across the library, holding onto bookshelves as he went. 'Shhhh, don't tell anyone, but she loves me and we ... we ... we're gonna get back together.'

'In your dreams, Liam. How many times do I have to say it's never going to happen,' Madeleine chided.

'I think the lady wants you to leave,' Bandit snarled as he gave Madeleine a reassuring squeeze, before picking up a shocked and anxious Liam from where he slouched.

'But I don't want to leave.'

Bandit inhaled deeply and looked at Madeleine who nodded her head in agreement that Liam needed to go. 'It wasn't a request. I think you've overstayed your welcome.'

Liam quickly looked back at Madeleine in the hope that she'd come to his rescue.

'Maddie, Maddie, don't you dare let him do this. You'll be sorry if you do.'

Liam's feet seemed to run in mid-air as Bandit picked him up with ease and carried him across the room.

'Maddie, call off the gorilla. I'm warning you. You're not going to get away with this. I won't let you.'

Bandit launched him from the library door and into the parlour where he landed in an undignified heap. 'The lady asked you to leave. You don't want her to have to ask again. Now get out.'

Madeleine could hear Liam's disgruntled Irish accent get louder and louder as once again Bandit picked him up and carried him, kicking and screaming, towards the front door. A crunch on the gravel indicated that he'd landed heavily and she couldn't help but laugh.

Bandit stood in the stone arched doorway of the hall watching Liam as he curled up on the grass, pretending to sleep. A taxi had been ordered and he had every intention of ensuring that Mr O'Grady got in it and left.

During the past week, he'd barely had time to speak to Madeleine. Yet each day he'd admired her control, compassion and dignity from a distance. She'd immediately realised that her father's death affected everyone and had taken the time to speak to every member of staff individually, ensured that they were all right and had everything that they needed to do their jobs. Each one had been given lighter duties during the aftermath, time off when they'd needed it and had been encouraged to spend time together, relaxing between chores.

'Your taxi's here,' he said as he poked Liam with his foot. 'Come on, get up.'

Liam could be heard grumbling. He'd curled up in a tighter ball, a little like a hedgehog without the spikes; his snores vibrated and he continued to sleep.

Bandit looked over his shoulder. He could see Madeleine watching from the library window. She had changed her clothes, no longer did she wear the black attire she'd been in all day but was now wearing a fitted white T-shirt along with a pair of tight fitting blue jeans that accentuated her shape.

Picking Liam up from the grass, Bandit dragged him to the taxi and threw him into the backseat. 'If he doesn't give you an address, take him to a Travelodge or something,' he said as he passed the driver a twenty pound note, closed the door and watched as the taxi left the grounds.

'I put him in a taxi, he's gone,' Bandit said sheepishly, walking back into the library. 'I hope I didn't overstep the mark? It's just, well, I was walking past and I heard you shout.'

'And you thought you'd save me?' She smiled. 'Thank you.'

Bandit looked down at the floor. 'You've got changed.'

Madeleine smiled again. 'I did. I needed to check on Poppy and Jess. They're both fast asleep, so I slipped into these and came back down to see you.'

Madeleine blushed. She'd liked the way he'd protected her and found his new chiselled look appealing. She'd also observed during the past week how he'd supported other members of staff, helped them with their work as well as doing his own. He had an admirable kindness and had even taken over the duty of walking Buddy through the grounds and in the woods, ensuring all her time could be spent not only looking after Poppy, but running a hotel that she knew nothing about.

'Would you like a drink?' she asked as she walked to the bar. 'I think we deserve one.'

Bandit nodded. 'Why not? I've got a morning off tomorrow. Chef doesn't need any fresh game, you know, with the lack of guests. So I'll get a lay in, for once.' He paused, looked towards the inglenook and then shyly continued, 'Shall I throw another log on the fire? We could sit for a while.'

'I'd like that.' It had been a long time since anyone had fought for her honour. It had amused her and had made her feel quite special that Bandit had made the assumption that she needed protecting. She looked over to the fire, where he stood. He was currently in the process of lifting away the fireguard and throwing a fresh log on top of the already glowing embers. It was probably a log which he'd cut, from a tree which he'd felled, from the gardens which he tended. It seemed only fitting that, for once, he should sit in front of the fire and enjoy the fruits of his labour.

'Is wine okay?' she shouted through from the bar. 'What do you drink? Red or white?'

'Red would be good.'

'Good.' She smiled. 'Same as me.' She picked up a bottle, along with two fresh glasses, and made her way into the parlour to stand beside him.

'Shall we?' He indicated the settee and sat down with a satisfied thud. Madeleine looked between the two settees before sitting down opposite him. She placed the glasses down on the table between them and listened to the glug, glug, glug as the wine was poured into the glass.

'Do you mind?' he said touching his beret which he still wore, 'It's been a long day.'

'No, of course, please take it off. Even though I must say it does suit you.'

For a while, they both sat silently, sipping the wine. The candles that surrounded the room flickered and the flames which danced haphazardly in the fireplace glowed with warmth that surrounded the room. There was a peaceful calm to the house, a stillness not often felt in the hub of a busy hotel and it occurred to Madeleine that they were both comfortable enough in each other's company to sit without trying to make conversation. She reached over and switched off the small table lamp that stood beside her, allowing the tawny ambience of the firelight to take over the room.

Bandit stood up, walked to the fire and threw another log into the embers. Then he turned back to the table, poured more wine into each of the empty glasses and then consciously sat back down on the settee beside Madeleine.

'Are you okay?' he asked as he picked up the glass and passed it to her. The ruby red liquid swirled around the crystal, sparkling in the light from the fire.

'I guess I will be,' she whispered. 'I still can't believe he's gone. That he'd, you know, do that.'

'It seems very out of character for him. I've known him for a while and I wouldn't have thought it would be something he'd do. None of it really makes sense. Will there be an inquest?'

Madeleine nodded and looked up into his eyes. 'As you say, it doesn't make sense. Just a couple of days before he said we had plenty of time to get to know each other. He was making plans and had promised that we'd take a holiday, him, Poppy and I.' She paused, overcome with the enormity of her loss. 'We were going to do so many things. But we didn't get the chance and now I really wish we had.' Tears sprang to her eyes and she fought to keep them under control.

'Hey, come here.' His voice was shaking as he held out his arms for a hug, making Madeleine wonder if he needed the hug as much as she did and her mind cast back to the morning he'd held onto Poppy's hug as though his life had depended upon its existence. After all, he'd known her father for a long time and it was obvious that he must be grieving too.

Curling up under his arm, she felt his arms entwine around her. His hold was warm, welcoming and for the first time since her father's death she felt content, safe and protected.

'I can't believe that he left everything to me but his solicitor told me that he had changed his will to make me the sole beneficiary after Josie died. I don't know why but I never expected that. I have so many questions to ask him, about his life and running the hotel. So much I need to know, and now it's too late.'

'It's never too late. There are always ways for you to get the answers. Jack's been his right hand man for years, I'm sure he'd be happy to guide you.'

'Actually, that's what Liam thought he'd do, guide me. He really believed that he could walk in here, take over the running of the hotel and I'd automatically fall into his arms.'

'Would you?'

'Not a chance. I hate him so much. He was horrid and cruel. He changed the moment that Poppy and I moved in, like Jekyll and Hyde. One minute he'd be lovely, the nicest person ever and then he'd turn and become the nastiest man in the world. He shouted at Poppy when she needed me, wouldn't allow her to play with his old Lego and I had to be careful with every single thing she touched in the house. It was as though he hated anyone being close to me, except for him. But then he cheated on me,' she paused and choked back the tears. 'I couldn't believe it and it was the final straw. I actually caught him, you know, in the act with a woman in the hallway of our house. I couldn't forgive him, not after that.'

She looked up; her eyes locked onto his for just a moment before looking back down at the table where her wine now stood.

He pulled her close. His eyes, black and shining had locked

firmly upon hers, his lips pursed as a rush of excitement ran through her body. His hand gently lifted to stroke her cheek, then hesitated and dropped back down to his knee.

Simultaneously, they both sat forward and picked up their wine.

'I'd better check on Poppy,' she finally said, draining the last of the wine from her glass before heading towards the stairs.

Chapter Twenty-Three

I have the most exciting news. I cannot tell anyone, not yet. This morning Eddie declared his love for me. It was the most perfect day. The summer is almost with us, the sun was shining, leaves were forming on the trees and a hundred birds were singing the most delightful tunes. We were strolling down by the lake, watching a squirrel that scurried around collecting nuts and burying them in the ground. We'd laughed at his antics, knowing that he'll most probably come back in the winter and dig them back up, when, out of nowhere, Eddie dropped down on one knee. He looked almost childlike with nerves as he held out a ring box and proposed. He said the most beautifully practised words; words that I'll never forget and words that he must have thought about for weeks. This is what he said:

'My darling, Emily. If I counted every grain of sand on the beach and multiplied them by every fish that swims in the sea, you'd have some idea of how very much I love you. It would be impossible to count, which only goes to show that there would be no number on earth that could quantify my love.'

He then opened a ring box, which held his grandmother's antique engagement ring, which he took out and placed on my finger. I'm not sure that it's gold, but it is so very pretty with a dark blue stone. I'm in so much shock that I look at it almost once every minute, to make sure I didn't dream the proposal.

Eddie then stood up and kissed me so very gently. I felt warm inside and felt a trembling that began in my stomach, before it travelled up through my body. It was a feeling that I've never felt so intensely before and I'm positive that it's a feeling I'd like to have again.

I wish I could tell Mary what happened, but she hates men and since she's stopped seeing Benjamin she refuses to believe that anyone else can be happy. I'm sure it makes her happy to be miserable, to moan all day and to be cruel to the male servants.

I've now gone to hide in my room while Eddie asks my father's permission.

I hear the dinner bell ring. We always have pheasant on a Wednesday and I normally look forward to it. But, until I know if Eddie has spoken to Father, I doubt I will be able to eat. My stomach is turning with nerves. In fact, I'm not sure I'll be able to do anything until Father indicates his decision.

'Why the hell is Liam O'Grady eating breakfast in the dining room?' Madeleine shrieked as she bounced into reception where Jack was organising the staff rota for the next week as guests were due to start arriving at the hall later that day.

'He's a paying guest, miss. He's entitled to breakfast, isn't he?' He looked confused and began straightening his tie.

Madeleine closed her eyes, took in a deep breath and mentally punched the air.

'I'm sorry. Do you know him? Is he a problem?' Jack asked as he picked up a stapler from the desk and clipped two pieces of paper together.

Madeleine raised her eyebrows. 'He's the man I left when I came to live here.'

'Ah, I see. I didn't know.' Jack put the paper down, walked over to the computer and tapped on the keyboard.

'It says here that he asked for a room at the back of the house, specifically asked for room nineteen, above the kitchen?' He shrugged as Madeleine walked over to the computer and looked over his shoulder. 'Maybe he likes to hear Nomsa sing.'

'He's up to something. The hotel's practically empty. Why on earth would he specially request that room?' Madeleine sighed. 'When did he check in?'

Jack once again referred to the computer. 'It must have been between nine and half past last night. Hannah would have been on a break, and it looks like one of the bar staff checked him in. He's paid for two nights.'

Between nine and half past would have been the time when she and Bandit had been sitting in the great hall. He'd have walked straight past them on his way up the main staircase, heard what they'd said or maybe witnessed the hug. She mentally kicked herself for not having heard his voice, for not realising that he was there, listening, snooping and watching.

Madeleine hadn't yet told Jess about the hug with Bandit. She didn't want to think of it as something that it wasn't. They'd both had an emotional day and who knows what Bandit would think today.

The night before, Madeleine had crept up the stairs, one step at a time, choosing the right part of the step to stand on to make minimal noise and it reminded her of the many late nights she'd sneaked in as a teenager, risking the wrath of Mother, who would lecture her for hours if she thought Maddie had been out late with Michael. But the night before had been different and the last thing she needed after one hug was getting the third degree from Jess. She'd have pummelled her for information to the very last detail which after the day she'd had would have been the last thing she needed.

She looked up at the wood panelling that surrounded the entrance, wishing her father was here to ask his advice. He'd have known what to do about Liam, how to manage the situation without causing a scene. But, in his absence, she needed to think quickly. Jack had said that he'd paid up front and what's more he didn't appear to be doing anything wrong. She could hardly throw him out for sitting nicely and eating his breakfast and she was sure that Liam would know that.

Picking up the phone, she buzzed her room. 'Jess, when you come down to breakfast, avoid the public rooms for me, will you? In fact, why don't you take Poppy out for the day?'

'Sure will, Maddie. Anything wrong?'

'It's Liam, he's checked in as a guest. He's staying here, Jess, room nineteen and I really don't want Poppy running into him.'

'Yeah, sure. But look, Maddie, I could do with going home.'

Madeleine panicked. 'Jess, you can't leave. Please, I need you here.'

'Hey, let me finish. I'm not leaving. I could do with going home to get some things, that's all. I did kind of drop everything when you called and I'm not sure if you've noticed, but most everything I've worn for the past week has come from your wardrobe. All I was thinking was that Poppy and I might go and camp at my flat for the night. It'd be fun. We could take Buddy with us.'

Sighing with relief, Maddie agreed. 'Okay, okay, don't have too much fun without me, and Jess, launder my clothes.' She laughed as she placed the phone back in its cradle and walked through the back of reception and into the kitchen.

'Now then, young lady, what can I be getting you for breakfast?' Nomsa's voice rang out as Jack appeared in the kitchen and washed his hands.

Madeleine shook her head. 'I'm not hungry, Nomsa, but thank you. Can I just have a mug of tea?'

Madeleine made her way to the door that separated the kitchen and the dining room. She peeped between the two. There were only two tables occupied at the moment. She recognised a woman who'd been at the funeral: tall, thin and blonde. She definitely didn't look like she came from the Pocklington side of the family and Madeleine felt embarrassed for not knowing if or how she was related.

The woman looked down at the boiled egg and toast that had been placed on the table in front of her.

'Waiter, excuse me.' She called out while clicking her fingers in the air. 'Could you take the top off my egg for me? There's a dear.'

Jack politely walked across to her table, his clean white serviette hung over his arm. 'Of course, Mrs Stone,' he said politely, picking up a knife from her table and removing the top from the boiled egg. 'Is there anything else I can do for you, madam?'

She shook her head and smirked, before cutting her toast and dipping it into the yolk that much to her disgust overflowed onto the plate.

In the other corner of the room, next to the window, sat Liam O'Grady. He was reading a newspaper, sipping at his tea and occasionally glancing out at the gardens through the huge bay window, which stood to his side. Jack walked over to his table and removed his empty plate and toast rack.

'Can I get you anything else, sir?' Jack asked.

'Another pot of tea would be good and I'll have some more toast, if it isn't too much trouble for ya, son?'

Madeleine could hear his dull Irish accent as she stood hiding. She needed to speak to him, find out what he was up to and, if at all possible, force him to leave.

She stood and waited patiently, until, after what seemed an eternity, the woman with the soft boiled egg managed to slurp the last of her tea, stood up and left the room.

Madeleine took in a deep breath and walked over to the table where Liam sat, still reading his newspaper with a twisted smirk on his face. She knew this conversation was going to be awkward, knew he wouldn't go quietly, and knew she had to be assertive, but the last thing she needed in the middle of the dining room was a first class showdown. She sat down opposite him.

'What the hell are you up to?' she whispered as she pulled the paper down from in front of his face. 'You were asked to leave.'

He looked amused, folded his newspaper and placed it carefully on the table. 'Up to? I'm not up to anything, Maddie, darlin',' he said, with a genuine look of hurt at the suggestion.

'So why the hell are you here?'

He seemed to think for a moment. 'Well, last night your guard dog put me in a taxi and I asked the driver to take me to a hotel. He brought me here, and, as far as I'm aware, he was absolutely right. This is a hotel.'

'Don't be bloody smart, Liam. You could have gone to any of a hundred hotels in Scarborough, so why here?'

'Well, I kind of like the place, especially after the amazing hospitality I received here yesterday.'

'Don't be clever, Liam. It really doesn't suit you.'

'Then don't ask stupid questions, Maddie darlin'.'

'I've told you before, don't call me darling. You have no right.'

A couple walked into the dining room and waited to be seated, and Jack discreetly steered them across to a table in the opposite corner of the room. He looked over at Madeleine who nodded in approval before turning back to where Liam sat.

Liam was aware that the dining room wasn't so big that the couple wouldn't hear their exchange and leaned closer to Madeleine as he spoke. 'Look, Maddie. We need to call a truce.'

'And why the hell would I want to do that?' Her nose was almost touching his as she stared into his eyes. She broke away, glanced back towards the couple and then back to Liam who had grabbed her hand and pulled it down onto his knee, making her lean closer to him as he spoke.

'Because you really don't want to know what I'm capable of if you don't.'

'Get off me,' she growled under her breath. The last thing she wanted was for the other guests to be disturbed and again she checked over her shoulder to ensure they hadn't heard.

'Maddie, face it. You need me. A hotel like this needs me, it needs a master who will care about it and nurture it. You need to be cared for. You need someone to look after you.'

'And you'd be applying for that job, would you, Liam?' Madeleine threw her head back and laughed.

'Unless you have someone else in mind?' he said with a sneer. 'After all, you know it makes sense, Maddie.'

'It makes sense, over my dead body.'

'Maybe that could be arranged. So many things can go wrong in a house of this size. Electrics, water, God forbid there could be a fire with all those guests sleeping in their beds. Just think of the tragedy.'

'What the hell are you implying, Liam?' Her voice had risen and she immediately looked around again. 'Are you threatening me?'

She tried to move her hand, but his grip was firm.

'I'm not implying anything, Maddie, darlin'. All I'm saying is that I think you should consider my offer. We'd be good together. With a bit of tender loving care we could turn this place into a palace. It could be made into something really special.' His eyes travelled around the room.

'Go to hell, Liam.' She finally pulled her hand from his grasp. 'Firstly, don't you ever dare threaten me again and, secondly, this house is how my father refurbished it and it is really special, just the way it is.'

His face turned to stone as once again he grabbed her wrist and tightened his hold.

'You'll be sorry, Maddie. Don't say I didn't warn you.'

Chapter Twenty-Four

Bandit ran through the woods. He loved running in the early morning sun, while listening to the sound of the birds and the clatter of water falling over the rocks as it flooded down to the stream. His blood pumped through his veins. His heart felt as though it would burst through his chest, yet still he ran.

He hadn't slept. Everything about the hall had changed and all he could think of was the evening he'd spent with Madeleine. How he'd held her in his arms as they'd sat before the fire, how they'd sipped wine, took silent pleasure in each other's company and how she'd looked up at him with those deep, beautiful eyes.

They'd parted awkwardly and he was sure that Madeleine had felt the tension that had passed between them just as much as he had and now he thought about it, it had always been there. Since that very first night when he'd pinned her to the driveway, which was now a night that seemed so very long ago, when in reality it had been little more than twelve days.

Stopping on the track, he picked up a fallen branch and tossed it away from the path. A startled blackbird shot out from behind a bush, tweeting angrily as he went. Bandit shouted an apology, and once again he began to run. Heading through the trees, over the stream and down past the ha-ha at the front of the house and then, when he felt as though he couldn't run any more, he turned and headed to the back door.

'Morning, Nomsa.' He walked into the kitchen and leaned for a while on the door frame to catch his breath. He looked between Nomsa and Bernie, realising that the normal buzz of the kitchen was missing. They were both silent and Bandit raised an eyebrow at Nomsa who indicated that something was happening in the dining room. Holding her finger to her lips, it was obvious that they were trying to listen to whatever was going on.

Peering through the small crack between the doors he could see Madeleine sat with her back to him, nose to nose in an intimate chat with her ex-boyfriend. They held hands under the table and they stared into each other's eyes. Liam looked over in his direction, caught sight of him, winked, then smiled. Liam pursed his lips and pouted at Madeleine and for all Bandit knew, she could have been pouting right back.

Walking back into the kitchen, he punched the utility wall. Immediately wishing he hadn't, he turned on the tap and ran cold water over his knuckles and then walked to the far end of the kitchen, pacing up and down. He had no idea why he was so frustrated. Madeleine wasn't his and it really wasn't any of his business what she was doing with Liam, but he couldn't help but feel a streak of jealousy as it raged through him.

'Sit down, my boy. I'll make you a nice breakfast,' Nomsa whispered as she placed a steaming mug of coffee on the table before him. 'How would you like some nice pork sausages?'

Bandit stared at the steaming, golden fluid. It swirled around in the mug, like a whirlpool with milk.

He was exhausted. He'd been on such a high after the night before, really happy, content. He thought they'd shared a moment together. Thought it had been the start of something new, an amazing new beginning, but should have known that life wasn't that simple.

Again he slammed his fist down on the table, making his coffee slop over the side of the mug and the cutlery jump up into the air.

'I'll not bother, Nomsa. I'm not hungry, but thank you,' he said as his eyes stared at the back of the dining room door. 'Bernie, do you need any duck or pheasant before tomorrow evening? If not, I might go into York, see my father.'

Bernie shook his head and wiped his brow on his sleeve. 'No, you're fine. I've got plenty for tonight. You get off and see your dad. I'm sure he'll be pleased to see you.'

Standing up, Bandit walked out of the kitchen, through the back door and allowed it to slam shut behind him. Besides, it was about time he went to see his father, he hadn't been since Morris had died. He hadn't known whether he should tell him of his death or not, after all his father had been to the hall, had met Morris many times, but he wasn't sure how much he remembered or understood and hadn't wanted to upset him unnecessarily.

Chapter Twenty-Five

May 21st, 1942

I've arranged to meet Eddie after dark. I'll hide on the secret staircase and then we'll take the tunnel that leads to the woods. At least there we can be alone together and now that the summer is coming, it's warm enough for us to stay out in the gardens, even after dark. It's the most perfect route and, as far as I'm aware, the previous owners may have had it built during the First World War as a way to get away from the house should the Germans invade England and take over the hall.

Eddie has made a wooden house in the trees. It's a summer house; it has a kitchen, a bedroom and a living space. Eddie say's it's a special place for us to be alone and undisturbed and tonight he's taking me to see it for the very first time. I'm so excited.

Mother is pregnant and, again, there will be another addition to our family. I do hope it's another brother; they're so much fun when they are babies, much nicer than little girls. It is, however, such a shame that they grow up and end up like Jimmy. So maybe a brother wouldn't be preferable after all, except of course that I wouldn't ever be expected to share a room with a boy, even if we had a party and lots of people came to stay. Mother says the baby will come in the late summer. I just dread the new nanny that will reside in the house to look after it. But, then again, whoever my parents employ, she can't possibly be as bad as the nanny that came to look after us as children. She was bad tempered, strict and expected us to bath every day.

Madeleine flicked over the page, looking to see what Emily had written next. But the next page had more of her sketches on it.

She thought back to the part of the diary that had spoken of Eddie going to ask Emily's father for permission to marry. It was hard to believe that this had really happened in years gone by, but the diary hadn't mentioned it since and Madeleine wondered what Emily's father had said.

Had her father given his permission or not?

Madeleine laughed, remembering how she and Michael had run away to the register office. They'd both known that they'd been far too young and that their families would try to dissuade them. But they hadn't cared; they were in love and hadn't been able to wait a moment longer to get married, which made her feel all the sorrier, after all that had happened, that she hadn't asked her father to walk her down the aisle.

Life had been so different for Emily Ennis. She may have had a big house to live in, posh clothes, and servants, but her choices had been so very limited, her lifestyle restricted and her actions were very much accountable.

Madeleine's laugh turned to a sigh as she walked through her room and stared at Poppy's bed. Jess had taken Poppy for the night, and although they'd only been gone a few short hours, the place seemed quiet and empty without her.

'I really need to do some work,' Madeleine said out loud as she walked through the room and sat down at her desk. Switching on her laptop, she checked through her emails. There was still no word from or about Bridget and, after two whole weeks, Madeleine wondered if she really might have gone on a last minute holiday without telling anyone. But according to the policeman who'd phoned, they didn't think so. She felt helpless, but being just one of Bridget's many clients didn't give her any right to ask the police for information.

She stared at the screen, but all the words blended together. None of them made sense. Her writing didn't seem to have the edge that it normally had and she realised that she hadn't been motivated to write since she'd moved out of Liam's house.

She thought about how different episodes in her life had influenced her writing. After Michael's death, she'd managed to throw her anger into her work. But her father's death had affected her differently and she couldn't concentrate for a minute. Perhaps her spark had gone because she no longer had to make a living from her writing, as she was now a wealthy woman with a hotel to run. But she couldn't think about that now.

She looked across to Emily's diary. Reading it had become a part of Madeleine's day, a time she looked forward to. It was an escape and gave her an insight into the history of this house, the people who lived here and how their lives had been. It was even more special that she had the story in Emily's own words. Emily mentioned so many things about Wrea Head that she didn't know, things that even her father hadn't known, which made her wonder just how many secrets one house could really have.

She picked the diary back up and flicked back to the page where Emily had mentioned the staircase, but on this occasion she'd also mentioned a tunnel; in fact what she'd said was that she'd taken the tunnel that led to the woods.

'There must be more than one tunnel. If Emily was taking the one that led to the woods, where did the other one lead to?' she whispered to herself. 'If there are tunnels, where are the openings?' She put the diary down. If there was a staircase or tunnels she had every intention of finding them. But not today, today she wanted to avoid Liam at all costs. He was only booked in for two nights, which meant that tonight would be his last and tomorrow, after breakfast, he'd be gone. She'd left strict instructions with reception never to allow him to book in again.

Pushing the laptop back across her desk, she looked out over the gardens. She'd been scanning them for most of the morning and even though Bandit had told her that he'd be off all day, she'd still hoped to catch sight of him pottering around.

A knock on her door made her jump. She went to answer it.

'Hi, Jack. All okay?'

'No, Mrs Frost, we seem to have a problem. It's the electrics in the kitchen. They don't seem to be working and Nomsa is right in the middle of tonight's desserts.'

Madeleine ran behind Jack and followed him down the stairs.

'Have we called an electrician?' she asked as she entered the corridor between the kitchen and the office.

'No need, I'm sorting it,' Liam's voice echoed. He appeared to be half in and half out of the cupboard where the fuse box was. 'There you go, all done. Nothing serious.'

Madeleine stared at his smug face. 'Really. It seems quite convenient that you repaired it so quickly, Liam O'Grady.'

'Maddie, darlin'. Seriously? What are you suggesting?'

'You really don't want me to answer that, do you?' She looked him up and down, at his perfectly pressed shirt, his shiny shoes and his slicked back hair. 'What the hell did I ever see in you?' she blurted out without thinking.

'Would you excuse us, Jack, I'm sure you have work to do,' Liam ordered.

Jack glanced at Madeleine but she nodded her head at him. She didn't want Jack caught in the crossfire between her and Liam and Jack immediately retreated into the office, closing the door behind him.

'Oh, so now you think you have a right to tell my staff what to do, do you?'

'You should be grateful that I was here,' Liam said as he continued to look at the fuse board. 'I did tell you that you need a man around the place, Maddie. I did say that things go wrong with electrics and, what's more, you know it makes sense for us to get back together. I've apologised for what happened. You've made me suffer enough by leaving me. But now it's time to sort things out.' He paused. 'As for my telling the staff what to do, they need to get used to it and so do you.'

Madeleine was stunned. He seriously believed that he could walk in here and take over. He was delusional and obviously totally unable to take no for an answer.

'Liam, first and foremost, stop calling me "Maddie, darlin'". I've told you before I don't like it, and second, I want you to leave my house and I want you to leave it right now,' she screamed so loudly that Nomsa ran into the corridor, broom in her hand.

'What's going on with you, mister, making Mrs Frost scream like that?' she shouted, the broom held up in her hand as though ready to strike.

'Hey, kitchen girl. Put down the broom and get back to work. Everything's fine. Isn't it, Maddie?'

Nomsa looked between Madeleine and Liam, the tension in the air could be cut with a knife.

'For your information, mister, I is not a kitchen girl. I may work in a kitchen, but first and foremost, sir, I is a lady and if I hear Mrs Frost yell again, I'm gonna show you how this lady's gonna whoop your ass with her broom,' she shouted as she shook the broom in the air. 'Do you get that?'

Chapter Twenty-Six

'Maddie, you need to come and get Poppy. I've been burgled. The whole flat is a mess: there's glass everywhere,' Jess shrieked down the phone. 'Everything's broken: the telly, the music centre and ... oh my God, my jewellery. Maddie, my jewellery, it's all gone.'

'Calm down, Jess, I'm coming.' Madeleine looked out the window and into the darkness that rolled in with the night.

'Maddie, I ... I ... I think your locket has gone too.'

Madeleine choked back her tears as she pulled on her jeans, bouncing around the room with the telephone held tightly in one hand. The bedpost was ideal to lean on and she managed to pull the jeans on quickly followed by a hoodie, which she zipped up over her naked breasts. There was no time to organise, no time to think of what was or was not appropriate.

'Jess, you left hours ago. Have you only just got home?' She needed to get to Jess and she needed to do it quickly. Her flat was over thirty miles away, but driving over the North Yorkshire moors at night could not be done at speed. Sheep wandered loose on the moors and often ended up on the roads, meaning a journey that would take forty minutes to drive in daylight could easily take anything up to an hour at night.

'Poppy wanted to go to the creamery for lunch and ice cream. There was a fair and we ended up walking through the village to take a look before heading home. Poppy won a goldfish. What the hell do I do with a goldfish, Maddie? My flat is wrecked.'

'It's okay, Jess, don't worry. Have you called the police? I'm on my way,' she said as calmly as she could. 'And just stick the fish in a bowl of tepid water, it'll be fine.'

'Yes, I've called them, but a neighbour says my window has been open for days. She thought nothing of it, thought I'd wanted the fresh air, so whoever's been in is long gone.'

'Okay, why don't you put Buddy in his cage and take Poppy to the café over the road. You'll all be safe there while you wait for the police. If you sit by the window, you'll see them arrive. I'm on my way.' She clicked off the phone, pulled on her trainers, ran out of her room and down the stairs.

'Hannah, I've got to go out,' she shouted to the receptionist as she ran past the front desk and out through the huge front doors.

The rain had once again begun to fall. The raindrops bounced on the gravel, the trees swayed in the wind, their last remaining leaves fell onto the drive and large puddles were beginning to form. There was a chill to the air that only came with the onslaught of winter and Maddie pulled the zip of her hoodie up as high as it would go, already regretting her lack of clothes and underwear.

She wondered how come her evenings of late seemed to change at a moment's notice. Only ten minutes before, she'd been planning a hot steaming bath followed by reading Emily Ennis's diary and now she was out in the cold, the wind and the rain.

Turning the key in the ignition, she slammed the door and began to chug away from the house. The Mazda's engine whirred, clunked, and then the car began to die. It rolled down the slope, picked up momentum and cruised down the lane, before it clunked and whirred again.

'Come on, Maggie Mazda. Don't do this to me. Not tonight,' Madeleine said as she punched the steering wheel with force. She once again turned the ignition. Again and again she tried, whilst desperately trying to see the petrol gauge in the dark.

Had she run out of fuel? Had the timing belt gone? Could it be the clutch? A tapping on the window startled her, making her jump. Looking up she saw Liam's face. And before she could lock the door, it opened.

'You got some trouble there, Maddie, darlin'?' he asked, with slight Irish sarcasm.

'Not at all, I normally sit on the drive, pedalling the clutch and hitting the steering wheel with so much force that the air bag could explode at any given moment,' Madeleine growled as once again, she depressed the clutch and turned the key.

Nothing happened, not even a clunk.

'Here, move over. Why don't you let me try?' he said as he slid in beside her, almost sitting on her knee, leaving her no alternative but to move across and into the passenger seat.

He turned the key once, fiddled with something under the dashboard, pumped the clutch and then turned the key again. To Madeleine's relief and frustration, the engine miraculously started. Clear as a bell and purring as though nothing had happened.

'Look, thank you,' she said as appreciatively as she could. She looked towards his knee, trying to see what he'd fiddled with as it crossed her mind that his mending the car, just like the electrics in the house, had been just a little too easy. 'What was wrong with it?' she said, pointing to the place under the dashboard.

'Where are you going?' he queried ignoring her question and without moving anything except for his fingers that he began drumming heavily on the dashboard in an irritating manner as his foot tapped the accelerator. It made the engine roar and Madeleine wondered what he would do next.

'Please, Liam. I appreciate what you did, but I have to go. Could you get out of the car now?'

'I asked where you were going. It's only polite that you tell me, Maddie. Especially after I've just repaired your car.'

'A little too easily, I think,' the words left her mouth before she realised what she'd said and she immediately saw annoyance cross his face. She felt vulnerable. She was all alone, on a lane hidden by trees, in a car with a man who'd acted strangely ever since she'd left him and she didn't like it. 'Liam, please.'

'Ah, please, now you say please. Wasn't that what you said to gorilla boy the other night?' He smirked, nodded and then sat back in his seat as though settling in for the night. 'You see,

I heard you, Maddie, darlin'. You were begging another man to hold you. It was quite pathetic, even by your standards.'

'It was just a hug and I did not beg,' she snarled as she reached for the door handle. His hand grabbed her other wrist making her scream as she struggled to release herself. 'Let me go,' she shouted using her other hand to try and release his hold, but his grip tightened.

'I'll never let you go, Maddie. Do you hear that?' His words were venomous, spat out through gritted teeth, showering her face with his saliva. His hand tightened again, making his nails sink into her wrist, deeper and deeper.

Madeleine screamed. 'Liam, get off. You're hurting me. Stop, stop now.' Fear took over. She stared into Liam's eyes, which now bore no emotion.

Even though he was now shouting at her, his facial expression didn't change making her realise that never before had she seen him so angry or determined. 'I won't let you go, Maddie. Not now, not ever!'

Madeleine began to shake with fear. The words 'not ever' terrified her and she suddenly realised that his words were of obsession and not of love. She had shooting pains in her wrist that were travelling up her arm. She had to think. She had to get away from him and she had to do it fast. Her eyes shot around the car.

'Arrgh, Liam a spider, there's a massive spider. Right above your head,' she screamed as loud as she could and kept her eyes fixed on an area of the Mazda's roof above where he sat. She knew he was terrified of spiders, knew he'd panic, knew he'd let go of her and watched as his arms splayed above his head in a frantic attempt to stop the imaginary creature from landing upon him.

She took her cue, jumped out of the car and quickly looked between the hall and the gatehouse. The gatehouse was closer and she headed straight for it. It was still raining heavily and within seconds of jumping out of the car, her hair was soaked, along with her jeans, which were much too long and were dragging in the puddles as she ran. Looking over her shoulder, she could see the car. It was still parked, still pointing towards the gates. The headlights were on full, making it impossible for her to see what Liam was doing, but the engine revved over and over and it crossed her mind that if he wanted to, he could aim the car right at her and end it all quickly. Her heartbeat pounded through her entire body, her head spun and her legs turned to jelly as she just managed to propel herself over the fence, launching herself into a full blown assault upon Bandit's door.

'Bandit, please. Please help me.' She ran around the house, banging on windows and doors as she went. 'Bandit. Are you in? Come on, come on, answer the door.' She pounded as hard as she could. Even if in a deep sleep, he'd have woken and it suddenly occurred to her that even though a lamp was on in the lounge, he might not be there at all.

Had he said that he'd be going away? Was he up at the hall? She knew it was his day off, but hadn't thought to ask what he'd normally do in his free time. Why would she? She wasn't his keeper.

'BAAANNNNDITTTTTT...!' she yelled in the hope that he'd be in earshot.

It was dark and Madeleine was terrified. It was more than obvious that Bandit was not there and she had no idea when he'd be coming home. She began to shake. She'd never seen Liam so angry before, never seen his eyes so wide, never heard that much anger in his voice and never wanted to hear it again. She thought back to things that had happened, the broken locket, the teddy bear, the electrics at the house, her car breaking down and, dare she think it, Jess's flat being broken into. There had been too many things happening, too many things going wrong and, right now, she was sure that Liam was at the centre of them all.

She heard the sound of the car revving again, making her

look around, wondering what she should do. Was it better to run or hide? The moon was covered by the dark clouds, making the night seem blacker than normal. It was raining and she still hadn't had time to explore the woods which stretched out as far as she could see. Even though the trees were bare, she didn't fancy trying to navigate her way through them – especially with Liam on her trail, but did she have a choice? She was sure he'd gone mad and hadn't liked the way he'd looked, the way he'd gripped her wrist or the way his words had spat out from his mouth in a definite threat. He'd meant to scare her, meant to hurt her and he'd succeeded. She had no idea what he was capable of next.

Looking behind the gatehouse and into the gardens beyond she saw a rickety old shed, which probably let more water in than it kept out, a low wooden frame, which may or may not have been a compost heap, and a whole group of bushes that looked thick enough to hide in. She ran down the path, trying to be careful with her step. To each side of the path were muddy patches of ground that looked like areas where vegetables could be grown in the spring.

Then she slipped. Tumbling to the ground, putting her hand out to save herself, she landed heavily on a patch of gravel. Gritting her teeth, she tried not to yell, but dared not to look at what damage she'd caused as she heard the noise of the car get closer. Pulling herself quickly to her knees, she crawled and used her hands to feel her way through the darkness towards where the old shed stood. It had a small brick base and she found herself cowering down between the shed and a bush, lying flat on her belly in the wet, sharp gravel as she hoped and prayed that the darkness would hide her.

The car had parked and stopped. She heard footsteps as he got out. Her heart pounded in her chest. Her breathing echoed in her ears and her whole body shook uncontrollably with fear. Her fingers were numb with the cold and the wetness of the mud soaked through her jeans and into her skin.

'You can't hide, Maddie.' Liam's voice reverberated through the rain that still poured down with a vengeance. 'I'll find you and when I do, you will come back to me, I can promise you that.' His voice paused and Madeleine could hear him walking around the gatehouse, every step bringing him closer and closer to where she hid. Every second felt like a minute. His boots stamped so heavily, she could almost feel the ground shake in mini earthquake tremors.

Peering above the wall, she could just about make out his silhouette looking through the windows of Bandit's empty gatehouse. He tried the windows and the doors, making Maddie wonder if he'd actually go in if one were open.

Oh, Bandit. Why, oh why couldn't you have been home? she thought to herself as she once again spread herself as close to the ground as she could.

'I know where you are, you bitch. You may as well just come out and we can sort this, once and for all.' Again, his voice grated in her mind and even though she'd never been religious in her life, she began to pray that he'd go away. 'Your boyfriend isn't home, Maddie. He left, right after he saw us cuddling up at breakfast. He knew we'd get back together, knew that I was the better man. Me, Maddie. That's right. Me, I'm the better man. I always have been. I'm the only man you'll ever have; why can't you understand that? As for your boyfriend, why do you think he isn't here now? He's left, Maddie. He isn't coming back.'

Madeleine pressed herself even closer to the ground. The gravel was uncomfortable, it pressed into her skin, but she dare not move, barely dared to breath and wished she'd worn clothing more suitable for rambling. But then she'd thought she was going to help Jess, thought she'd be in the car. Her heart was now pounding in her head, booming like a bass drum, first steady and rhythmic, then it sped up, going faster and faster making Madeleine grab each side of her head in the hope that it would stop.

Had Bandit really seen them together that morning? She'd been in the dining room talking to Liam. He'd held her hand under the table, restricting her, ensuring she couldn't move while they spoke. Bandit must have seen and thought they were being intimate; thought they were getting back together just like Liam had said. She felt nauseous as the ground began to move.

Had Bandit really believed she'd gone back to Liam, especially after all she'd told him and after the evening they'd spent together?

Suddenly, she heard Liam's footsteps stamp away. The car engine continued to run but still Madeleine dared not move. A distant noise came from inside the car. 'Paperback Writer', the ringtone on her phone. She listened as it rang and rang, stopped and then rang again. It was probably Jess, checking on her whereabouts, wondering where she was. Each time it rang, she mentally sang the song and wondered how many times Jess would try before realising that something was terribly wrong.

Closing her eyes, she thought of how Jess would be coping. She'd be waiting for the police, hopefully she'd gone to the café, but if not she'd be looking after Poppy and Buddy and doing her best to keep both away from the glass that she'd said was all over the floor. But Madeleine knew that Poppy would be safe. She knew, without doubt, that Jess would protect them and would ensure that no harm came to either Poppy or Buddy.

Madeleine wanted to move. Her whole body was shaking. She was afraid, cold and wet. Every instinct she had made her want to run to the car, go and protect Poppy, she had to get to her at all costs, but she couldn't be sure where Liam had gone and knew that he could be waiting in the car. With no other choice, she made slow determined moves and managed to crawl towards the edge of the woods, where she began making her way inch by inch on her belly through the trees and back to Wrea Head.

Chapter Twenty-Seven

Liam ran as fast as he could back up the lane to where his own car stood. He knew that Madeleine was hiding somewhere around that cottage and no matter how clever she thought she was right now, he was determined to find her.

He looked in the back seat, grabbed a rucksack and opened the zip. He studied its contents and pulled a knife out of the depths of the bag. He nodded at his choice, zipped the bag back up, started the car and with no headlights he drove slowly back down the lane, all the while scanning the fields which contained horses, sheep and pigs. A movement caught his eye and he stopped the car, climbed out and leaned against the fence while his eyes became accustomed to the dark.

He slowly looked towards the cottage, to where he'd left her, where he knew she'd been hiding, cowering in the dirt. He laughed at the thought, after all it was her fault. She'd started all this when she'd first moved in. He'd loved her for so long but he'd wanted her, alone. Not the mother to a whining child. She'd cared about the brat too much, hadn't put him first and had spoken out of turn, challenging him, which had disappointed him. She'd not done as she was told. She'd refused to put all her money into a joint account, didn't understand that she was not to touch his things, nor should she have allowed Poppy to play with his childhood toys. He'd done everything for her, shared his house, played the game fair, but she hadn't. He shook his head as he reached the cottage and, as quietly as he could, walked around its edge with his eyes wide open, looking for Madeleine.

He walked up the path to the shed. She had to still be there, he thought as once again the rain began pouring in torrents. He looked up at the sky, wondering if she were stupid enough to move, stupid enough to leave her hiding place and head into the woods, where untold dangers would be. He looked over to the trees and shook his head. No, not Maddie. She wouldn't go there; she'd be too scared.

He held the knife up in the rain and watched as trickles of water ran down its blade. But then he stopped in his tracks and threw the blade at the shed. 'Stupid, stupid, stupid. You didn't wear the gloves.' He then fell to his hands and knees and crawled along the path, searching for the blade that had landed in the long grass that surrounded the edge of the shed. 'You're getting too confident, you're making mistakes, you're a stupid, stupid boy.' He slapped himself across the face, a form of punishment he'd learnt to give himself over the years. 'You're so stupid,' he screamed.

He stopped in his tracks. Wasn't that what his mother would say, hadn't she called him stupid each and every time he'd done something wrong, every time he'd left his toys out all over the floor? Wasn't it always his fault, always him that was stupid and always him that got into trouble, even if it was Freya that had stood on or fell over things?

He found the blade and grabbed at it, stood up and looked down at his mud stained clothes.

'Oh, no. Not good. Not good.' He thought of how he looked, of how he hated being dirty and of how Madeleine had brought him to this.

'You shouldn't have lied, should you? You should have been out that day.' He thought of how all his clothes had tumbled down the stairs, of how he'd had to launder them all and iron them again before he could place them back in the wardrobe, where they belonged. 'You did that, Maddie. You did that to me and now, now you have to pay.' He looked down at the knife, knowing that it couldn't be used. 'You're normally better than this,' he berated himself as he bounded round the corner of the shed and searched behind. He usually planned meticulously, thought things through from every conceivable angle but tonight Madeleine had made him shake with anger, made him lose the control that he normally kept on a very tight leash.

He stopped, listening to the dark night and finally realised that Maddie was not there. Somehow she had escaped him again. Tonight would not be the night that she paid. That night would come. It would come soon and when it did, he'd get his revenge.

Chapter Twenty-Eight

Dusk was falling as Bandit ran along the side of the River Ouse. Mud squelched underfoot and once or twice he felt his foot slide beneath him. He'd been running for miles. It had been the only way to burn off his energy. The only way he would sleep that night. He had to find a way to stop himself from thinking of Madeleine. But he'd run further than he'd thought and only now did he begin to recognise the area. He passed the Lombardy trees which lined the path on which he ran and could now see both the York Minster and the National Railway Museum in the distance. A women's quad scull crew sailed past him at speed and he knew that he'd soon be approaching Clifton, where he'd left his truck. An intended visit to The Elder Lodge Nursing Home had turned into what must have been a twenty mile run. He just hoped that his father hadn't noticed the truck, watched him run off or waited for the past four hours for him to walk through the door.

Bandit slowed down, caught his breath and walked the final mile. Visiting his father took energy and he needed to ensure that by the time he got there, his mind and body would be rejuvenated. He reached Water Lane and the path ended. Here he stopped for a moment, pulled his soaked T-shirt over his head and dried his body with it. Opening the truck, he reached for a can of deodorant, grabbed a clean jumper and pulled it over his head. He then reached for the box of fudge that he'd brought for his father to eat and ventured inside to the sitting room where he knew his father would be.

'Now then, Dad. How are you doing? You okay?'

His words were lost. His father's eyes were closed. Deep in sleep, his hands were clutching a teddy bear to his chest, while his legs were curled beneath him. He resembled a small child in a chair that looked far too big for his needs. His chair stood in its normal spot by the bay window; a table stood by its side littered with magazines, picture books and chocolate. An elderly woman, much older than his father, sat close by. Bandit had noticed her many times before. She was often sitting beside his father and her chair almost always touched his. Once or twice he'd noticed her tenderly holding his father's hand. But each time Bandit entered the room she'd tenderly pat his father on the arm and then stand up to leave. She took hold of the Zimmer frame that stood by her side and slowly disappeared out of sight and into another room.

Bandit smiled at the peaceful sight. It was good that his father had a friend, someone to talk to during the long repetitive days. He moved closer and then wrinkled up his nose at the smell of disinfectant, bleach and plug in air fresheners that was overpowering his senses.

Taking a seat beside his father, Bandit sat quietly and closed his eyes, contemplating his father's life. He'd been in the home for years. He went out occasionally, but most days he was too tired and ill to move, yet too well to die and Bandit wondered if it would have been kinder all those years before to have let him go. He had his own world in which he lived, it was primitive, but it was his own. He didn't have a care in the world and Bandit sat for over an hour wondering whether he or his father actually had the better life.

Was it better not to know what was happening in the world around you? To be oblivious of it all and not to know the worry, or be affected by the stress and the heartache that surrounded life. Or was it actually better being capable and independent? Both had an argument in their favour and this had been his overwhelming thought when he'd set off for his run. He'd only stopped running once he'd come to the conclusion that he needed both the happiness and the heartache, whatever that might mean. It was both the happiness and the heartache that made his heart beat as though it would burst out of his chest, that made him feel alive and without the occasional heartache, you didn't get the happiness.

'Would you like a drink, Mr Lawless?' a young nurse asked as she walked past the door. 'We have some fresh tea brewed, if you would like?'

Bandit shook his head preferring to sit peacefully while his father slept. A gold clock with ornamental spikes hung on the wall and ticked loudly and just as it struck five o'clock his dad opened his eyes, looked up, yawned and then smiled broadly as he saw his son.

'Hey.' The word was simple, but to Bandit it meant a lot. It meant that today was a good day and the child within his father had recognised him. He held out his hand and took his father's hand in his.

'You okay, Dad?'

He smiled. 'I've been to sleep.'

'Yes, you have. Did you have a good dream?' Bandit asked, watching as his father struggled with his thoughts.

He nodded. 'Went to see the lady. She'd made cheese sandwiches and cream cakes for our tea.'

'Which lady did you go to see, Dad?'

'The lady. I went to see the lovely lady. Love the lady, she's so nice.'

Bandit smiled. His father often talked of the lady and a life he thought he'd had. But the truth was that he'd been adopted soon after birth and his Nana Lawless had died when Bandit had been only three years old. She'd only ever been called Nana, never referred to as the lady. But other than her, Bandit had no idea who his father was talking about.

Bandit lovingly stroked his father's hand. Did it really matter if he imagined her? He wasn't hurting anyone else if he lived in a place that no one else recognised, was he?

Bandit shook his head. 'Is the lady nice to you, Dad?' he asked as his father broke into a broad smile and in a very child-like manner, nodded his head.

Bandit leaned forward and kissed his father on the forehead. 'That's good, then, isn't it? We like nice, kind people, don't we?'

His father slipped back into his sleep, the teddy bear still clutched in one hand as his other held on tightly to Bandit's.

'That's right, Daddy. You have a lovely new dream.'

Chapter Twenty-Nine

I'm happy and sad all at once. Tonight, I'm going to sneak to the summer house at midnight. Eddie has a plan and says he has enough candles to light up the woods. I'm excited to see him but also I'm really worried because the war is getting worse.

Men are being recruited and I'm terrified that Eddie will be called up too. All single men aged between eighteen and twenty-two years old are liable to go. They call them the 'militiamen'.

It is soon to be Eddie's birthday. He will be eighteen years old in July and I've begged him to go and work in the mines, just until the war is over. The 'Bevin Boys' are expected to mine for coal. They are expected to keep the mines working and wouldn't be expected to go to war. But Eddie won't have it and watches the drive daily for the postman arriving with his letter of conscription.

Not only do I fear for Eddie, I fear for both Mary and I. Women are being enrolled into the war effort too and I just hope that if Eddie gets called up, so do I. Even though I'm sure that Father would find a reason why I couldn't go.

Rationing has gotten worse. The use of coal, gas and electricity has now been tightened along with both tinned tomatoes and peas. So, I'm pleased that we grow our own vegetables. Father has taken to hiding them in the cellar wrapped in brown paper and kept in the cold. There is word that sweets will be rationed and Jimmy is distraught. He does love his chocolate and I know that he's asked cook to hide some for him in the pantry.

Eddie and I still see each other as often as we can, albeit

Father now watches for us meeting. He's forbidden that we see each other, has refused to allow us to marry and has threatened to throw Eddie's mother out of the gatehouse if our dalliance continues. But I love him so much, how can we possibly stop?

Father has now insisted that I go to London for the summer even though with the rationing of fuel I have no idea how he intends me to get there. He says that a new environment will sharpen my mind and improve my manner and has insisted that I'll be leaving within the month. I fully expect that the conveyor belt of single, eligible men will be churned out before me, the moment I get there.

I don't want to go; it's far too warm to be in London. I'll have to dress correctly at all times, just in case a suitor drops in to visit. I'd much rather be here, wearing our light summer dresses, but what can I do?

Madeleine propped herself up against the pillows as she read the words of Emily's diary. She sat forward and sneezed, wiped her nose on a tissue and then collapsed back against the pillow, coughing. Every inch of her body shook with cold and then moments later was overheated from within. It had been two days since she'd ran to Bandit's cottage, lain on the floor beside the shed and hidden herself in fear for her life, while Liam had screamed and shouted. She'd been shaking, terrified, wet and emotional and her hands and knees had been shredded against the gravel that had covered the path. All she could remember was crawling on her hands and knees through the woods for what seemed like hours, hiding every time she heard a noise and holding her breath, waiting for Liam to find her.

She pulled another tissue from the box, just in time as she sneezed again. Feeling hot, she threw back the covers, only to drag them back over her a few minutes later in an attempt to stop the shivers. She'd taken everything at Nomsa's insistence from hot whisky to Beechams powders and wondered what she needed to do just to feel normal again. Her eyes glanced towards the bathroom and she wondered how much energy it would take for her to crawl into a deep, hot bath.

A knock on the door made her sit up and pull the blankets closer to her.

'Who is it?'

'It's me, Nomsa. Can I come in?'

A feeling of relief flooded through her as she lay back and began to cry. Every time there was a knock on the door, every noise in the corridor, every sound outside made her panic that Liam was back.

'Sure, but use the key, it's locked,' she sobbed as she heard the key in the door and Nomsa walked in holding a huge bunch of wild flowers in a vase.

'I picked you these from the garden.' She smiled as she placed the vase on Madeleine's bedside cupboard. 'I thought they'd cheer you up. How are you doing, my girl? Do you want me to make you some nice parsnip and sweet potato soup or some pancakes, I have blueberries?'

'I'm okay, Nomsa. I'm not hungry,' Madeleine said, shaking her head, 'but thank you. I'll be fine once this damn cold goes.'

Nomsa sat silently for a few moments. 'Maddie, my darling girl, you don't fool me. You are not fine at all. I saw you come back that night. How you crawled in from the woods, covered in mud. You looked horrendous and I hate him for what he did to you.' Her voice was full of concern. She looked down, and bowed her head. They'd become close since her father had died. Nomsa now acted like a mother figure to her, Poppy and Jess.

'Oh, Nomsa. It's such a blur. He grabbed my wrist, hurt me and said nasty things and I really didn't know what he would do next. I really thought he'd kill me.' She fell into Nomsa's arms and sobbed. 'I was so scared, but all I could think about was getting to Jess. All I could think was that he'd go after her and Poppy too.'

'Well, he'd better not show his face around here 'cause my broom is ready and waiting for him. I swear, Maddie, I'll whoop him good if he ever goes near you again.' Nomsa's eyes filled with tears and Madeleine knew that she meant what she said.

'Is Poppy okay?' Madeleine pulled a tissue from the box and looked at Nomsa for an answer. With her being so ill, Poppy had been staying in Jess's room since the night of the break in and Madeleine missed being with her.

'She's having her breakfast in the kitchen with Jess and Jack.' Nomsa nodded as she replied to her question.

'Did Bandit come back yet?' Madeleine managed to say as a series of sneezes overcame her and the tissue she'd pulled from the box came into use.

'Oh yes, he's around, my girl. He'd been over to York to see his daddy that day and had stayed in town overnight.'

'His father? Of course, why didn't I think of that?' She sat back, relieved.

'Well, if it helps, he was furious when I told him what had happened. Swears that if ever Liam O'Grady steps foot in the grounds of Wrea Head Hall again, he'll be gunning for him. And what's more, you need to get yourself better soon, because he asks about you all the time. I've had to feed him twice as many scones these past two days.'

Madeleine smiled at the thought of Bandit eating all of Nomsa's scones. 'Really?'

'Yes, really. I'm sure he keeps dropping by the kitchen in the hope that you'll be down there.'

Madeleine smiled and shook her head. 'Oh, I doubt he'd want to see me looking like this.'

But Nomsa gave a knowing nod, kissed Madeleine on the cheek and disappeared back down the staircase and to her kitchen.

Chapter Thirty

July 12th, 1942

The worst has happened.

It was Eddie's birthday last week. He's now eighteen years old and this morning the postmaster delivered his conscription letter. This time next week, he'll be gone. He has to do some training for just eight weeks, following which he will go to war.

My poor Eddie will be sent to a battlefield where grown men will want him dead and I can't bear to think of it.

He says he will go, won't do anything to get out of it and even though I've begged and begged for him to work down the mines, he's not having any of it, says he won't work the mines and definitely won't be seen as a coward. Besides, now that the coal is rationed, even the Bevin Boys are being called to war.

We're going to meet at the summer house tonight. Father is still watching us closely and I don't want him to see me walk into the woods, so I'll use the tunnel to get there and back.

I have to make a plan. I have to do something to keep him here in England. Whatever it costs, I want to keep him where he is safe but I have no idea what I can do.

Jimmy is home from school again. He's already up to mischief and I need to watch him carefully. The chambermaid he took to chasing has now left Father's employment, but a new one is here and his attentions have moved to her. I caught him on the upper landing, outside the room where the maids go to take a bath and I'm sure that he waits until the coast is clear and goes in there with them.

I think that Mary and the valet, Benjamin, are once again on talking terms. He now seems to like her more and notices *her every time she walks past. They tend to disappear after dinner a little too often and he actually left Father waiting for his coat the night before last and Father had to get it for himself. Benjamin said that he'd been taken poorly, but I'm not sure that Father believed him. If he found out the truth, he'd be furious.*

I overheard Father speak to our mother about the need for a valet and suggest that it was time to keep less staff. Life has changed in big houses, more household members now do their own chores and I'm sure that Father thinks that Mary and I should do more work, but I doubt that I could, especially the gardening. It would be awful if, when Eddie comes back from war, there was no job here for him to come home to. And, if he had no job, what would become of his mother and her gatehouse? It's tied to the hall and I fear she'd have to move out.

Mother's baby will be due soon. She's getting bigger by the day and her moods have changed. We're told that it will come late in the summer, but, by the size of her, I suspect that the baby will come sooner than she thinks.

Madeleine inhaled deeply.

'Poor Emily,' she whispered as she pulled the covers back and stepped out of bed. She'd been reading the diary and looking at her sketches and pictures for hours. Walking into the bathroom, she grabbed a towel, washed her face and glared at her bright red nose which shone back at her in the mirror.

'You look damned awful,' she said, pulling a face, before turning around and walking back into the bedroom. She tidied the quilt and puffed up the pillows. 'Won't be long before I'm back to normal,' she said as she turned to the wardrobe and dug through her clothes until she found a pair of clean tracksuit bottoms, thick fluffy socks and a knitted long sleeved top.

'Pull yourself together; you have a daughter and a puppy to look after,' she said sternly to herself as she pulled on the clothes. 'You can't expect Jess and Nomsa to do it all,' she added, knowing that they'd both minded Poppy for the past two days while she'd insisted that Madeleine should take to her bed.

Madeleine picked up her hairbrush and began dragging it through her knotted hair. 'You're sure not going to win any beauty contests,' she continued as she sat back down on the bed with a sigh, 'but I think it's time to face the world again.'

Madeleine used the back staircase to take herself down to the kitchen. She was not dressed appropriately for the hotel and was keen that she didn't bump into any guests. At least Liam was gone and if Bandit or Nomsa had anything to do with it, he'd never dare show his face here again.

'There you are, my girl. It's good to see you out of your bed. Now, let me get you a hot drink,' Nomsa's voice rang out and Madeleine slumped in the chair and felt Nomsa's hand immediately attach itself to her forehead. 'You're still feeling warm to me, though, so take it slowly.' She walked through the kitchen, switched on the kettle and lifted some bacon onto a crisp white bread roll. 'Eat this up, you need to get strong again.'

'I can't. I need to see Poppy. Where is she?'

'She's fine. She's out there on the grass with Jess. I believe young Jack could be out there too.' Her eyebrows lifted as she said the words making Madeleine jump up and look out of the window. Jack sat next to Jess with both Poppy and Buddy bouncing around them. They looked fondly at each other and were sitting so close that not a blade of grass could have grown between them, making Madeleine raise her own eyebrows and look back at Nomsa, who smiled.

'A lot can change when you're not watching,' Nomsa said as she pushed the bacon sandwich firmly under Madeleine's nose, before turning to pour the tea.

'Wow. When did all this happen? I should go get Poppy. Give them some privacy.' She smiled at the thought that Jess had found a friend and wondered how far the relationship had gone. They did look extremely affectionate towards one another and Madeleine approved wholeheartedly. Jack had never done anything to worry her, he'd always been the perfect gentleman and although he was a few years older than Jess, Madeleine secretly hoped that he'd be the catalyst that kept Jess from going back on the ships. She knew she was being selfish and protective, but after all that had happened and all that she'd lost, she wanted to keep Jess close and here at the hall.

She took a bite of the sandwich.

'Poppy's all right, trust me. The child gives them a reason to be together in the garden. Shall we say they're watching her play?'

Madeleine nodded.

'Oh, ouch. Wow, you look like crap.' Bandit walked into the kitchen, held up his fingers like a cross and sat down opposite Madeleine at the table. 'Am I safe to sit here or do I need one of those surgical masks, you know, the ones all the Japanese wear to protect them against pollution?' he said with a grin as he reached over for the teapot and poured himself a drink.

'Thanks. I've felt better,' Madeleine said sulkily. She knew she looked a mess, knew her nose was bright red, but she really didn't need reminding. 'It's your fault. I wouldn't be this poorly if you'd been home the other night,' she said as she stuck out her lip. 'You should have been there.'

Bandit laughed. 'So now it's my fault that your ex is totally deranged?'

Madeleine turned her back to where he sat, turning her attention back to where Poppy played and noticed that she was trying to teach Buddy to catch, but each time she threw the ball it hit the puppy square on the nose and he'd give her a puzzled look, as though wondering why on earth she'd thrown the ball at him in the first place. She watched as Poppy found this hysterical and threw herself to the floor repeatedly, laughing, each time it happened.

'Have you read any more of Emily's diary?' Bandit enquired as he moved around the table to sit beside her, nudged her arm and slurped his tea.

Madeleine turned to face him. 'Of course. I can't put it down. Emily talks of underground tunnels that go between here and a summer house. Have you been to the summer house?'

Bandit nodded. 'Of course. It's right in the middle of the woods. Quite a distance from the house, I'd say a good half a mile.'

He pointed and Madeleine sat back and stared towards the trees. 'The tunnel must be huge. I mean, you couldn't really crawl that far, could you? So it would have to be a tunnel that you could walk through, right?' She stood up, walked to the window and tried to estimate how far away the nearest trees were. 'I doubt Emily Ennis would have crawled that far. Trust me, I did it. It hurts like hell.' She pointed to the trees and thought of the night she'd crawled through the woods.

'It must ... It just has to be in the cellar.'

Madeleine turned to watch Bandit as he disappeared down the cellar steps. 'Where are you going?'

'To find the tunnel. Are you coming? It's got to be down here. Where else is so far below the grass? It's the obvious starting point.'

Madeleine turned to Nomsa who smiled and shooed her to the cellar. 'Go, I'll look out for Poppy. If she starts driving the lovebirds mad, I'll bring her in. The Aga's warm, we can do some baking.'

Madeleine thanked her and ran down to the cellar to follow Bandit and help search for the secret tunnel.

Together they walked through the arched rooms that were

below the house. An old coal chute and coal room stood to the left, the wine cellar to the right and the room before them was full to the roof with Christmas decorations, pieces of wooden furniture and piles of boxes all neatly labelled.

Bandit walked around carefully looking at the structure. 'There has to be a clue,' he said pulling the boxes from their pile and moving them to a new one behind him.

'Which direction are the woods?' she asked as she spun around on the spot.

Bandit thought carefully for a moment and then pointed towards the wine cellar. 'That would be the outside wall facing the woods.'

Madeleine stood with her hands on her hips. 'Then isn't it logical that if the entrance is down here, it would be in there?'

They both moved quickly into the second room. Every wall was full of wine racks, every rack overflowed with bottles that were all stacked on their sides. Each rack was dated, each bottle dusty.

Bandit cast a glance over at Maddie. 'Listen, I'm sorry. I wish I'd been there for you, you know, at home when you needed me.'

Madeleine stopped in her tracks and breathed in. Since the night she'd hid in Bandit's garden she'd managed to distance herself from everyone's sympathy and had felt that she could just about cope with what happened. But here, now, Bandit's voice had softened and she felt herself begin to shake as memories of that night flooded back.

Bandit's hand was immediately on her shoulder. 'Hey. Come here.' He turned her to him and pulled her into a hold that surrounded her whole body with a tenderness and warmth that she hadn't felt for years. Her tears began to fall. She could hear Bandit's soft voice that sounded as though it came from somewhere in the distance. His hand rested on the back of her head and his slow, deep breaths pulled her into an almost trance-like state for what felt like an eternity.

'It's okay, shhhhh, let it all out,' Bandit whispered as he pulled a tissue from his pocket and gently wiped away her tears and Madeleine knew that he'd known by the distant look in her eyes that she'd been suffering from within. She'd seen the trauma in his own eyes that day he'd pulled Poppy from the greenhouse and knew that he knew how she felt, knew what trauma could do to you.

'I'm so sorry I wasn't there for you.'

Madeleine watched as he moved his body into a sitting position against the wine rack and she relaxed in his hold. The cellar probably wasn't the best place to be and she knew she'd be much better up in the kitchen where it was warmer, but the last thing she wanted to do was to move. She felt safe in his arms. Her whole body now felt calm as he pulled his jacket tightly around them both and for the first time in days, she was warm without overheating.

After what seemed like an age, Madeleine looked into his eyes. 'I'm so sorry,' she managed to say as she took the tissue from his hand and blew her nose. 'It just got the better of me and, as though I didn't look bad enough before, I bet I look a right state now.'

'Maddie, you always look perfect to me,' he said sincerely as he pushed the hair away from her face.

Maddie knew she didn't look her best. Knew his words were kind and knew that she wanted him to kiss her, but not now, not here. It wasn't right, not like this. She pushed away from him abruptly making them both stumble and they crashed back against the wine rack in an undignified heap. A loud noise filled the cellar and the wine rack began to move.

Bandit jumped towards Maddie once again, catching hold of her in a protective gesture. 'What the hell?'

'Oh my goodness, Bandit. We did it. It's ... it's the tunnel. We found the bloody tunnel,' Madeleine squealed as she grabbed hold of Bandit's hand and dragged him to the opening that had suddenly appeared within the wall.

Chapter Thirty-One

'For God's sake, Bandit. Why can't we just walk down the damn tunnel?' Madeleine said for the umpteenth time as she impatiently stamped from one foot to the other while she waited for Bandit to repeatedly check the contents of his rucksack.

It was now two hours since they'd found the entrance and two hours since she'd run upstairs with a tear stained face, yelling and screaming for everyone to come and look at the tunnel that had most probably been hidden for over fifty years.

Each and every member of staff had rushed down the cellar steps, peered into the darkness of the arched tunnel, taken photos on their mobile phones and made jokes about going in there and never coming back out again. This, of course, had sent Bandit into what Madeleine could only have described as military planning mode and every possible scenario had been thought of and every item of safety equipment had been packed into the small rucksack that he now lifted onto one shoulder. Madeleine stood with her arms crossed, watching and waiting for the moment he'd stop discussing possible problems, synchronise watches and pass the written time plan to Nomsa.

Even Poppy had been into the cellar to look at the tunnel. She'd stood as far back from the hole in the wall as possible, pulled a face and then conveniently remembered that Jess had mentioned the Sea Life Centre, insisted that Jess had promised that they would go and disappeared back up the cellar steps as fast as she could. They'd both now gone for the whole afternoon, totally unimpressed with the happenings in the cellar.

Bandit once again stood in the entrance and assessed the tunnel. Then he turned and picked up the two hard hats and three torches from the bench behind him.

He passed one of the hats and a torch to Maddie. 'Are you coming?'

'Thank God for that, you bet I am.' She turned on the torch and marched into the darkness beyond.

'Maddie, go slow. Keep checking around you and if there's any sound or movement, I want you to retreat as fast as you can back to the house.'

'Yes, sir.' She stamped her foot as though on parade and then shone the torch directly at him. 'Can we go now?'

The first thing she noticed were the brick lined arches that rose above her like a giant underground semicircle. 'Bandit, these are the tunnels that Emily Ennis talks about. Isn't that exciting?' she said thinking of the diary which still lay on her bed. 'I'm surprised, though, that the cellar being the starting point of the tunnels hadn't occurred to you before.'

'I could say the same,' he asked as he shined his torch under his chin and pulled a face.

'Oh, they did. I actually looked down here when I first began reading the diary. I came down to get some wine, searched all around but I didn't notice anything beyond the small rooms and the shelves. I would have thought a tunnel would have been a little more obvious than it was.'

Bandit's laugh echoed. 'It's a secret tunnel, you dummy. You didn't expect it to have a sign and an arrow pointing to it, did you?'

Madeleine slapped his arm, making Bandit turn to her. 'Ha, ha. You're so funny.'

'Am I?' he whispered as he took a step through the darkness towards her.

She looked up, immediately captured by the deep, volcanic sparkles that were his eyes. 'Well, I … I … was kind of being ironic,' she stumbled over her words as his fingers reached out and touched her cheek.

'Were you?' He stepped closer still and Madeleine could feel his breath on her face. She caught a drift of his musky aftershave and stared into his eyes, not daring to look away. She could barely breathe as his face came towards hers, slowly at first. Then without warning, she felt the hard thud as both hard hats crashed together.

They both laughed nervously and hesitated before removing the hats. Madeleine reached her hand up to his face, gently touching the side of his cheek as though guiding his lips to hers and just for a moment they touched, soft and gently as though both were waiting for permission from the other. They moved in unison, slowly at first. Both teasing the other as their mouths parted, hands roamed and breathing became laboured. Every touch of Bandit's lips sent short sharp sparks of desire burning through every part of her. His hands moved over her shoulders, caught the back of her neck and pulled her firmly to him sending mini electric shocks flashing through her entire body as his lips unexpectedly left hers and began searing a path across her cheek and down her neck. She could feel his breaths coming faster, could hear his heart beating in his chest and then as suddenly as the kiss had begun, he stepped away and turned around. And Madeleine watched as his hands shot up to run them through his hair.

'I ... I ... think ...' He looked around the tunnel. '... we shouldn't do this here ... it's really not the most romantic place and ... and ... I'm sorry, it shouldn't be like this. You deserve better, you deserve romance.' He stepped away, replaced his hard hat, turned back in the direction they had been walking and held out his hand.

Madeleine felt cold, stunned and disappointed at the abrupt ending of the kiss, but she put her hat back on, took his hand and followed him through the disused tunnel. Of course he was right, but that didn't stop her stomach doing somersaults, while her cheeks burnt with embarrassment. Why had she allowed that to happen, why had he kissed her at all and why here?

After all she'd read in the diaries, of the love between

Emily and Eddie, she'd thought of the tunnels as romantic, but instead it was dark, cold and endless.

She thought about the past. She knew it had been complicated back in Emily Ennis's time but she hadn't realised the trouble that she and Eddie had gone through just to be together. Surely Emily would have had to walk along this tunnel alone, she'd said so in the diary. But on occasions, Eddie would have walked with her, which made her wonder if they too had shared a kiss down here? Had they shared the heat of passion that she'd just felt or had they walked platonically hand in hand, just as she and Bandit did now?

'It's been a long night. I thought you could do with some food and a drink,' Bandit said as he stood in the entrance to the office, tray in hand. He lifted a glass of wine from the tray and passed it to her. 'Are you working? Where's Poppy?'

He sat in the spare chair, crossed his legs and looked at her.

'Yes, I'm working. Trying to understand how the hell a hotel runs. As for Poppy, she's in with Jess. I've let her move into Dad's old bedroom, you know, till we sort things out properly.'

'I brought sandwiches too,' Bandit said with a smile.

Madeleine eyed up the thick granary bread with what looked like a generous amount of tuna mayonnaise sandwiched between. 'Looks amazing, did you make these yourself?'

'Mmmmm, if I said yes, would you believe me?' He winked and passed the sandwich to her. 'Nomsa, she was worried that you hadn't eaten since lunchtime.'

Madeleine laughed, picked up the bread and took a giant mouthful of food. Nomsa was right, she hadn't eaten since the bacon sandwich and what's more it was only now that she started to eat that she realised just how hungry she really was. 'I should have known better. Having Nomsa around is like having another mother.'

He nodded in agreement. 'Were you surprised that there were two tunnels?'

'Mmmmm, not really,' she managed to say between mouthfuls of sandwich. 'The diary kind of hinted that there might be.'

'Such a shame the tunnel came to an abrupt end. Who do you think bricked it up?'

She picked up Emily Ennis's diary that lay unopened on her desk and began flicking through its pages. 'Emily said that one went to the summer house. But the other, that's confusing.'

'It seemed to head out to the gates, towards the gatehouse,' Bandit said, thoughtfully. 'Which kind of makes sense. My father keeps talking about going through the tunnel to visit the lady? And he lived in the gatehouse.'

'Do you think that lady could have been Emily Ennis?' Madeleine sat excitedly upright in her chair.

'I guess she might have been.' Bandit picked at the fluff on his jumper and then pointed to the diary. 'It has to hold the answers.'

July 19th, 1942

My whole life is falling apart and there is nothing I can do except lie in my bed and allow my heart to break. I've cried now for so many hours, yet still I can't seem to stop.

My Eddie has gone to war and I don't know when he'll ever come home. I begged for him to stay and even tried to change his mind but he is not a coward and wouldn't even consider the idea that he could hide until the war was at an end.

On the last night that he was home, we went through the tunnel to the summer house. I'm so proud that he would build such a house for us both and even though it's made of wood, Eddie has made such a lovely job. The house is beautiful, curtains have been hung and a small kitchen stands in one corner. There's no gas lighting or running water, but it didn't seem to matter, we had a candle that lit up the room and added to the romance and, for the first time, we made love.

It was beautiful and part of me wishes that we'd made love many times before. Eddie must have known what it meant for me to give myself to him and I only hope that the war is over soon and he comes home safe. Even though I'm happy that we had our one special night, it now makes it so much worse that he's been taken away from me, but Eddie has promised that the moment he comes back from the war, he'll do all that he can to convince Father to allow us to marry. The problem is that Father seems pleased that Eddie has gone. So what are the chances that he'd agree to a union?

Both Mary and I still have to go to London and even though I don't want to go, it's Mary that has put up the biggest protest. I could hear her wailing and screaming at Mother, but I doubt Mother cares how unfair it all seems to my sister. After all, finding us both good marriages has been something her and Father have spoken of for years and I'm sure somewhere they've kept a book and written down the names of suitable young men that have crossed our path since we were born.

Rationing is still a problem. Meat is rare and tinned vegetables are hard to come by. Father actually gave the village butcher one of our biggest pigs and told him to keep the carcass hidden and to only give the meat to the people local to Scalby. Now everywhere Father walks, the villagers are patting him on the back, shaking his hand and giving him knowing smiles, albeit no one actually mentions the meat.

I gave Eddie a chicken to ensure that both he and his mother got meat too. If Father can give away meat, then so can I. Eddie told me that his mother had cried, carried the chicken like gold dust and had promised to cook a good dinner for them both before he left.

So now I wait. I wait to hear from Eddie. I wait to be taken to London and I wait for our parents to parade us before bachelors, well at least the ones who are not in the forces and away fighting. I just know that the coming months will be the worst of my life and there is nothing I can do to stop them from happening.

Chapter Thirty-Two

Madeleine woke and immediately looked through the window and out over the fields to where the summer house stood.

She thought of Emily Ennis's words, the ones she'd read the night before and wiped the tears from her eyes. Emily had been so young, so naive and so desperate to be loved. She'd fallen for a man who her family disapproved of, a man beneath her station, a man so anxious to be recognised as a hero that he went to war at just eighteen years old to become a soldier, yet he was still a man that her father didn't deem worthy.

Madeleine needed to know what had happened to Eddie. The next page of the diary had shown pictures, drawings and had clippings from newspapers folded into envelopes.

The telephone rang and she answered. 'Hi, Jack, is all okay?'

'Mrs Frost,' Jack's voice sounded nervous. 'You seem to have a delivery.'

'Jack, you sound anxious. What is it?'

'It's a bed, Mrs Frost. In fact, it's quite a large, Victorian four-poster bed. Do you know anything about it?'

Madeleine's mind flashed back to her father and the conversation they'd had about the new bed that he'd found. Following his death, she'd totally forgotten that it would be arriving and, with all that had happened, room four, where it was intended to go, still hadn't been finished. She placed the phone down in its holder and went into Poppy's room.

'Come on, sleepy girl, we've got to get up. Let's go see Nomsa.'

Jack was right. The bed was indeed one of the largest she'd ever seen. It was currently standing on the back of a truck, covered in bubble wrap and cardboard.

'Where do you want it, miss?' the lorry driver asked as he lowered the tailgate.

Madeleine looked at Jack. 'Do you have any idea what my father would have done?'

'Of course, Mrs Frost. Would you like me to take care of it for you?' Jack said as he immediately jumped into action. He not only began organising the deliveryman, but also the staff within the hall. Within an hour, the bed had been offloaded and placed in the rose room where it was to be kept until room four was ready.

Madeleine went into the office and searched through her father's computer for phone numbers. There was a file on the desktop labelled 'refurbishment'. Opening it, she found the most comprehensive filing system she'd ever seen. Inside the main folder, there were sub folders: one for each room, and in each of these were colour boards and pictures of wallpapers, furniture, curtains and carpets. Each room had its own supplier list and priority lists for which jobs came first and what had to be added into each room.

Madeleine noticed that her father had been laying new water pipes between the rooms that were not yet connected, new heating systems and fire detection equipment. It was only now that she realised how admirable her father had been. All of this was for the future of the hotel and what's more it was foresight into his future. It certainly wasn't the actions of a man who hadn't planned to be here, a man who would take his own life.

'Look at this, Jack. Do you know about any of this?' She showed him the file, the colour boards and the plans.

'Of course, Mrs Frost, let me show you.' He went into a room next to her father's office and returned with a full-sized colour board. It was adorned with pieces of material, pictures of settees, beds and phone numbers. Each phone number had an arrow that pointed to a different part of the board; this indicated which supplier was responsible for which job.

'Thank you, Jack. I can see now why Father relied on you so much. You're a star. Oh, and while you're at it, if you're dating my sister, you'd probably better start calling me Madeleine.'

Madeleine smiled as Jack turned away and blushed.

'Yes, Mrs Frost ... er, Madeleine.'

Her father really had relied on him and now her sister trusted him too and she not only approved of Jess's choice, but envied them both.

Chapter Thirty-Three

'Poppy, come on now eat your sandwich, or there will be no cake.' Madeleine looked at her daughter with her best face of authority, but within moments her eyes had softened and her lips turned up at the corners into a gentle loving smile. She looked out of the window in the hope that Jess would hurry up and arrive at the café soon.

She was late, but for Jess that was normal.

The café was quaint and cottage-like and reminded Madeleine of her grandma's farmhouse kitchen when she'd been a small child.

'What's under there?' Poppy asked as she pointed to a small dish that had been placed on the table. A circle of material covered it and had small beads attached to its edge.

'It's the sugar cubes.' Madeleine laughed as she picked up the material to reveal small cubes of brown and white sugar beneath. 'The cloth is to keep the flies away.'

Poppy had immediately lost interest and her eyes now stared impatiently at the huge oak sideboard which stood next to them, with cake domes littering its surface.

Madeleine watched Poppy eyeing them up over the top of her food, knowing full well that she was carefully choosing which one she would ask for once the chore of eating the sandwich was complete.

'Hey, are you waiting for me?' Jess asked as she bounced in through the door twenty minutes late and sat down at the table. She picked up the teapot and poured herself a drink into the spare cup that Madeleine had put ready for her. 'Oh, I need this. That journey over the moors gets worse and worse. I got stuck behind the slowest tractor in the world and those roads, they're so bendy.'

'I know, they drive you mad, don't they?' Madeleine said as

she kissed her sister on the cheek. 'Good to see that you got here safely though.'

Jess tickled Poppy under the table. 'Now then, young lady, is that sandwich lovely?'

Poppy shook her head and held up the sandwich, showing her how much of it she'd already eaten, whilst dipping her head behind the teapot and pointing to the cakes.

'Poppy, I can see you, you know. The teapot isn't big enough to hide you.'

Madeleine looked over to where the waitress stood.

'Do you think we might have three pieces of that lovely carrot cake, please?' she asked, knowing that carrot cake was the favourite of both Poppy and Jess, both of whose eyes lit up at the request and Poppy immediately dropped her sandwich on the plate making it obvious that the task of eating it was over, especially now that the battle to get cake had been won.

Pulling off her coat, Jess hung it on the back of the chair and then reached into her handbag and pulled out an envelope.

'Maddie, I have a confession to make,' she announced. 'When my flat got broken into I said that I thought your locket had gone. Well, that's only partly true.'

Madeleine watched as Jess emptied the envelope onto the table. One oval piece of locket fell out and Madeleine picked it up. 'Where's the rest, the other side of the locket, the chain?' Closing her eyes, she knew the answer before she'd finished her question. 'It's gone, isn't it?'

Jess nodded. 'I've searched and I can't find it anywhere. I'm so sorry, Maddie.'

Holding back the tears, she turned the piece of locket over and over in her hand. A single, dated picture of her father remained.

'Why, Jess? Why would anyone steal half a locket? I don't get it.'

Jess shrugged her shoulders and watched as the waitress placed the three plates of carrot cake on the table before them. 'Thank you,' she said, waiting till the waitress had gone before she continued. 'Maddie, it's really strange. There were lots of things broken, but such odd things taken. Nothing that you'd have expected. They didn't take the laptop or the television, they just smashed it. In fact, they took nothing of any value whatsoever.'

'So, what did they take?'

'The whole flat looked like a nuclear war zone. They took random stuff, really weird bits of jewellery, an old photograph album, a few DVDs and that picture frame that you gave me last Christmas.'

'What use would any of that be to anyone?'

'I have no idea. Especially the DVDs. I only realised that some had gone when I looked for the one where I swam with the dolphins last year.'

'The ones in the Dominican? You probably loaned it to someone to watch.'

'Not a chance. It cost me a hundred dollars, so I protect it with my life. I'd been telling Poppy about it and told her I'd let her watch it.'

Madeleine thought for a moment before she spoke. 'Do you want to hear some good news for a change?'

'Go on then, spill the beans.' Jess sat upright in her chair.

'Well, without going into too much detail because little ears are listening, but in the tunnel there was a ... well ... what you might call an incident.'

'What are you talking about?' Jess raised her eyebrows. 'You might have to give me just a little bit more of a clue, Maddie.'

'Okay, this morning I had a delivery of flowers.' Madeleine blushed as she thought of the flowers that had arrived and the note that had simply said, 'You deserve romance.'

'What flowers? Who are they from?'

Madeleine looked at Poppy who continued to eat her cake. 'Well, you know.'

'Oh no, please don't tell me Liam sent you flowers.'

Poppy burst out laughing. 'No, silly Aunty Jessie. It was Mr Bang'it man. He sent my mummy some pretty flowers, the chocolates were yummy too.'

Jess fell silent and Madeleine giggled. 'Through the mouths of babes,' she whispered as she watched Poppy, who had now eaten all of her cake and was eagerly watching Jess in the hope that she might get to share hers.

Chapter Thirty-Four

October 29th, 1942

Father made me go to London right after Eddie left for the war. I spent eight long weeks being paraded like a prize heifer before every man that my father thought suitable. They were awful. Complete snobs and most of them spoke as though they still held a plum in their mouth. Besides most of the rich boys all seem to have the most awful spotty chins, I blame it on them spending all their days indoors, they're not out in the weather, not like my Eddie and I wouldn't have wanted any one of them to come near me. I rejected them all.

Rationing was worse in London than it is in the country, however Father seems to be able to buy anything that he needs. But then again he's rich, whereas the poor go without and barely have any food to eat at all. Most of the men who were too old or infirm to go to war walk around in jackets with elbows that have been patched with old pieces of leather, their boots don't shine like they used to and the women's dresses look old, faded or like they were made from old drapes.

Mother's baby was born, so thankfully we had to come back to the hall. It's a girl. They've called her Rose after Mother's favourite flower and both Mother and Father sit beside her crib, watching her for hours. The new nanny should arrive very soon and I often wonder what she will be like, but as long as she stops Mother and Father from drooling all over the child, I don't care.

I've felt poorly now for a number of weeks. At first I thought I might have the flu, I was tired and couldn't wake up of a morning. But then, I woke up too quickly and the sickness arrived. My stomach is hard, like a rock and I know that I'm carrying a part of Eddie within me, but what will happen to me if my parents find out? Will I be forced to abort my sweet innocent baby? I can't allow them to take Eddie's child away from me, besides I'm sure it's illegal. I've heard talk of how it's done, of the horrendous pain that follows and of how many women die shortly after. Is the shame really so bad that it's worth dying for?

I fear the actual birth and have no idea how I will cope. I overheard Mother telling our Father of the torment she went through, the pain she endured. She said that she thought she would die, it had been so bad and that was with her fourth child, not her first.

I pray daily for Eddie to come home. I need him here before the baby is discovered. Father would have to allow us to marry now. Just think of the shame if he didn't. But until then, I will hide myself away. I'm lucky it's turned cold and wintery outside. I wear loose clothes, a pinafore, and even a large jumper to cover my shape.

I've been spending time walking to the summer house during the day. I sit and read while there's light or look out over the woods. At least there I can act normally without drawing attention to myself. Whereas when I'm at the hall, I just stay in my room and feign tiredness of an evening. I've even convinced cook to allow me to take some of my meals in my room too and she doesn't seem to care. I actually think she prefers this to me being in or around her kitchen.

Mother is so taken with baby Rose she doesn't seem to notice anything that I'm doing. But I watch her carefully, when I can. I watch how she holds the baby, changes her and feeds her. I've even taken to folding the towelling squares for Mother once they're washed and dried, just so I can learn how to do it.

The nights are drawing in, and as the weather turns colder Father will expect us to sit around the log fire in the great hall. He's decided that it's cosier that way and has forbidden us to use hearths in mine or Mary's bedroom. He says it's far too dangerous in that wing of the house and that if ever a fire were *to break out, the whole house would burn like a tinderbox. Of course, I expect it's because of the fuel rations, even Father's supplies must be running low by now. The war has caused so much heartache; our men are fighting for freedom but in the meantime we will all freeze during the winter.*

Every day I watch for the postman. Every day I hope for news from Eddie, but after the first letter I received, there has been nothing. I read that letter daily and digest the words. I think by now, I could repeat all the words from memory.

I need him to come home and pray every day that he will find a way.

'Would there be a way?' Madeleine looked up to where Bandit sat on the settee in her room. He'd taken as much interest as she had in the diary and over the past few days Madeleine had taken to inviting him up whenever she knew Poppy was busy elsewhere, so they could read it together.

'I'm not sure. I doubt it. The only way they got to come home once trained was if they were injured, in a box or if they ran away. But if he did run away, he'd have most certainly been court martialled.'

Madeleine closed the diary. 'But why would they do that? If the men ran, surely they'd know how frightened they were. It's barbaric to make men fight, especially when they don't want to.'

'The men took their chance in the hope that they wouldn't be caught. They hadn't had a choice about signing up; most hadn't wanted to go in the first place. They reached eighteen, got called up and were sent to war. Most of them saw things that they could never have imagined. There are things in war that still give men nightmares. He would have seen his friends killed right before his eyes. They'd have known that if they ran, they at least had a chance of freedom. If they stayed, they were almost certainly going to die.'

* * *

Bandit felt his face constrict as he spoke of the nightmare of war. His breathing quickened and he noticed his hands clench together in fists, so tight that cramps immediately shot up both arms. He tried to release them, clasp them in and out, but failed as once again they gripped tightly together, as though ready to go and fight.

Forcing himself to stand, he picked up a glass of water, took a sip and walked to the window. Opening it, he gulped in the air.

A crash, an explosion, the screams that still rang in his ears and continued to pierce his mind even after all this time.

He leaned as far out of the window as he could. Sweat dripped down his face and he grabbed at a box of tissues and pulling one out, he wiped his brow. A flash of pain crossed his face, his eyes suddenly closed tightly and he held his breath, just for a moment. Then his mind returned to the present. He took deep controlling breaths, turned and opened his eyes to see a look of horror on Madeleine's face.

She watched as Bandit lived through an internal nightmare; she knew that he must have seen things that he'd rather forget and stood, helplessly wondering what she could do to help.

'Are you okay?' She rested her hand on his arm, moved it down to his hand and prised his fist apart, to place her hand in his. 'I'm here, Bandit. I'm here. Do you want to talk about it? I know you saw things. Do you want to tell me what they were?'

His eyes opened wide and he stared into her eyes, picked up Madeleine's glass and took a huge gulp of wine.

'There was an explosion. One of many, but this one killed my friends, my girl and the rest of my team.'

'Oh my God, that must have been awful for you. Did you actually see it?'

He nodded. 'Not only did I see it. I should have been on board that truck. I should have been with them.' Once again he took a gulp of wine, picked up a tissue and wiped his face leaving small pieces of tissue behind on his bristles. 'I had to clean up after it. It was my job. I spent the whole day picking up the body parts of my team, my friends, and of Karen.'

It was more than obvious that Karen hadn't been just one of the team. 'Did you love her?'

Again he nodded, looked up and stared into her eyes. 'Of course I did. But Karen was like the most beautiful orchid that I could find and I knew that no matter how much I cared for her, how much I loved her, I knew that one day, especially with the job that we did, I knew that one day I'd lose her, or that she'd lose me. I just didn't know which one of us would go first, or how awful it would be.'

Madeleine gasped. 'Oh, Bandit.' She knew it must have been bad for him and he was right, love didn't always last forever but it didn't mean that you didn't allow yourself to love. She'd have had to be blind not to have noticed his reaction when he'd saved Poppy from the greenhouse, how he'd grabbed her in the thunderstorm when she'd slipped in the mud and how he'd reacted in the tunnel just a few days before, insisting on safety, checking everything and ensuring that every step taken had been checked with military precision. But never had she imagined that he would compare his love to a beautiful orchid, nor had she imagined in her wildest dreams that he'd had to pick up the body parts of the woman he'd loved.

'Have you been to see anyone, you know, professionally?'

Bandit shook his head. 'What, a shrink? I saw the military ones before I left the marines, but no one since. They can't help me. Nothing can erase what I saw. It's down to me. I just have to deal with it.'

Madeleine held out her arms. 'You don't have to deal with it on your own. I'm here for you,' she said with a nervous laugh. 'You know, maybe we could be here for each other.'

Bandit pulled her into his arms. 'Why would you need

anyone to be there for you? You're beautiful, strong, you have the world at your feet. I mean, look at this place, you're the owner of this beautiful hotel now.'

She looked thoughtfully around the room. 'I'm not the owner of this house, Bandit. No one ever owns a house like this, they just keep it till the next keeper comes along and, to be honest, I may have all of this, but at what price? It's mine because my father died and if I'm a hundred per cent honest, I don't believe for one minute that he killed himself.' She looked at Bandit. 'I need to find out what really happened to him. Will you help me?'

Bandit picked up the diary that had been resting on her bed. 'Deal, I'll help you and tomorrow, we start looking for clues. If your father didn't kill himself, and I too don't believe for one moment that he did, then there must be something to tell us what really happened.' He turned the page of the diary and pulled an old crinkled piece of paper from an envelope. The envelope had been glued to the page and looked tissue paper thin with age.

'What is it?'

Bandit unfolded the paper. 'I think it's the letter that Eddie wrote to Emily. You see, there are always clues to what happened in the past.' He paused. 'Do you think we should read it?'

They glanced at each other and then back to the letter. It was really tattered and torn from the obvious reading and re-reading that Emily had done and Bandit carefully unfolded it, placing it on the bed.

'I daren't hold it in my hands, it might fall apart,' he said as he stared down at the words.

'Read it to me,' Madeleine said as she lay back against the pillows.

'The words are hard to decipher. Some of them have disappeared into the creases of the page.'

'Just do your best.'

My dearest Emily,

I can't give too much in the detail. I can't mention places or dates. My letters are censored and I just hope they will get to you.

I left with three other lads. We travelled by train and arrived late in the evening. We were met by the Training Centre Staff and were marched to our barracks. Once there, we were all given our numbers. Mine is 14259331 and I have been given the rank of Private. I'm not sure that I like being a number, but here we don't have a say in the matter. If you write to me, put this number on the envelope of all my mail, otherwise it could go astray and they wouldn't know where to send it.

We went to the Mess Room and were given a meal. It looked like slops; all of our food was served in a tin. I think tomorrow, I will buy my food from the NAAFI. I have a little money and can do that for a few days, but doubt that the money will last long and once it runs out I will have no choice but to eat the slops again. I have come to appreciate, however, that the slops will look much more preferable once I have no other choice and it does put a fear into me that if the food here is this bad, what will it be like when we go to war? Will there be any food and, if there is, will the food be digestible at all?

After dinner we were taken to be kitted out with a uniform. Nothing fits us properly. We were given shirts, trousers, underwear, boots, puttees, webbing, mess tin, gas mask and a helmet. It's all just a little too big, coarse and uncomfortable against my skin and it makes me wish that I could hold your soft body against me, just one more time.

A bird flew past me today, it was so close that I could almost touch it and I watched it till it flew far into the distance and out of sight. All I can say is that I wished that I were that bird. If I were, I'd fly back to you.

I miss you every second of every day. There is nothing I

wouldn't do to once again be in the summer house with you and I promise you now that I'm going to work hard, try and improve my rank in the hope that I can impress your father and he will allow us to marry.

Tomorrow we will be given tests. This will decide which branch of the army we will be most suitable for. I hope to join the Royal Armoured Corps, as I don't much fancy being in the infantry as many of the men in that branch never return home. Besides, there is much more chance of advancement if I get in the Corps.

I wish for the day when I get to return to you. Even if your father refuses me your hand in marriage, it would be enough just to see you each day.

I promise, my love, that I will do my best to come home to you as soon as I can.

All my love.
Eddie xx

Madeleine watched the reaction on Bandit's face. He looked distant, thoughtful and emotional, as he stared at the letter as it lay before him.

'They really did love each other, didn't they?' he said as he walked over to the window. It was still before lunch but it had been raining persistently all day and with the onset of winter, a dark greyness was already overtaking the grounds.

Madeleine admired his physique. It wasn't the first time she'd watched him, wasn't the first time she'd noticed his toned body, but ever since the kiss in the tunnel, she seemed to notice him more. His hair was all ruffled, in no particular style, yet still it looked perfect, suited him and she couldn't imagine it any other way. His T-shirt was pulled tight around the top of his muscular arms, which now stretched out before him as he leaned on the windowsill, and his jeans hugged his backside so tight that they emphasised its exact taut shape.

He was so attractive.

He turned to look at her and her eyes held his as she watched him take in a deep breath. A look of indecisiveness flashed across his face and Madeleine could tell that he was deciding what to do and whether he should kiss her or not. Since the day in the tunnel, he'd brought her flowers every day, but hadn't kissed her or held her at all and she'd felt sure that he'd been as indecisive as her. He walked over to the bed and she felt his hand as it lifted to touch her cheek before resting behind her neck. She held her breath with anticipation and felt him pull her towards him as his lips grazed hers. She responded eagerly, parting her lips to accept the kiss.

Madeleine caught the strong scent of his aftershave – a deep, earthy, manly smell – as his lips left hers momentarily and began to work his way over her neck and shoulder blade. She moaned with desire as a heat seared through her. His lips re-captured hers. He was strong and demanding and his tongue sent shivers racing through her body as he pulled her onto her side and his fingers traced the curve of her spine.

Madeleine gasped. It was more than obvious that this was more than a simple kiss as desire swept through them both.

'Are you sure?' The words were simple, yet had demands of their own. She could feel his breath heaving in his chest; the kiss was temporarily stopped as he searched Madeleine's eyes.

'Poppy, what time will she be back?' He knew that Poppy was with Jess, who since the break in had now moved into the hotel on a more permanent basis. She helped look after Poppy during the day while Madeleine worked, but it was now late morning and he knew that at some time soon Poppy would be looking for her mother, and the last thing she needed was to walk into her bedroom to find her in bed with a man she only met just a few weeks before.

'Er, let me call Jess.'

* * *

Bandit stood up and walked around the room. He could hear Madeleine on the phone, heard that Jess would be taking Poppy out and they'd be gone for hours. He and Madeleine had the whole afternoon to themselves.

He looked at where she was lying on the bed, phone in hand, leaning against the pillows. He loved the way she arched her arm up above her head as she talked, loved the way she curled her legs up beneath her and wanted more than anything to believe that she wanted him and needed him as much as he wanted her. But he was afraid. He knew he still suffered from traumatic stress, knew the flashbacks could happen at any time and knew that it would be easy for him to become attached and end up being hurt again.

Yet something told him that Madeleine was different. She was probably the most honest person he'd ever met, which was quite a statement as he'd only known her for a few short weeks. The one thing he could be sure of was that he wanted her in his life.

'Bandit, I … I don't do one night stands.' It was as though Madeleine had been reading his mind. Her words were enough for him and he climbed onto the bed and his lips touched hers. He lingered. He'd thought about kissing her again for days, he'd thought of how she'd feel in his arms and knew that the moment he took her to bed, he'd want to make love to her and he wouldn't want to stop.

Bandit once again looked into her eyes and Madeleine threw her head back from his face. 'Now, are you going to make love to me or not?' she whispered.

Bandit responded immediately and pulled her to her feet.

Madeleine felt the buttons of her blouse begin to open. The soft material slipped from her shoulders and to the floor with ease, quickly followed by her jeans. Her feet left the floor as Bandit picked her up and she felt the coldness of the sheets as he pulled back the duvet and laid her down. She gave an involuntary shudder as the last of her underwear was removed and finally her naked body was his to see. He sat up; his eyes admired her slender body as his hands slowly moved over her stomach and up to her breasts with the expertise of a masseuse.

'You're so very beautiful,' he whispered as his hands worked reverently.

'You're beautiful too,' she managed to say as she felt him lean forward to place gentle kisses up and down her stomach. She gasped, caught her breath and then pulled him towards her.

'Not so fast,' he whispered with a smile and then pulled away, to stand beside the bed.

Madeleine stared longingly and lovingly as she watched his clothes fall from his body, revealing his taut chest and defined muscles. Everything about him was chiselled and perfect. She pulled at the sheet to cover herself from his view as he turned and pulled the curtains closed over the greyness of the day, leaving the room dark and shadowy. The deep sparkle of his eyes shone back at her through the darkness as he moved over her, pressing her body beneath him and she allowed his mouth to reclaim hers. Taking his time, he kissed her while allowing his hands to gently arouse her and then suddenly without warning, he was deep inside her. Their bodies began to move as one. At first they moved slowly, but then rhythmically and passionately together in a fierce, yet powerful tempo. A scream of ecstasy left Madeleine's lips as simultaneously Bandit became still and moaned with pleasure, before using his hands and mouth to ensure that Madeleine completely surrendered too.

'Are you all right?' he whispered in her ear as he pivoted above her.

She nodded, unable to speak as she gasped for breath.

He searched her face. 'I've wanted to make love to you since the first night I met you.'

Madeleine's eyes lit up. 'Met me? You mean the night when you grabbed me from behind and launched me to the floor.' She giggled.

'Yeah, that would have been it.' He moved his weight from above her and lay to her side.

Madeleine sat up against her pillows. 'Have you really wanted this, you know, since then?'

'You know I have.' He smiled as he once again pulled her towards him, making her feel every inch of him as he pressed against her body. 'Do you need to sleep?' he asked as his arms protectively enveloped her body.

'Oh, no, don't you dare sleep, it's still daytime, it's not allowed.'

It was an hour later when she lay completely sated in Bandit's arms. He'd slipped into sleep and she simply lay watching and listening to his deep, steady breaths. He twitched, making Madeleine watch more closely as the corners of his mouth moved into an involuntary grimace. Suddenly, his arm shot out, thrusting into the air, as his body began to shake and his head began moving rapidly from side to side.

'Nooooooooooooooooo. Don't .... don't .... Please, don't ....!' The yells came from a voice so full of emotion that she barely recognised it. His reaction had been of terror, fear and the pain and anguish in his voice had been soul destroying. Her heart leapt out of her chest as she watched his arms suddenly cover his face as though protecting himself from harm.

'Shhhhhh, it's okay. Bandit, it's okay,' she whispered calmly. She really wanted to get him to talk about the explosion, about his time in the marines, but she also knew that now was not the time. But one day it would be and she knew she'd have to bring up the subject and ask him more about the living nightmare that he endured. But for now, all she could do was hold him in her arms.

November 5th, 1942

Today I will write to Eddie. I've waited and waited for a letter to come, for some indication of when he'd be home but when none came I knew I'd have to write once more and tell him about the baby. I would have liked to tell him in person, but now I don't feel that I have any choice. I really want him to know that he'll soon be a father and that when he gets home, there will be a wedding. Not so grand as the one Father had thought I would have, but I don't care as long as it's Eddie that I marry.

After all, Father really can't refuse us now, can he?

I'm hoping that once Eddie knows he's about to become a father, he will find a way to come home. I'm sure there must be a way.

I feel so very alone and Mary is too mixed up with Benjamin to notice me. She has her own ways and up to now I don't think she's noticed my change of mood. She's distant and has taken to sleeping in her own room. I fear that she's meeting Benjamin after dark. And when she's not with Benjamin, she spends a lot of time in the kitchen. It wouldn't surprise me if she isn't making food for him and his family. After all, we still seem to have plenty here with our own vegetables and game. In fact, rationing doesn't seem to have affected us much at all except for the bread which now has so little yeast in it that it comes out of the oven a little flat.

Jimmy is back at school, which is a blessing in disguise. He is far too observant for his own good and would be sure to realise that my shape has changed especially when I refuse to play rough and tumble games with him. Jimmy will be at school until the end of term and should only come home at Christmas and by then I hope that I'll have worked out what to do.

Chapter Thirty-Five

Liam stood in the centre of the bedroom. It was the room that stood at the bottom of the landing, the one that he'd told Madeleine had belonged to his parents and that he kept locked. It was the room that she'd never been in and the room which had held his secrets for so many years.

Each wall was wallpapered in tattered, crude woodchip paper. It was painted in a pale washed out green emulsion and covered with large, wooden framed cork boards. Seven of the nine had pictures, photographs, personal items and pieces of clothing pinned to them. Each had a name above it, and each had photos or items hung from pins that were stuck into the cork below.

Black lines had been scribbled through the people's eyes in the photographs, partially obliterating the pictures, making it difficult to recognise who some of them were.

He laughed as he spun around in the centre of the room, admiring his work and his perfect murders. His sister had been the first, quickly followed by his mother and his father. His laugh turned into a hysterical screech.

'To think Maddie believed that you'd gone back to Ireland,' he said as he poked at his mother's board. 'Everyone believed me.'

He then turned and looked at a board that hung alone. 'You had to die. She loved you too much, when all I wanted was for her to love me.' It was a picture of a man trapped in a car. The car had crashed and his head was slumped backward in the darkness, his mouth hung open and blood spilling from his nose as water surrounded the car, spilling in through its windows.

Liam laughed. 'It was just too easy to get rid of you, wasn't it, Michael?' He walked to the window at the back of the house. 'Of course she missed you, she cried for you. But I was there for her. It was me that comforted her when the time was right after your death.' He thought of the night he'd waited for Michael's car. Of how he'd laughed hysterically, watching as it sped around the corner. He'd known that Michael would have to hit his brakes. Known that he'd swerve to avoid the broken timber that had been strewn all over the road. And had been in awe of his own ingenuity when Michael lost control on the bend and the car left the road in exactly the spot that he'd predicted and cascaded over the bridge and into the water below.

His board was the only board with just one photo stuck in the middle. There were no other photos, no items of clothing, no articles that had belonged to him. 'She shouldn't have loved you, don't you see? I had to get rid of you, just like her mother who interfered after your death. It was so easy to feed her the nuts, discharge the Epi-pen and walk away. Far too easy, she was far too trusting.'

There were two boards to the right of the room. The first was of Bridget, Maddie's agent. 'You, you too interfered and gave too much advice. I wanted a joint account, I needed Maddie's money. But you advised Maddie to keep her own money, keep her independence, but that was a mistake. A really big mistake.' He then moved to the next board along and sat in the middle of the floor with his head held in his hands. He rocked back and forth, his eyes fixed on Angelina's board as he looked at each photograph in turn. Most were of her at work, of them both at work, laughing and joking and he thought of how much effort he'd put in to keep her on side, to keep his job. On one photograph Angelina's eyes still managed to peer out, making him grab a black marker pen that lay on the windowsill. Ferociously he scrawled a line across the picture, this time completely eradicating her eyes.

'You shouldn't have made me redundant, should you?' he finally continued. 'You should have been nice to me when you had the chance. But you chose the others over me. It wasn't fair. I worked hard, but you couldn't forgive me, could you?' He stood back from the board and thought of the time he'd brought her to the house, the time Madeleine had caught them and Angelina had stamped off, glaring at him as she'd gone. 'Well, I bet you wished that you hadn't done that now, don't you? Cause I had the last laugh, didn't I?' His voice trembled as he spoke, and then turned into a soft, gentle sound as he threw the marker pen down. 'Well, you can't watch me now, can you? That's why you had to wear the blindfold; after all you couldn't watch. Not when I killed you. It wouldn't be right.'

He liked the chase, to capture and torment, torture and maim. He'd spent years creating the perfect murder, yet still he couldn't bear them to look at him and had never wanted to visualise how their eyes had looked just before they'd closed for the very last time.

He looked up at the two newer boards. One was covered in pictures of Madeleine, some large, some small.

'You too, Maddie. You turned against me, just like the others. You shouldn't have left me,' he said as he flicked at the broken locket that hung from the board. It was held there with a pin and showed the small picture of Madeleine within the gold oval. He stroked it carefully and seductively while looking up at the hundreds of other photographs that adorned the board. One or two were recognisable as Madeleine looked now, but the others were much older and dated back to when she'd have been between twelve and eighteen years old. One of her on a bike, one in fancy dress and another was a picture from secondary school; her black framed glasses were perched on her miserable face, her hair had been pulled back in a tight ponytail and her school tie had been wrapped around itself so many times it was almost as wide as her neck.

'Didn't know the school photos were being done that day, did you, Maddie?' He laughed and stroked the photo.

'You'd have worn make-up and done your hair if you had. That's right, you just hated having your picture taken without notice, didn't you?'

He stepped back and studied her other pictures. All were staged. All had a look of Madeleine's perfect pose, perfect hair and perfect smile.

'You didn't like me at school, Maddie, did you?' A tear fell down his face. 'And I waited such a long time for you. I watched you every day, every morning outside your form class.' He paused. 'But you walked past me with your friends. You didn't even know that I existed, did you? But, Maddie, I did exist and just like the others who ignored me, annoyed me or left me, you're going to have to pay.' He looked across at the seven discarded boards. 'You're going to realise that I exist, Maddie. I will punish you, and you will pay for your mistakes, just like they did.'

His eyes flicked to the second new board that he'd erected. Another laugh left his throat as he looked at the photos of Jess that he'd begun to collect. There were only a few but he'd get more. His collection of her possessions had already started; the break in at her flat had been easy and the photo album had been a jewel. The DVD had been an obvious choice. He could play it over and over. Watch how she moved, laughed and played. She hadn't owned much jewellery, but the odd pieces that he'd found were now hung up on pins. And central to the board there was a large picture of both Jess and Madeleine; they had their hair in braids and were smiling, cuddling and wearing soft pastel bikinis.

The photo had been taken during a holiday they'd shared during their time at school. It had been around the same time that he'd watched Madeleine outside her classroom; she was two years below him and had smiled once or twice as she'd walked past. He'd felt sure that the smile had meant something, felt sure that she was waiting for him to make his move and had risked everything to walk across the canteen to speak to her. But she'd turned her back on him, ignored him and had carried on speaking to her friends.

And then, with good planning on his side, everything had fallen into place. He'd waited for hours in the snow, watched for her to emerge from her flat and had then performed the act of his life, crashing into her at just the right moment. Oh, she'd been sorry. He'd been hurt and just as he'd predicted, she'd invited him in. The rest had been history as he'd slowly become her friend, her confidante and she'd allowed him to manipulate her life, not realising for a moment that they'd been in the same school and he hadn't thought to tell her. There would have been no point.

He'd given himself a second chance. She was going to be his and for once in his life he was going to have what he wanted: a normal loving relationship with someone who wanted him too.

He looked at the holiday photo and then between both Madeleine and Jess's boards wondering which one it truly belonged to. Stepping back his foot stood on a discarded photo album making him slip and twist his knee.

'Damn you!' he screamed as he stared down at the object that had been tossed on the floor, next to an ornate photograph frame that he'd stamped on to break it in two. Cursing, he kicked them both to one side of the room as he walked over to a picture that lay on his desk. Madeleine's father looked up at him. 'Do I class you as murder too?' He picked up the picture and tossed it in the bin. 'No, you were too easy, just one little sachet in your drink, one dose was all it took and, with a little bit of persuasion, you flew like a bird. So, was it my doing, or yours? Besides, you didn't play fair. I didn't get to torture you, maim you or blindfold you.' He shook his head. 'No, you don't get a board, though I'm glad that you're gone. You tried to take Maddie away from me and no one takes her away from me.'

He moved back to Madeleine's board.

'You think you can run, but you can't hide, Maddie, darlin'. You should have loved me at school.' The words fell from his mouth as he grabbed at his face and a sob reached his throat. 'You almost made up for it, Maddie. I was happy, we were normal, we were a family. I almost forgave you. You should never have left me.'

He picked up a large camping knife. It was pointed with a long serrated edge. He pressed the tip against his thumb, testing the sharpness of the blade. A bright red drop of blood ballooned up. Pushing his thumb in his mouth he began to suck away the fluid. The suckling gave him comfort like that of a mother giving comfort to her child.

'You didn't love me either, Mummy, did you?' he sobbed as he looked over at the second board that he'd hung. Old black and white pictures of his mother covered the board. Again black marker pen obliterated her eyes. 'I needed you to love me, but you loved her instead,' he said as he stared at the board containing pictures of his younger sister.

He'd never liked her. Never wanted her in his life and had no idea why his mother had needed a second child. She'd taken his place. Special they'd called her. Well, she was special now.

The pictures stared back at him: a child of five, young, and tiny for her age, smiled for the camera with a vacant, dreamy and innocent look, that only a blind child could give. The photographs remained unmarked and unlike all the others, her eyes stared back.

Walking over to the picture of Jess and Madeleine, he used the knife to separate the two. 'Soon I'll make sure that you're parted forever, Maddie. You don't need a sister and neither did I,' he said as he pulled the half that contained Madeleine and walked across the room to pin the picture on her own board. He chose a place near the locket, picked up a pin and pushed it through her face. 'Not so pretty now, are we? You bitch.'

A knock at the front door made him jump. Following his normal routine, he locked the door carefully behind him, all three Yale locks. Opening the door to the servants' staircase, he picked up the small pouch, hid the keys inside and then tucked the pouch carefully under the top step. He looked up and smiled as he saw the cage. That's where most of them had ended up. Where they all begged for their life and where they'd all eventually died. He then shut and locked the door to the servants' staircase with three keys on his keyring, then went to open the front door.

Two figures stood waiting and he saw a hand rise up as they knocked again.

Opening the door, two policemen stood before him, dressed in their traditional black uniforms.

'Mr O'Grady?' one of the policemen questioned as he placed a foot forward stopping Liam from slamming the door.

'Yes, sir, what can I do for you?' His Irish tone came over as gentle, friendly and composed.

'We're following up on the disappearance of a Miss Angelina Corby. Could we ask you a few questions, Mr O'Grady, please?'

Chapter Thirty-Six

December 25th, 1942

It is Christmas Day and the worst Christmas I have ever known. Yesterday morning Eddie's mother was told that he is missing in action. Neither his commanding officer, nor his comrades know of his fate. All I can hope is that he is safe and well and that if he was killed in action that his torment was over quickly.

I can't bear to think that he has either died, or is out there alone, or even worse that he's a prisoner of war and that he's being tortured daily to find out the secrets of our country that he wouldn't know. It could even be that he ran away from the war. He's not a violent man and I know that he would not have enjoyed killing other human beings, but if he ran in an attempt to get home to me and has been caught, will he be court martialled?

I pray that I'm not responsible for whatever has happened to my wonderful man. I honestly believe that my letters will have reached him by now and even though I can't be sure, I will never forgive myself if the news of his unborn child was too much for him to bear and have nightmares that I may well have been in part responsible. Did he feel happy or sad to know that by the spring he'd be a father? Whatever went through his mind in those final days before he went missing, I only hope that my letters may have brought him some small comfort in the knowledge that he was very much loved.

I am now left with a huge dilemma. The life within me is so small and defenceless and only has me to protect it. Already I feel a sense of overwhelming love and devotion to it and promise that once my child is born I will show it a photograph of its father every day in the hope that one day my Eddie returns to us. If he doesn't, I need to ensure that the child grows up knowing who his father was and that he would have loved him just as much as I will.

My dilemma is one of choice. Shall I run, take my baby and go? It's an option that I have to consider, but I have no idea where I would go. Everyone I know is a friend of either my mother or my father, which means that turning to them is impossible and to leave with nothing would mean that I'm penniless and without a home. Father would abandon me, disown me and expect everyone else to disown me too.

I could go abroad. But both America and Europe are out of the question. The war is too dangerous and America is too far. I have to be sure that if Eddie does come home, I will be here with his child to greet him, which means that my options are limited.

Madeleine looked up at Bandit who still lay beside her. 'That's awful, she had nightmares too, just like you do.' She grabbed for a tissue, wiped her eyes and blew her nose.

Bandit held Madeleine close and dropped a kiss lightly on her forehead, just as the bedroom door burst open and both Poppy and Jess burst in. 'Mummy—'

Jess stopped in her tracks. 'Oh my goodness, Maddie. Err, I'm so sorry, I'm so sorry,' she shouted as she immediately closed her eyes, grabbed Poppy and pulled her back out of the room, slamming the door behind her. 'We'll just go get a cup of tea. Come on, Poppy, let's go see Nomsa, I smell cake.'

Madeleine could hear the panic in her sister's voice and held her hand over her mouth to stop herself from laughing out loud.

'But I wanna see Mr Bang'it man.'

Jess coughed. 'Poppy, you have no idea how much of Mr Bang'it man you almost got to see.' Jess's voice echoed through the corridor and Madeleine could hear Poppy protesting loudly as she was being dragged towards the stairs.

Madeleine looked at Bandit and finally burst out laughing.

'I'd better go,' he whispered as he dropped a kiss on her lips, pulled back the sheets and began searching for his jeans.

'No you don't,' she said as she dragged him back beneath the sheets. 'You don't think they'll come back any time soon, do you?' She shook her head. 'Besides, they've seen us now. Secret's out, I'm afraid. Come back to bed.'

'Really, you're quite the temptress, Mrs Frost. Now, do tell, what do you want me to come back to bed for?'

'Well, actually, I thought we could read some more of Emily's diary.' A saucy giggle left her lips as she picked up the book and dropped it in his lap.

Chapter Thirty-Seven

'There you go, my girl, eat up your soup,' Nomsa said as she placed a steaming bowl of beetroot and apple soup down on the table in front of Jess.

'Thanks, can I have some of that yummy bread too?' she asked, pointing to some crusty bread buns that stood on a cooling tray next to the range. Steam still rose from them, making the kitchen smell all warm and homely.

'Of course you can, my lovely girl.' Nomsa laughed as she walked to the tray, picked out two rolls and passed them to Jess.

'Nom Nom, we came to see you,' Poppy shouted as she took one look at Jess's soup, turned her nose up and immediately jumped up beside Jess, cuddling in.

'You want some of my soup?' Jess asked as Poppy frantically shook her head and clamped her hand over her mouth.

'If you ask Nomsa nicely she might find you something yummy to eat or we could go out and play with Buddy. Would you like that?'

Poppy nodded.

'Jess said we had to come for cake, but I wanna go play on the bed with Mummy and Mr Bang'it man,' she announced loudly as she picked up the glass of juice that Nomsa had put in front of her, took a gulp and wiped her mouth with her sleeve making everyone else in the room turn around and stare.

Jess shrugged her shoulders, stifled a giggle and picked up a mug of tea that Nomsa had put before her. Lifting it to her lips, she began to sip it slowly in the hope that she could blend into the surroundings and no one would question her as to what Poppy had meant.

'I'm going to go and get Buddy,' Poppy ran straight to the back door and jumped up to grab the key.

'Oh, no you don't, madam,' Nomsa said as she stopped Poppy from pulling the key from the door, grabbed her by the arm and sat her back at the table. She locked the back door, pulled the key out from the lock, held it up in the air for Poppy to see and then placed it in her pocket. 'You're not going out there, young lady, until you've had something to eat.'

'Jess said we could take Buddy out while Mummy was playing with Mr Bang'it man.'

'Poppy, enough, for goodness' sake. I think you've made it very clear and I think everyone heard you the first time and the second time and I'm sure your mummy will be very pleased how enthusiastically you just told everyone.' Jess picked up the bowl and wiped her bread around it to soak up the soup.

Poppy smiled and looked pleased with herself until Nomsa placed a small sandwich before her, making her frown. 'Eat the sandwich, or you get no cake.'

'Huggle me, Nom Nom,' Poppy asked as she raised her arms up to Nomsa for a hug.

'Cupboard love, that's what you give, my girl,' she said with a smile as she sat on the edge of the bench to cuddle the youngster, just as she felt Poppy's hand reach into her pocket to grab the key.

'Oh, no you don't.' She spoke a moment too late. The key flew up into the air and as though in slow motion, it spun and spiralled before clattering down behind the Aga. 'Poppy, where did it go?'

Poppy shrugged her shoulders and began to sheepishly eat the sandwich as both Nomsa and Jess got on their knees and began looking in and around the chimney breast where the range stood. The floor was clean and tiled and a key would have easily been seen if it were there.

'Bernie, you are going to have to pull this out. It must have got trapped behind there.' Nomsa pointed to the chimney breast.

Bernie's eyebrows rose up. 'If you think I've got time to dismantle that right now, you're kidding yourself. Besides, it's hot and I've got sixty people to feed and they are not going to feed themselves. You are going to have to wait till after dinner.' He stood with his hands on his hips. 'Now, I could use some help with chopping the vegetables, if you don't mind.'

Jess's mobile began to ring and she turned away to answer it.

Jess closed her eyes. 'Not again. Has someone broken in?' she paused and listened. 'But the place is almost empty. It can't be that bad. Can it?' She opened her eyes and held her head in her hands. 'Thank you, I'll be right there.' She looked up at Nomsa and thought for a moment. It had been half an hour since she'd left Madeleine and Bandit alone upstairs and knew that they'd have followed her down by now to find Poppy if they weren't in a position where they didn't want to be disturbed. This was Madeleine's time to be happy, she deserved it and Jess had no intention of interrupting her.

'Listen, Nomsa, can you watch Poppy till Maddie comes down? That was the police. Sounds like someone broke into my flat again.'

'I sure can, my girl. When are you going to finish emptying that nasty place and come live here permanently?' Nomsa asked as she smiled hopefully. 'Leave her with me. She can help me make the chocolate cookies for us to eat after tea.'

Chapter Thirty-Eight

I know it's been a while since I've written in my diary, but so much has happened, I barely know where to begin.

My baby arrived last week and I have named him Edward Arthur after his father.

I didn't know what to do or what was happening to me when the pain hit like a battering ram. I've never felt pain like it and now I understand what Mother had meant. I was so cold and so very alone and to make it worse, it began to snow.

I took the secret staircase and hid in the room by the bell tower. It was the only place I could go where I knew I'd be safe. Where I could scream and be sure that no one would hear. I have no idea why the room was built, the only thing that I know for sure is that whoever built the house designed the room in with the plans and needed it to be secret for a reason.

The room was my perfect hiding place. Except for when the bell chimed and the whole room shook along with the staircase. For some time following Edward Arthur's birth, I hid him up there, wrapped in towels and blankets, and no one suspected a thing.

That was until Father returned from London and discovered me sneaking to the stairs.

Up until then, I thought I'd got away with my deceit. I'd sleep with him each night beneath the bell tower, then creep down early in the morning and wait until both Father and Mother had busied themselves with Rose. Then I made excuses of needing air or exercise, but one day it had been raining and I knew that I'd already left Edward Arthur alone for far too long and that he'd be both wet and hungry. But I'd suffered badly after the birth; every part of me was in pain and as I got to the staircase entrance and my hand reached for the door handle, I remember my body doubling beneath me. The next thing I knew Father had hold of me. He helped me up to the room and lay me on the bed where a fever took over my body and I must have slept for days.

When I finally woke, Edward Arthur was by my side. He lay in an old, but newly painted crib, all white with pretty little yellow ducks. The bed that I slept on now had blankets and all I can think is that Father must have bought them for me as I don't recognise them from the house, nor did I recognise the patterned curtains or the huge rag rug made from brown and cream squares.

My father looked after me at a time when I least expected him to, at a time when I'd have thought he'd disown me rather than look at me and for a while afterwards, I couldn't understand why he'd do any of this at all.

Chapter Thirty-Nine

A loud bang, followed by a shrill alarm, a continuous beep ... beep ... beep ... beep noise came from somewhere in the distance as Madeleine woke up with a start. Her chest felt tight and she began to cough. It was dark and her hand reached out to her side but Bandit had already jumped out of bed.

She reached for the light but the electric failed and she began to panic as her breathing became heavier and more laboured.

'Bandit, what ... what's that noise?' She coughed again, caught her breath and tried to take a deep breath but pain seared through her lungs.

Bandit had run to the door. He opened it to reveal a bright glow from the stairway.

He slammed the door shut, leaned against it for a second and took a moment to think. 'Jesus Christ, Maddie, we have to get out. It's a fire. It's blocking the stairs.' His words were controlled yet Madeleine could tell that he too was struggling to breathe. He began to cough and covered his mouth with his hand. Then he scrambled around the room in the darkness, grabbed at the sheets and pulled them into the bathroom, where he turned on the taps, dropped them into the bath and soaked them before throwing them across the gap at the bottom of the door.

'That should help.' He pulled on his clothes and threw Madeleine hers. 'Get dressed, we don't have much time,' he shouted as he grabbed a rucksack from the side of the bed. 'Right, what can you not live without?'

'What?'

'Maddie, this is serious. That fire is coming up that stairway, fast. You have one rucksack; fill it with anything you can't live without, you have five seconds.' He grabbed her laptop, data sticks, her reading glasses and Emily's diary. 'Is there anything else you have to have ... your work Maddie, your books? Is there anything you can't manage or continue without?'

'Poppy. Oh my God. I can't live without Poppy. I need Poppy. Where is she?' She felt her heart bang in her chest as once again she began to cough. Pulling away the sheets from the door, she pulled it open and saw the flames coming towards her. Slamming the door tightly closed, she quickly replaced the wet sheets across the bottom. 'There's fire, it's coming up the staircase. Why aren't the sprinklers working? Bandit, what happened to the bloody sprinklers? We're trapped.'

'Well done, Sherlock, I did tell you there was a fire and I think someone sabotaged the sprinklers. Now, come on, we need to get out.'

'But what happened to the sprinklers?' She was still half asleep and hadn't understood.

He grabbed her by the shoulders. 'Maddie, wake up. I told you, someone sabotaged them, and we have to get out. NOW.'

He opened the window and looked down at the drop. It was at least twenty feet down and nothing but flowerbeds, pathways and concrete below them. The flowerbeds were under the windows, each one full of sharp, prickly roses. The lawns were set back behind them and would be impossible to reach in one jump.

Madeleine stared down at the drop in horror.

He tried to smile. 'Don't worry. I'll get you out, I promise.'

He pushed towels in the rucksack to cushion the laptop before throwing it from the window and into the flowerbed below. The branches of the rose bushes broke its fall and he cursed the day that he'd ever planted them, vowing that as soon as they were safe, he'd dig them up. But right now there was no time to think, he had to save them. He hadn't waited half his life to meet a woman as wonderful as Madeleine just to lose her in this way.

'Maddie, listen to me. We can't jump. We have to try and climb our way out. Wait here, I'll try and find us a way.'

He climbed onto the windowsill and disappeared from her view.

'Bandit, I'm scared. Where's my Poppy? What if she's hurt? Oh my God, what if she's trapped?' She leaned out of the window, looking both up and down in an attempt to see where he'd gone. 'POPPPPPYYYYYYYY ... POPPPPYYYYYY ... where are you, baby? Oh my God, please, please ... please let her be okay.'

This side of the hall was quiet. It was the private quarters and was about as far away from the guestrooms as it could be. She closed her eyes and thought of the room plans that had been on her father's computer. She remembered the new sprinkler system, along with the fact that it had been fitted in the main hotel but this was the family wing, this area would have had to wait until last, until the rest of the hotel had been finished.

She closed her eyes and thought of the guests and hoped they'd all got out safely. They should all be at the meeting area at the front of the house. All the staff would have gone there too, meaning that no one would come to the back of the hotel to look for them and since her father had died, no one else resided in this part of the house, no one except for Jess.

Bandit reappeared and climbed back in through the window. 'The room that's above this one, what is it?'

'What room? I don't think there are any rooms above here.' Madeleine leaned out of the window. 'There can't be a room, and how would you get to it? The staircase stops out there.' She pointed to the door.

'Seriously, Maddie, there's a room. I think it's the room

next to the bell tower. Do you remember in Emily's diary? She mentioned that the noise of the bell could be heard on the staircase.'

Madeleine looked around the room. 'Where's the diary? It might give us a clue.' Her coughing got worse and she leaned out of the window to gasp at the air.

'I threw it out the window. Now come on, we have to get to that room. It just has to lead us out.'

There was a loud bang, followed by a distant scream; glass shattered and another scream. Bandit ducked briefly as though waiting for a second explosion. He then stood up and looked out to see if he could see where the scream had come from. 'If we can hear them, they should be able hear us.'

'Okay, we need to shout together.'

'HEEELLLLLPPPPPPPP ...' they both yelled as they leaned as far out of the window as they could.

'Did they hear us?' She coughed again, her breathing was becoming laboured and she knew the smoke would soon completely fill the room. If they didn't get out now, it could be too late.

Bandit shook his head. 'I don't think so. Are you okay?'

'I think I'm gonna be sick.' She climbed up onto the ledge, caught her breath and began to vomit.

'It's the smoke. I know you feel ill, but we have to keep moving.' He held out his hand. 'Here, let me help you.'

Madeleine wiped her mouth on her sleeve. Her head spun but she began to move slowly. The windowsills were wide but she could feel the danger in every step. Her legs felt like jelly as she inched her way across from one sill to the other. Her hands worked their way along the wall until she reached where the house came to a corner, where it jutted out in a right angle that branched out over the kitchen and, above it, Madeleine could just about see the bell tower.

'Here, it's easier to climb up the corner.' In one swift movement, Bandit pulled himself up onto the roof; lay spread-eagled on the wet slate tiles and then leaned forward, holding out his hand and arm to where she balanced.

'I can't, Bandit, please, can't we just break through one of the other windows?'

'Madeleine just grab my arm and, for God's sake, don't smash a window. You'll cause a backdraft, the last thing you need is a fire ball throwing itself at you.'

Madeleine looked up to where he balanced. Stone ridges lined the edge of the tiles. She took hold of the tile, but felt it immediately slip through her hand and crash to the floor.

She held her breath and looked down to where the tile now lay in pieces on the concrete and began to shake with fear. Every millimetre of her body froze, she knew that she couldn't stay where she was, but was too afraid to move, too afraid that she'd fall too.

'Madeleine, grab my arm. NOW.'

Madeleine looked up at Bandit. 'I swear to God that if we get out of here I will dig up the concrete by myself and lay that bouncy stuff that they put in children's playgrounds. That has to have a soft landing, right?'

'Right, but what you really mean is you'll ask me to dig up the concrete and lay that soft bouncy stuff. Now do as I say, grab my arm. I'll pull you up. Trust me.'

Madeleine hesitated before reaching up and then felt her whole body suspend in mid-air as he pulled her towards him. The next moment, she was lying on the roof and Bandit dropped a kiss on her forehead.

'Well done. Now, do you see the window, the one right there?' He pointed to a small window that stood to the left of the bell tower. It would have barely been noticeable from the woods and she'd certainly never noticed it from the ground.

'If Emily's diary is right, this room is separate to the rest of the house, not only is it separate, it has its own staircase. We should be safe from the fire and, let's hope, from backdrafts.'

Pulling an army knife from his pocket, Bandit pulled out

the blade, slipped it between the wood and the lock and prised the window open.

'Come on.' He once again grabbed her hand and pulled her to the window. 'Put your foot on there.' He pointed to a concrete sill and Madeleine stepped forward, her foot slipped and she landed with a crash in the cold, dark room. She wasn't hurt and tried to adjust her eyes to take note of her surroundings. It was dark and dusty. She sneezed.

'My goodness, how dirty is this room?' She wiped her hand across an old dressing table that stood to the side of the window and could physically feel the dirt move beneath her fingers. There was an old glass mirror, which reflected the moonlight and lit the room just enough to show a baby's crib. It too was covered in layers of dust and stood by a single metal-framed bed, a paraffin lamp and an old dark wood wardrobe, which had long since lost its doors.

'I have to come back up here in daylight,' she said as Bandit climbed into the room and began feeling his way around the walls. 'Do you see the crib? This is the room she talks of; this is where Emily hid her baby.'

He continued to feel his way around the edges of the room. 'Here, there's a door.' He pulled at a handle; a firm thud told them both that the door was locked and he fiddled around until he found a key. 'It's stuck,' he said as he pulled. The door was swollen and stiff. Bandit stood back, assessed the situation, pulled his knife back out of his pocket and began prising at the hinges until the door fell from its frame and landed on the floor, sending a plume of dust high up and into the air.

Madeleine saw the darkness beyond and a staircase that led downwards. Smoke drifted up to where they stood and she looked up as she continued to cough. 'That must be the bell tower Emily mentioned. I can still smell the smoke ... can you see the fire?'

'Staircase looks clear,' Bandit said. 'Come on, we need to

get out.' Bandit led the way and Madeleine watched as he placed his foot carefully down on each tread, checking its yield before trusting it to take his weight.

'This really is where she came to have her baby, isn't it?' she said excitedly as she tried to look up to where the bell hung above them both. 'Jesus. I do hope that's secure.' She pointed to the bell. 'Shall we ring it, just once? It would let people know we are here.'

Bandit shook his head. 'What if it isn't secure and it falls to the ground? It could damage the staircase which we are about to escape down, couldn't it?'

Madeleine looked up once more. 'Okay, okay. You have a point, we'll do it another day, keep going.'

Bandit kept moving down the stairs with caution. 'We're at the bottom. Stand back, I'm going to open the door. I need for you to lie as close to the floor as you can, on your belly. There could be a backdraft and, Maddie, if anything goes wrong,' he paused and dropped a kiss on her forehead, 'Remember, I love you.'

Nomsa cowered in the cellar with Poppy. 'It's okay, baby. It's okay. Someone will come soon, I promise.' Once again she repeated the words that she'd continually muttered for the past twenty minutes, but no longer believed. She looked at her watch for what seemed like the hundredth time. It felt as though she'd been down there for at least an hour and listened desperately as the sound of crashes, bangs and screams echoed down the staircase.

Both she and Poppy had been in the kitchen when the fire alarm had sounded. Nomsa had immediately run to the back door with the child in her arms, as both Bernie and Jack had run to the front, through the house and past the flames.

The back door had been locked and Nomsa remembered the lost key that had fallen behind the Aga. In desperation, she turned and ran back through the kitchen, but stopped dead in her tracks and froze as she saw the flames advancing towards her.

'We'll be safe down here, Poppy. Smoke rises.' Nomsa looked at the wine racks, remembered the tunnel and used her hands to feel for the opening. She wished she'd paid more attention when Madeleine had shown her the entrance. When she'd been told of how it had opened. All she knew was that the wine rack had moved. 'Do you remember where it was, honey?' she asked Poppy.

Poppy shrugged in a matter of fact way. ''Course I do, Nom Nom, you push the rack right here,' she said as she ran to the rack that stood right at the back of the room.

Chapter Forty

Bandit pushed up at the grate above his head. The entrance to the stairway had brought them out below ground level and at some point, someone had put metal grates above the stone steps that led down to the door, either to hide it from view or to stop anyone from gaining access.

'No wonder I couldn't find the door, it's hidden down here,' Madeleine said as she looked around for something to push the grate with. 'We need to make a noise. Should we both scream together?'

They mentally counted to three and began to scream and shout as loudly as they could. Madeleine reached for Bandit's hand. 'I've not climbed out of windows, over roofs and found secret staircases to die in a horrid smelly hole in the ground.' She balked at the smell and turned back towards the stairs. 'Keep trying, I'll be quick. There has to be something up there that can help us.' She looked back over her shoulder, gave Bandit a smile and then disappeared up the stairs, while Bandit continued with his attempts to move the grate, to no avail. It had probably been there for over seventy years, with seventy years of rust, seventy years of dust and seventy years of rain that would have fallen above it.

'Damn you.' He swore directly at the grate, shook it and pushed at it with every ounce of strength that he had. 'Come on,' he screamed. 'You son of a bitch, move. Arrrghhhhhhh!' The bellow left his lips, his voice full of anger and emotion as his taut muscles flexed against the grate.

He had no idea what to do next, but he knew that Madeleine was right. Tonight was not going to be the night that they died. He hadn't been to Afghanistan, watched his friends and lover die and spent the past years coming to terms with what was left of his life only to die in a storm drain below the ground level of the house.

Besides, he had Maddie now. He'd only just found her. Had made love to her for the first time and he knew that she was worth fighting for. He had to stay strong. He had to survive, had to ensure that she survived too and all of that was going to take some planning. He assessed the situation, used his penknife to work its way around the edges then forced the blade up as far as he could to create a wedge.

Anger took over as once again he pushed against the metal. 'Arrrrrrrrrrrghhhhhhhh, come on!' he screamed as the grate moved a fraction.

'Maddie, it moved. Quick, I felt it move.' He listened intently for her returning footsteps, but all he could hear were the crackling, banging and explosions that came from within the house. His thoughts went back to Emily Ennis's diary; she'd said it would burn like a tinderbox and she'd been right. He felt helpless, the house was burning down, and from down here there was nothing he could do about it.

'I found this,' Madeleine said as she suddenly appeared behind him carrying a long wooden pole. 'It was in the wardrobe. I'm sorry I was so long, I had to break the wardrobe to get it out.'

Bandit took the pole from her hands and pushed it under the grate at an angle. As slowly as he dared, he inched the pole higher and higher, a millimetre at a time until he felt the grate once again begin to move.

'When I shout, help me push the pole higher,' he said as he grabbed the grate in both hands. 'NOOOOWWWWW...!'

Madeleine pushed with all her strength. Bandit screamed with pure emotion, the grate lifted and then dropped back into the position it had been in for all the years before as the pole twanged and snapped in half and both Madeleine and Bandit dropped to their knees.

'No, no, no, it can't. It can't break,' she sobbed as Bandit threw his arms around her. The smoke had reached their prison and again they both began to cough and choke. Her thoughts went back to Poppy, of all the happy days when they'd played with her doll's house, ran through the woods and rolled around with Buddy.

'Buddy, that's it. Shout for Buddy.'

They both began to shout as loud as they could. A dog's hearing was so much better than a human's. He always came when Madeleine called and she knew he'd hear her voice; she just knew he'd respond.

'What if he's trapped in his kennel?' she began to cry. 'What if ... what if ... Buddy, come on, boy, please, Buddy, come on,' she continued to cough, cry and shout all at once.

Then as though he was just out for a walk, Buddy appeared. His nose poked down the grate, his whole body waggled as though bending in two and he tried to lick at Madeleine's hand through the metal.

New tears fell down her face, tears of joy and relief. Buddy was still alive.

'Okay, Buddy. Sit. Sit down. Now, Buddy, SPEAK, BUDDY, speak!' she shouted as the pup took the hint and began to bark repeatedly and louder than normal. 'Good boy, Buddy. Speak for Mummy. Come on, Buddy, do it again. SPEAK!'

She closed her eyes and began to pray. She'd taught him this as a way to get Poppy to eat and right now she may just have got him to save their lives.

'It's times like this that I wish I'd trained him to retrieve or bring help. I mean, did you ever watch *Lassie*?' she said trying to lighten the situation as a new coughing fit began to overtake her body.

'Listen.' Bandit held his finger to his lips as the sound of people's voices could clearly be heard as they got closer.

'Okay, Buddy. Do it again. Speak, speak for Mummy.'

Chapter Forty-One

Madeleine felt overwhelmed with relief, yet distraught with anguish as she was dragged out of the ground, forcibly taken to an ambulance and laid on a trolley bed.

Fire engines surrounded the hall and firemen ran around spraying water towards reception where flames jumped out from the window frames and shot up to the roof of the house.

'Bernie, Jack, where's Poppy, where is she?' Madeleine felt the panic flood through her as both Jack and Bernie shook their heads.

She'd been so sure that as soon as they escaped the house someone would have brought Poppy to her, but they hadn't. Why hadn't they brought her?

'Maddie, she's with Nomsa. Jess left her with Nomsa. They were in the kitchen,' Jack said as tears streamed down his face.

Madeleine felt a moment of relief. 'That's good, right? If she's with Nomsa, that would be good. Nomsa would look after her, right?' she tried to find a rational explanation as Jack crumpled before her.

'We haven't seen them, not since the fire broke out,' he sobbed like a child and stared directly at Bandit. 'I didn't know what to do.'

'Where did Jess go?' Maddie asked. Jess wouldn't have left Poppy without a good reason. Where would she have gone without her? Had Jess gone into the house, was she in her father's old bedroom? Was she trapped in the fire? Maddie's heart rate accelerated and her breathing sped up. Both were at a rate that made her feel as though her chest would burst. The two people that meant the most to her were both missing and all she could see was their home burning to the ground before her.

She looked across at Bandit who'd already freed himself from the restraints of the ambulance.

There was no time to think. No time to plan. Choice didn't come into his thoughts. Poppy could be in that fire and if she were, he had to save her.

He grabbed hold of Madeleine's hands. 'Maddie. I promise you, I'm going to find her, they must still be inside. I'm sure that Nomsa would have done everything she could to get out, but if they are still inside, I'm sure she'll be protecting her,' he said looking directly into her eyes. 'I'll find her. I promise.' He knew he was making promises, giving her hope that the child would come out alive and that he would bring Poppy back to her mother.

All he could hear were Madeleine's screams as he ran towards the burning building. He dodged behind the bushes, past the firemen and straight for the main door. He'd never really been religious, never been one for the church but right now he looked to the sky that glowed amber with flames and began to pray before running in through the front door, heading straight to the kitchen.

Madeleine clawed at the bed straps.

'Let me off of here,' she screamed as she watched Bandit run into the flames. 'My baby, my baby's in there.' She launched herself from the trolley, just as the coughing once again overcame her.

'Mrs Frost, you need oxygen. Please, lie down, put this mask on your face.' The words of the ambulance man screeched through her mind like a firework tearing up and through the sky.

'LIE DOWN, lie down? Don't talk so stupid. My baby's in that fire.' She stood up again and stumbled towards the house but Jack caught her and tackled her to the floor.

'Maddie, please. Please don't. Bandit will find her. He

232

promised, he promised he'd find her,' Jack cried as he clung onto her as tightly as he could. 'He always keeps his word, you know he does. Please don't go in there. We can't lose you too.'

'Jack, get off me,' Madeleine screamed as she prised his arms from around her only to find Bernie pinning her down too. 'You don't understand,' she began to sob. 'I have to help her, I'm all that she's got. Please, Jack, Bernie, please let me go to my Poppy.' Her sobs turned into hysteria as she continually tried to escape their clutches and tried to claw her way across the grass, her fingers digging deep into the soil as she did. Seconds turned into minutes. Minutes turned into what seemed like hours. She held her breath, not daring to breathe as her eyes searched every window for any tiny sign of movement within.

Firefighters shouted to each other and one moved forward, breathing apparatus attached to his back. 'He's got her, he's got the little girl,' came the shout as the firemen all ran to the back of the house.

Confusion struck and Jack let go of Madeleine, allowing her to stand. She ran to the side of the house and saw Bandit running from the direction of the woods and across the grass. Poppy was in his arms and Nomsa was at his side.

Chapter Forty-Two

'I still can't get hold of Jess,' Madeleine said as once again she hit the red button, turning off the phone and dropping it back down on the table in Bandit's kitchen.

It was dark outside, but from the gatehouse she could still see the blue flashing lights that still surrounded the hall, while firemen continually worked to try and save her home.

She looked down at where both Poppy and Nomsa slept peacefully on Bandit's couch. 'I have no idea how to thank you, and I can't believe you found them both.'

Bandit shook his head. 'They'd gone down the tunnel and guess what? There's a false floor in the summer house. Eddie must have built the summer house right over the top of the entrance.'

'But it was bricked up, how did they get to the summer house ...?'

He held a finger to his lips, leaned forward and kissed her. 'Over the past few days I've been working to open up the tunnel. It was supposed to be a surprise for you. It seems that Poppy had worked me out, as always. She showed Nomsa where the tunnel was and led them both to safety.'

A tear dropped down Madeleine's face. 'My brave, clever girl,' she whispered and then looked up to where Bandit stood. 'Thank you so much for trying to surprise me, your surprise has saved their lives.'

The night before still seemed surreal. The main part of the house including the grand staircase had been saved, but the reception, and the bedrooms above were all destroyed and, at this moment in time, Madeleine had no idea what insurance cover her father had had. She'd never thought to check it after her father's death but right now, she didn't care. Poppy was safe and all she had to do now was find Jess to complete her family circle.

'I should go see what's happening at the hall. It's almost daylight,' she said as she grabbed one of Bandit's coats and he rose to go with her.

Burnt and broken, the hall rose up before them as Madeleine made silent promises to do everything she could to bring it back to its former glory.

'Mrs Frost, can I speak to you please?' a fireman asked as he walked towards them. 'Mrs Frost. I'm Fire Officer Hanwell. Could I ask, do you recognise this pen knife?' His words were simple, yet Madeleine looked at the knife and caught her breath. It lay protected in a plastic bag.

She nodded. 'It ... it ... belongs to my ex-boyfriend. Where ... how did you get it?' She searched his eyes for an explanation, but already knew what he was about to say. 'Was he in there?' She paused as the answer hit her all at once. 'Did he do this? Is he dead?'

Fire Officer Hanwell shook his head. 'No, miss, there is no body. But we believe the fire was started deliberately and the knife was dropped by the site of where it was started.'

Madeleine began to shake. 'He did this, didn't he?'

Bandit's arms surrounded her as her legs gave way and she collapsed into him, sobbing and cursing all at once as she remembered the sprinklers and the word 'sabotage' that Bandit had used. Her head spun as every imaginable reason for Liam's penknife, that he kept on his keyring, being at the site of the fire flew through her mind. He'd started the fire. He'd said she'd pay for leaving him. He'd said she'd be sorry. But, he'd gone ... she thought he'd gone. Thought he'd finally left them alone. So, why had he come back? Why couldn't he leave her alone and what's more, where was Jess?

The sun had now risen and Madeleine walked around the outside of the house alone, surveying the damage. She looked up at the window from where she and Bandit had climbed and then across at the rose bushes where her rucksack remained. Walking between the bushes, she grabbed the bag and threw it over her shoulder.

'Mrs Frost, word has it that the fire was started deliberately. What are your thoughts on that?' A young woman had suddenly appeared. She had a recording device in her hand and thrust it at Madeleine making her jump backwards.

'Do you mind, that almost hit me,' Madeleine shouted as she made her way out of the roses and back towards the house.

'I'm so sorry. I'd hate people thrusting things at me too.' She paused and flicked back her long auburn hair. 'Can we start again? I'm Ella Hope of the *Filey Chronicle*. I've always loved this house, my parents brought me here once for a treat and I just need a statement about the fire. It's my job. One statement and I'll leave you alone, I promise.'

Madeleine smiled at the woman. They were about the same age and Madeleine seemed to remember her from high school. 'All I can say is that at this point, I honestly don't know what happened. I'm just relieved that everyone got out safely.'

Ella flicked through a notebook. 'Could I ask one more question? Your sister, Jess Croft. She's missing, is that right?' she asked without waiting for permission.

Madeleine nodded. 'Yes, she left just before the fire. I haven't heard from her since.'

Ella picked up her mobile phone and began pressing buttons and then held a picture up for Madeleine to see. 'But, Mrs Frost, if your sister left, why would her car be parked right outside the gates of the hall? Do you think she could have gone back inside? Could she have started the fire?'

Chapter Forty-Three

Jess had stopped crying hours before. Her legs were screwed up tightly beneath her and cramp tore through her entire body, but she dared not move, she dared not try to stretch. The cage which imprisoned her hung precariously from a frail rope over a dark wooden stairway. Liam's words still haunted her mind.

'Don't move, you bitch, or the cage will drop and you will drop with it. It will kill you, just like it did the others.' She'd looked down, noticing damage and blood stains on the staircase and listened to his sickening laugh, making her body shake with terror.

She'd stared at him, trying to work out the man her sister had once loved. Maddie had only lived with him for a short time, but Jess couldn't believe that none of them had worked him out to be the monster that he was.

'Why are you doing this? What did I ever do wrong to you?' she pleaded, noticing that he turned his face away and avoided her stare.

'Don't look at me, just turn away, look away or I'll blindfold you,' he'd shouted as he'd smashed a wooden pole into the side of the cage. 'Turn away. I mean it, turn away now!'

She'd looked down, hoping and praying that he wouldn't hit the cage again. The rope didn't look that strong and his hitting the cage had made it swing violently from side to side.

'Please, Liam. Tell me why?'

'You said I was creepy, told Madeleine that you'd always thought so. Well, this will teach you not to speak badly of people or to swing golf clubs at them, won't it?'

'I'm sorry.' She had to try and weaken him, had to do whatever it took for him to let her go.

'You're just like my mother, she was cruel too. Well, I showed her, didn't I?'

'What about your mother?' Jess knew she shouldn't, but she prodded for the truth and then wished she hadn't as the pole once again struck the cage.

'She's down there.' He laughed and pointed down the stairs. 'Where she belongs. She's with the rest of them.'

Jess tried to see into the darkness. Was his mother captive in the cellar? Had she been there all along?

Liam poked at her through the cage making Jess scream out loud as her prison spun in the air and she caught sight of Liam's face, one whole side of which was bright red; his eye was closed and his skin was blistered and covered in burns.

'Liam, you need help. You need a doctor.'

He glared at her. 'Look away from me. I told you not to look.'

Jess felt her whole body tremble, the movement of which made the cage begin to rock uncontrollably. 'Let me out, I'll help you,' she lied.

'She's down there, my mother. She's dead. You see, she didn't love me enough, went and had another baby when she already had me. I should have been enough, she didn't need another child, did she? Well, I took care of them both.'

It was at that moment that Jess looked back up. She had no idea what sort of monster Liam was, but she knew that if a man could kill his own mother and sibling, he wouldn't hesitate about killing her too.

'Now, you be good and stay still, or you never know, that rope might snap. I'll be back soon. Just as soon as I've seen to that sister of yours,' he shouted as he slammed the door, leaving her in pitch darkness, unable to see, unable to move.

She knew where she was. Knew this was the staircase in his house, the one that Madeleine had never been allowed to see and now she knew why. She'd been to the house once or twice, but working away on the cruise ships meant that she'd not been here during the weeks that Maddie had actually lived here. However, she did remember telling her how weird she'd thought it was that Liam had locked doors in his house and had always thought him to be a bit strange, although never in her life would she have guessed the secrets that this house held.

Her mind spiralled. How many people had he killed? How many people were now buried at the bottom of this staircase, and how many of them had been squashed into this cage, hung from the ceiling and dropped to their death?

She'd been unable to move, unable to scream, knowing that if she did no one would hear. The house was old, Victorian, and every wall was made of solid brick. But how had she got here? She remembered Liam jumping in front of her car as she left Wrea Head, her slamming on the brakes and him opening the car door. She remembered screaming, his hand going over her face and then a hazy recollection of being folded up in the boot of a car. Then nothing until she woke up, squashed into this cage.

Suddenly there was a crash followed by a noise that echoed like a stampede. She could hear boots, many boots, which meant many men.

'Clear.' A man's voice shouted.

'Clear.' Another voice shouted. It was different from the one before and a voice she knew didn't belong to Liam.

'HELP ME,' she yelled as loud as she could. Suddenly there was a much louder, much closer crash, followed by a bang as the second lock was attacked. Daylight flooded in as the door to the staircase flew open and Jess finally closed her eyes and began to cry.

'I got one female. Alive. Get me an ambulance.'

She opened her eyes. The door was in pieces and so was the one beyond. Three armed policemen stood before her and one grabbed at the cage pulling it towards him.

'Tom, you grab that side,' he shouted and the second

policeman grabbed hold of the cage. 'It's okay, love. I've got you. It's okay. Tell me your name.'

She held her breath as the cage was lowered and finally touched the top step. Then the cage door opened and she struggled to move. Every inch of her was in agony and she gratefully allowed the paramedic to place an oxygen mask over her face, just as her eyes fixed on the open door of the bedroom beyond, at the noticeboard that hung on the wall facing her. Madeleine's broken locket swung from its hook and then suddenly fell to the floor as six policemen stamped into the room.

'My sister, Madeleine Frost, you've got to help her. I think he's going to kill her.'

Chapter Forty-Four

Father was being so kind and helped me without question or argument for weeks. He would bring food up to the room, light fires in the grate and would hold Edward Arthur as though he was his own.

He made it quite clear that neither Mother nor Mary were aware of his birth and that I understand that his existence was to be kept a secret and no fuss should be made at all.

But, now I know why Father has been so kind and so very secretive.

Edward Arthur is now just over five weeks old and today my father suggested that I go to the main part of the house and take a hot bath. He promised that he'd take care of my boy while I was gone.

The thought of a hot bath was too much and I almost skipped down the staircase with joy. Mother, Mary and Rose had all gone to London and much to my surprise the hall was empty of servants; everyone except cook and Benjamin seemed to have gone out, which seemed rather odd.

I went directly to my room on the first floor. I couldn't wait for the luxury of the bath, but knew that it would take a while for cook to boil the water and for Benjamin to carry it up to my room, so while I waited, I rushed back up the staircase, to the room beyond where my baby lay.

This is where my nightmare began. A woman dressed in a tweed coat and hat held Edward Arthur; she told me not to make a fuss, that he'd be much better loved by an adoptive family and that I'd be better off without him. Father went quiet and it was then that I realised he was having my baby taken away. I screamed as loud as I could and for a moment

241

*I was grateful for the tolling of the bell tower. The noise
unnerved the woman and I took the opportunity to grab
Edward Arthur from her arms. I ran from the house as fast
as I could in just my dress and my shoes and only managed
to grab my bag which contained my beloved diary and a few
of Edward's things, but there hadn't been time to take a coat,
not for me or for Edward Arthur. I didn't know where to
go. But my options were limited and eventually I ran to the
gatehouse, told Eddie's mother everything and she promised
to take us both in.*

*I now wait daily for news of Eddie. It's now months since
he disappeared and every day since I left the hall, I walk to the
kissing gate, hide behind the trees and watch as the postman
delivers letters to the hall.*

Madeleine read the words out loud as she turned the wafer
thin page of the diary.

'I can't imagine how I'd have felt if someone had tried to
take Poppy, or having to run away like she did. It must have
been awful for her,' she said as she held tightly onto Jess
who lay on the bed between her and Bandit, cuddling tightly
between them. They'd spent days like this, waiting for news.
They'd been asked to stay together, asked to confine themselves
to one room and not to leave the hall unless necessary.

Poppy was sleeping in her own bed and even though she'd
had no idea of the torment that Jess had gone through, she'd
been astute enough to build a wall of teddies around the edge
of her bed and hide behind them for safety.

A police officer had stood outside the front doors of the
hall for days. Liam still hadn't been found, but after what
he'd done to Jess, they wouldn't take the chance that he could
return to finish the job. After all, the police had no idea what
lengths Liam might go to. It was obvious that he was obsessed
with Madeleine and no one knew how far he'd go to gain his
revenge.

'How long are we going to be cooped up like this? It's like being a prisoner. I hate being inside. I feel like I'm in that cage again. I don't like it, Maddie. I hate it, it's horrible,' Jess whispered as she sat up against the pillows, looked down at where Bandit stared into space and pulled her knees up under her chin. 'Why haven't they caught him yet? I want to see Jack.'

Madeleine knew that Jess feared what Liam might do. She feared being trapped and enclosed and since being found, they'd all had to spend many hours just sitting in the middle of the garden with her, looking towards the woods, the summer house and the vast open fields that lay beyond. They'd all agreed that there was a certain safety in numbers, but Jess needed space and time to heal and until Liam was caught, neither the space, nor the healing was going to happen fast.

'I don't know, honey. All I know is that while the police are outside, we are all safe.'

'He'd killed both his mother and his sister, Maddie. They're buried in the cellar of that house, the one where you lived. They think he killed our Mother and Michael too and they even think he could have been involved in your father's death. Have you even thought about what that means?' Her voice still shook with fear. 'He's done all of this for years, killed them all. Even that girl you caught him shagging in your bloody hallway, Maddie. She's dead. I mean, why? Why would he do that and what was all that with the marker pen and the eyes?' They were words that Jess had repeated continuously, words that she needed answers to and words that spun around in her mind like a washing machine on full cycle.

Madeleine pulled her sister back towards her, caught Bandit's eye and silent words of compassion passed between them.

'Sweetie, please don't. Don't torture yourself. Whatever he did, it's done. We can't change it. All we can do is look after each other now, isn't that right, Bandit?'

She had no idea what else to say. It was true. Liam had killed them all. The police had confirmed that the bodies of three women had been found; all had been buried in the cellar. All had been tortured and just as he'd indicated to Jess, all had been dropped from a height that had broken almost every one of their bones. The identity of the third was still to be announced, but if the noticeboards were anything to go by, the third body would be that of her missing agent, Bridget.

There had been a picture on the desk of her father, the reason for which still hadn't been answered. But Madeleine suspected that she knew what had happened, just as she knew what happened to Michael, her mother, to the parents Liam said had moved to Ireland and to his little five-year-old sister, whose only misdemeanour had been being born blind. His mother had cared for her, more than she'd cared for him and the jealousy had begun.

Maddie's mind spun like a child's roundabout getting faster and faster, spinning out of control as it went, all the questions and answers were blending into one and she felt a constant feeling of nausea and stomach cramps. The deaths of Michael, her mother and father, even her agent, Bridget, were because of her – and she had so very nearly lost Poppy, Jess and Bandit too. Why did Liam hate her so much? He'd call it love but she was his obsession and she hated him with every fibre of her body.

She stood up, rubbed her stomach and looked over to where Bandit clasped the diary. His face had gone grey, but perspiration shone from his forehead as he stared at the wall, watching the clock that hung before him.

'You okay?' Madeleine asked as she watched him shake his head.

He stood up, walked to the bathroom and rinsed his face in the sink. 'The words in the diary, Maddie. Did you understand what they meant?' he asked when he came back into the bedroom.

Madeleine nodded. 'Of course, it meant that Emily went to live with Eddie's mother. What else?'

'My father, Maddie. His name is Arthur. Emily's baby was Edward Arthur. Put the clues together: Arthur, my dad's gatehouse and the lady he went to visit through the tunnel. What's the betting that Emily's baby is my father and all his ramblings are true? Emily Ennis is my father's mother – my grandmother – he just didn't know it.'

Chapter Forty-Five

May 8th, 1943

My Eddie has not returned and I presume him dead. I've had to make the heart breaking decision to have my Arthur adopted. Eddie's mother will bring him up as her own and I must admit, I do trust her to do this.

Father is pleased with this decision and I'm sure that he has made it worth her while to take the child. And from what I gather, the gatehouse is now hers to keep and he's also agreed that Arthur can be brought in secret to the hall, through the tunnels to the room by the bell tower. With this, I must be grateful. At least I still get to see my son, although he won't grow up knowing who I am.

With the war still in full force, there are many wounded soldiers, so many hospitals that have been set up to look after those who need medical care and I've decided to keep myself busy and enlist in the medical corps, where I will work in a nursing capacity and help wherever I can. As far as I'm aware, many soldiers need help with missing limbs, wounds that still haven't healed and problems of the mind that may never go away. It's the only thing I can think to do. I still pray that Eddie lives and I'm going to search every soldier's face for my Eddie in the hope that I find him and bring him home to the hall, where he belongs.

It will break my heart to leave my beautiful son behind. I live for every single smile that he gives and can't imagine not being with him every single day, not being able to hold him or put him to bed or even being able to watch him grow at the hall. He may only be at the gatehouse, but to me it's still so very far away.

The news channels had spoken of nothing but Liam O'Grady for days. His house had been searched and boarded up after the bodies of his mother, Angelina Corby and Bridget had all been found, buried at the base of the servant's staircase. And the body of his sister, Freya O'Grady, had been found weighed down at the bottom of the garden pond. The same pond which he'd told Poppy had had no bottom and anyone who fell in would never come out.

Following the evidence that had been found, the police were now making enquiries into the deaths of eight victims, along with arson and the attempted murders of both her and her beautiful sister Jess.

Madeleine watched the television as pictures of Liam's house flashed up on the news. Her heart was in her mouth. She had lived in that house with her three-year-old daughter. Slept there, made breakfast there, and lived happily there, in the place where, unbeknown to her, lived a deranged serial killer who she made love to, ate dinner with and had allowed her daughter to play in those rooms so close to where the bodies had been found.

She could barely breathe with nerves as once more Liam's photograph flashed up on the screen, making her heave and reach for a glass of water, taking a sip before replacing it on the bedside cabinet.

They'd taken up residence in room four of the hotel while the private residence rooms were refurbished and that part of the house rebuilt. The room was huge. The Victorian four-poster bed that her father had bought stood in one corner and the windows looked over the ha-ha at the side of the property, where sheep grazed on the autumn grass.

A knock at the door made her jump. 'Who is it?'

'It's Jack, Mrs Frost, I mean, Madeleine,' he said as the door opened. 'I have Inspector Johnson here, miss. I've seated him in the dining room.'

Madeleine noticed Jack's eyes connect with Jess and they sparkled with love and warmth.

'Jack, could you do me a favour?' she asked as she once again looked between Jack and Jess. 'Would you mind taking the rest of the day off, spend some time with Jess, you know, look after her for me. I think she'd like to stay in her own room tonight.' Madeleine smiled as she saw the two of them beam with delight. It didn't take a genius to realise how close the two had become, how their romance had blossomed and how they both radiated love the moment the other walked in the room, and even the protective big sister in her knew that time alone with Jack was exactly what Jess needed.

Jack winked at Jess. 'It'd be my absolute pleasure, Madeleine. Thank you.'

Looking in the mirror, Madeleine pulled a brush through her hair and added a touch of lip gloss. Satisfied with her appearance, she turned to Bandit and they walked out of the room and down the stairs. The inglenook fire was already lit and eerie looking pumpkins stood all around the floors and windowsills. Even though the private quarters of the house had been badly damaged by the fire, the rest of the hall had been miraculously saved and after a deep clean, most of the hotel had been allowed to re-open to guests; with Halloween fast approaching the pumpkins had been carved and lit giving the room a warm, atmospheric feel.

As she entered the dining room she saw that Inspector Johnson was already there. Bandit gripped onto Madeleine's hand as they walked towards him and sat down.

'Mrs Frost, the exhumation of your father and subsequent autopsy has brought new evidence to light and I need to inform you that we are now classing his death as murder, not suicide,' the inspector said as Madeleine noticed tears spring to his eyes. 'I knew your father very well, Mrs Frost, and, if I'm honest, I was very shocked to think that he'd taken his own life.'

'What's the new evidence?' Madeleine fought back the tears. She'd been right all along. He had wanted to live and had intended to be around for her, as he'd promised.

'I'm afraid I can't say, Mrs Frost. I'm sure that all will be revealed at the new inquest. All I will say is that your father was a good man. It was an honour to know him.'

At this, he stood up and walked to the door. Madeleine walked with him, leaving Bandit at the table with a look of shock on his face.

Madeleine took her time in reception, studied the walls and counted the ghosts. So much had already happened here. So many things had gone wrong.

'I think it's about time I did the right thing. It's time that the hall had new owners,' she announced as she walked back into the dining room and sat back down by Bandit's side.

'But, it was his dream. This whole place was your father's dream; why would you sell it?'

Madeleine could see sadness in Bandit's eyes. She thought back to the conversations she'd had with her father about the hall, about his wishes and his dreams. But now she had to think about Bandit; if his suspicions were correct, and she had no reason to doubt them, this house was part of his heritage and his father's heritage before him.

Chapter Forty-Six

August 31st, 1943

After my initial training with the 21st Army Group Medical Corps, I have been deployed to a hospital in London. It means that I can live in the London house but I'm hardly ever there as the suffering of the injured keeps me at the hospital doing what little I can to relieve them.

I look closely at every soldier that I tend. Not many of the nurses do this, but it's the only way that I can search for my Eddie, the only way to see the faces of those that are injured and know that he is not amongst them.

This war can't go on for much longer and I pray for the simplicity of Wrea Head Hall. I used to be bored by the daily routine, of spending hours in the kitchen chopping up vegetables for cook, or of the time I'd spend chatting with Mary, wishing for excitement and joviality or of how I'd moan when on a Wednesday, without fail, we'd eat pheasant week after week. But now all I wish for is to eat pheasant on a Wednesday, chat with Mary and curl up on my bed with my baby boy. I miss him so much. I need to hold him in my arms and go for walks with him in the meadows, but then I remind myself that he is no longer mine and my heart tears apart repeatedly as I think of him calling another woman 'mother'.

Will he ever know how very much I love him, how I live for his every smile? All I wish for now is that I might find my Eddie and we can go home to be one family, together.

December 24th, 1944

It is Christmas Eve and it is such a relief to be back at Wrea Head Hall.

Just before Christmas, I found my Eddie. There he was, just sitting in a corner of the hospital where I worked for so long, in a wing I'd never been in. It was a wing saved for those who have lost their minds, somewhere I'd never thought to look before and even though I am glad that he is alive, my heart breaks every time I look into his eyes. He is no longer the man that I once knew. He stares into space, doesn't recognise a soul and no longer seems to know who I am.

But all is not lost. I was allowed to go home and had permission to take Eddie with me. I'm sure that now he's home and is surrounded by the things he held dear, he will begin to remember.

I will take him to the summer house in the morning, to the room beneath the bell tower and sit with him on the secret staircase. Surely he will recollect the times that we had. After all, how can a man not remember his home, his mother or his loved one? But I am quite prepared that he might not and I fear that he will always live within his own mind. But if he does, he does. It does not matter to me, he is still my Eddie and I will care for him for as long as he needs me to.

It appears that in my absence, the whole house has fallen apart. Everything has changed and nothing is as it was. Mary married Benjamin. Of course, Father didn't approve, but they took themselves away, eloped to Gretna Green and married in spite of him. And only now that I'm home have they told me that my beautiful twin died in childbirth two months ago. I should have been there for her, should have helped her and I'm heartbroken and feel so guilty that she, and her unborn child, died without me at her side.

Young Rose is now walking, talking and causing havoc and Jimmy got one of the chambermaids pregnant and immediately ran away to fight in the war. Mother will have had a fit and the girl will have been sent away to bear the child and paid handsomely never to return and even though I can't judge, I've always known that this would happen.

I'm afraid that returning home with Eddie will push Mother over the edge. But I can't leave him alone and intend to care for him and if Father won't allow Eddie to stay with me at the hall, we'll live in the summer house. After all, it's cosy and Eddie built it out of his love for me.

Edward Arthur is happy. I went to see him the moment we arrived back at the hall. He is well looked after and now thinks of Eddie's mother as his own and, even though my heart breaks daily, to disrupt his life now would be cruel. Besides, would there be any point in telling Eddie of his son's existence, especially when ten minutes later he forgets who he is?

Chapter Forty-Seven

The days were passing and Madeleine needed to run.

Placing the diary under her pillow, she walked down the stairs. She smiled and looked out to where both Jack and Jess ran around on the ha-ha with Poppy, playing a game of catch. A police officer stood on the terrace right next to them, in the same place that he'd stood for the past few weeks. Always alert, always watching. At least the police had taken their security seriously and at one point had even offered to put the whole family into a witness protection programme, but to do that, they would have to leave Wrea Head Hall and every other single person and part of their life behind. She couldn't imagine leaving Bandit behind. Nor could she ever imagine not seeing Jack, Bernie or Nomsa ever again. She could have insisted that Bandit came with them, but again he would have had to cut all ties with his past and that would mean never again seeing his father. It would be asking him to choose between the two of them. And to do that would be unfair.

Christmas was almost upon them, and Madeleine felt excited that on Christmas Eve the new owners of the hall would be announced. Until then, the restoration continued and the beauty of the hall was beginning to return to its original state.

She closed her eyes and thought of Bandit. Of how hard he'd worked these grounds, of all the gardening, game keeping and general maintenance he'd done, just as his father and grandfather had done before him. She thought of all the weathers he'd worked in, the storms that were followed by rainbows and then sunshine.

'Come on, Buddy. Let's go.'

She'd long since stopped putting Buddy on a lead in the grounds of Wrea Head, there simply didn't seem much point.

The nearest road was around half a mile away, and Buddy had now learnt where he could and couldn't go. Besides, he'd saved their lives, so freedom was the least he could expect.

Running over the grass, Madeleine caught her breath and purposely slowed her pace. She looked over her shoulder to the gatehouse, where Eddie had lived and Edward Arthur had been left so many years before.

'Again, do it again, Aunty Jess. Again,' Poppy's voice came through the trees and Madeleine grinned from ear to ear. She knew exactly what Emily had meant by living for every smile; it's what she'd done with Poppy for years and she thought of the many times she'd watched her sleep, especially the months when she'd lived in Liam's house, and the new knowledge of what secrets that house had held made her shake. The police were now sure that Liam had been responsible for Michael's death and the inquest had proved that he'd drugged her father.

A nationwide manhunt was in place and each night Madeleine switched on the television in the hope that she'd see news of his capture, although she felt sure that if he had been caught, the police would inform her and the security around the house would probably be dropped.

Her lungs burned with adrenaline. It was a while since she'd last run and the exertion on her body was taking its toll. Slowing down, she picked up a stick, threw it into the trees and watched Buddy as he ran after it through the dried winter leaves. He picked it up, brought it back and dropped it at her feet, and now barked at her to throw it again.

Kneeling down on the grass she laughed as Buddy jumped up, knocking her to the floor. He wagged his tail as his whole body bent in two, backwards and forwards, licking in mid-air, taking in every stroke and tickle that Madeleine gave.

'Here, fetch the stick!' she shouted as once again she picked up the stick and threw it into the trees. Buddy ran off, ignored the stick and kept on running. 'Hey, Buddy. Come here.'

She looked at the tree line; the police had asked her not

to go in the woods. She looked back at the house to see if she could indicate to someone where she was going but all Madeleine could make out was Poppy running off towards the ha-ha and Jess running after her.

'Buddy, get here now. Buddy, Buddy, come back!' She tried to shout, hoping that the sternness of her voice would bring him running with his stick in his mouth and tail between his legs. She couldn't hear him, which was strange and she walked into the tree line, checking the floor for holes as she began to wonder if the earth had opened up and swallowed him whole.

'Buddy, where the hell are you? Buddy, come here, boy.'

Again she looked over her shoulder. The house was now beyond the skeletal trees. She inched deeper and deeper into the woods. Her heart began beating loudly in her chest as worry took over her mind.

Buddy always came back. He never ran off. So where had he gone?

Spotting him between the trees, she breathed a sigh of relief. 'There you are, boy, come here.' He sat, looked at her, tail wagging. But he didn't move.

'Buddy, for God's sake. Come here.'

Something wasn't right and Madeleine slowed her steps until she stood perfectly still. Buddy still sat in the distance, which disturbed her. She'd never known him to sit for so long, not in the same position, not when he didn't have to. She listened and waited before turning to the house in the hope that Nomsa or the police would now have realised that she'd disappeared. But no one looked in her direction. No one appeared to have noticed she'd left the path and it occurred to her that she hadn't told anyone where she was going.

A twig snapped underfoot, but she hadn't moved. She knew someone else was in the woods with her, but who?

'Bandit, is that you?'

Silence.

Again, she looked at the house. She knew someone was there. She'd heard the footstep and they hadn't replied when she'd shouted out. Every instinct she had within her body told her to run, but Buddy wailed and yapped.

She couldn't leave him.

She began to walk slowly in his direction. A tether could clearly be seen and Madeleine looked over her shoulder. Someone must be there, someone must have tethered him and it must have been someone he'd have known and run to.

Kneeling down, she began to untie the rope as quickly as she could while she constantly looked around her. Buddy bounced up and down, making a fuss. But his eyes were firmly placed looking over her shoulder making Madeleine tense up with fear.

Then darkness over took her mind.

Chapter Forty-Eight

Bandit leaned against the inglenook in the grand hall, picked up the long cast iron poker and stoked the remnants of the fire, which had almost gone out. Picking up a large log, he threw it into the flames along with five or six small pieces of kindling to give it a chance of relighting. He waited for the crackling to begin and for the flames to dance and spark, before picking up the coal scuttle and surrounding the log with small pieces of fuel.

The news that the hall would have new owners upset him more than he cared to admit. It had been the only place he'd ever settled, felt at home and had finally stopped running from the past. Of course the gatehouse would always be his, but the thought that things might change and that he might not come here for breakfast, sit around the table in the kitchen and see Nomsa, Jack or Bernie again tore through him.

He looked around it now: the great hall, where pictures lined the walls, ornaments stood around the windowsills and dark wood sideboards and tables were all decorated with pieces of arts and crafts. Madeleine had always wondered why there had been no family pictures, but the diary had said it all. Bandit looked up at the mantle; it was where there should have been pictures of his father, of Emily's son. But there were none and never had been. His father had been outcast and the family had had too many secrets which they'd felt should be hidden.

'Why haven't I paid you more attention?' he asked himself. His hand delicately stroked the deep blue chesterfield settee as he desperately tried to imprint the image of the room into his mind. He looked carefully at every piece of furniture, every inch of carpet and every ornament, knowing that each and every one held secrets to his father's heritage, to a life he should have had and hadn't been allowed.

Bandit planned to bring his father home for one final Christmas here at the hall, but wasn't sure how much he remembered of his past. His memories of the tunnels were vague, but he was quite aware that he'd been down them and had mentioned them many times in the past few months. Bandit had sat and listened more intently as his father had described the lanterns that used to be lit at each end, the ones that still stood in the tunnel now. While at the same time, he'd spoken of the nursery, the noise of the bell tower and the happy times he'd spent in front of the log fires.

Bandit wanted his father to see it all, just one last time, but didn't know how he would feel when nothing looked the same, when he realised that the lady, as he'd called her, was no longer there and whether he'd ask to see the tunnel which was now partially blocked and dangerous.

'Hey there, Buddy boy. What you doing in the house?' He bent down to fuss Buddy who'd just ran into the great hall, jumped up on the leather chesterfield settee and barked before jumping down again and running back and forth towards the door.

Bandit caught hold of his collar and noticed the strands of nylon rope that were tied to it. This was not a rope he recognised. He normally ordered the rope and tools for the hall and this was not one that he had previously used. So why had Buddy been tethered with it now?

'Jack, has Madeleine started tying Buddy up?'

Jack laughed. 'Seriously? Why would she? If anything he hasn't been in his run for days, takes himself in and out as he pleases and takes himself to the woods for walks. It wouldn't surprise me if he was sleeping in Poppy's bed every night.'

'Then why would he have this around his neck?' He held up the strands of rope for Jack to see.

Both stared, both shrugged their shoulders and both fussed Buddy who ran back and forth, barking for attention.

'Where's Maddie?' Bandit asked.

'Haven't seen her for an hour or two,' Jack replied as he collected the empty glasses that stood on the table, turned and walked back to the dining room.

Bandit took the stairs, two steps at a time. He needed to locate Madeleine, and for some reason he knew he needed to find her fast.

'Jess, Jess, where's Maddie?' he shouted as he burst into the bedroom where Jess knelt by the bath and Poppy jumped up from beneath the bubbles, arms above her head in the hope that Bandit would swing her out of the water and into a cuddle.

'I noticed her running shoes have gone. I thought she'd gone out with you.' Jess's face paled as both she and Bandit stared towards the window. 'Where is she Bandit? Jesus Christ, where did she go?'

Chapter Forty-Nine

Madeleine felt pain.

Every single inch of her hurt, yet she wasn't sure which part hurt the most. Her arms were stretched above her head. Her wrists were bound and her toes were barely touching the floor making pain shoot through her shoulders as they took the weight of her whole body.

She opened her eyes, just a slit at first. She knew she was in danger. She'd have been a fool not to have worked that out quickly, and she assessed, gauged, and calculated her situation.

She was indoors. The room she was in was dark, yet dim lighting came through a crack in a door. It was another room maybe, or the door could even lead to the outside. She could tell that the room she was in was built of wood, the smell unmistakable. She could only just make out the shadows of old wooden beams which seemed to hold up the roof and it felt as though there was no carpet underfoot, just rough planed floorboards.

From the light coming from the door she could just make out the silhouette of a chair. It stood in the far corner, near a window. In it sat a shadowy figure.

'So, you're finally awake.' His unmistakable Irish tone echoed through the room. 'I wondered how long it would take. Some people take longer than others. Your sister, she slept for hours in the boot of my car.'

'Why … why am I here? What did you do to me, you freak?'

'Now, now, Maddie, darlin'. That's no way to speak to me, now is it?' His voice grated through the air and she felt nauseous as he spoke.

'You're nothing to me, Liam.'

'Of course I am. We love each other, Maddie. Don't we, darlin'?'

'Liam, I've told you before, you lost the right to call me that the moment I caught you shagging that piece of skirt in our hallway. Now let me go.' She held her breath as he walked around the edge of the darkened room, studying her from a distance. 'They searched your house, Liam. They found the bodies, the room with the noticeboards.' She paused and tried to focus on his face, which he purposely kept turned to one side. 'Why, Liam? Why did you do it and why Jess, why were you going to hurt Jess?'

He stopped in his tracks and stared out of the window. Madeleine could make out the trees beyond. There was a swing seat that hung on the porch and she realised that her holding place was the wooden summer house, deep within the woods.

'They betrayed me, all of them.'

'Who did?' Madeleine tried to move her wrists, tried to stop the pains that shot down each arm. She almost dreaded the words that he might speak, knowing that the boards held photographs of both her and of Jess. Did he feel that they had betrayed him too?

'She betrayed me. She had that screaming baby. She didn't have to have another one, especially one with needs. Mother loved her more than she loved me. How could she do that?' He slammed his hand against the window, the pane shattering beneath his hand. 'Arrrgghhhhh, now look what you made me do!' He turned towards her, thrusting his hand in her face, leaving a crimson streak across her cheek.

Madeleine screamed. But it was not his actions that terrified her.

She saw his face. One side of which was destroyed by burns. Deep, red scars covered his cheek. He turned his face to look at her; his left eye was welded shut, and there was extensive damage to the whole side of his face and hairline, all unrecognisable as the Liam she'd known.

'Do you see what you did to me, Maddie? You did this, Maddie. It's your fault.'

She shook her head. Tears sprang to her eyes and began to fall uncontrollably down her face. Jess had said he'd been burnt, but she'd had no idea how bad it had been. She knew she had to buy time, knew she had to keep him talking, after all he had nothing left to lose.

Strangely, and for just a moment, she wanted to reach out and touch his face, heal his pain and take away the scars. For some reason she felt sad that his good looks had gone. But then she reminded herself of what he'd done. A man who had killed her beloved Michael, her mother, her father, Angelina and Bridget, not to mention his sister and parents. She shook her head from side to side. He'd almost killed Jess too and for that, she was glad he'd suffered unbearable pain.

'You should have died in that fire, not my face. The fire exploded in my face. I was hurt and it took me forever to escape, yet you and the soldier man, you both got out, unharmed. Well, it's your turn to burn, Maddie. You need to know how it feels.'

The words were venomous, making Madeleine close her eyes out of fear. She no longer wanted to look at him, no longer wanted to take away his pain. All she could think of was escaping, getting out of this nightmare. She had to get him talking, had to get him to concentrate on something else.

'Please, Liam, tell me about your sister. You've never told me about her. Why did you hate her so much?'

'My sister, that little toad. She was blind, born without sight and relied on Mother for everything. She was a leech. She clung to Mother and followed her around, making it impossible for Mother to love me too. But I needed her, I needed her to be there for me, but she never was.'

'That must have been awful for you, but I'm sure she loved you too, Liam. A child with blindness has to be difficult. I can't imagine how I would feel if Poppy had been born that way.'

262

Madeleine thought back to what the police had told her about the noticeboards. The victims had had their eyes blacked out, thick marker pen scribbled across them. All except for the sister, and no one had known why. But, of course, she'd been blind and couldn't look at him at all. She couldn't see the hate in his eyes, had no idea what danger she was in and probably didn't even understand what he was doing when he killed her.

Madeleine stared at the man she'd once thought she loved and wondered what kind of animal he really was. How could he hate a blind toddler so very much? How could he hurt her, murder her? Drown her in the pond and then kill his mother for having loved her? Had he killed the sister or the mother first? Or perhaps his father?

'Stop looking at me. I've told you, I don't want you to look at me.'

'Liam, please.'

'No, Maddie. It's the rule. You can't look at me.'

'Then, please, tell me, why did you kill Michael? He did nothing wrong to you, and my father. Did you kill him too?'

A loud, sickening laugh filled the room. 'Because they had you and I didn't. They had no right to have you. They had to be eliminated. Your father though, I couldn't call that as one of my own, not really, a couple of little amphetamines in his drink and he flew like a bird.'

Madeleine felt her heart break in two. He'd killed them both and in Liam's words they'd been eliminated. They'd died because they loved her.

'You self-centred, evil bastard. You don't eliminate people because they love someone else. What kind of a man are you?' her anger boiled over and she purposely stared at where he stood. She stared at his scars, knowing that the longer she looked at him, the more uncomfortable he became. 'Did you do all of that just to get me into your bed? Did you? I fell for you, Liam. I actually loved you. How the hell did that happen?'

She continued to stare as he began pacing the bare floorboards. She counted as he walked: ten steps in one direction and then ten steps in the other. 'Look at me, Liam O'Grady. After all you've taken from me, the least you can do is look at me, you coward.'

She kicked out at him, making herself scream with pain as the full weight of her body pulled heavily on her wrists, the coarse rope cut deep into her skin and deep red blood seeped into the blue nylon of the rope.

'You never did remember me, Maddie, did you? I knew you hadn't. I knew you couldn't possibly have remembered me,' he rambled on as he continued to pace up and down the floor.

'Remember you? What the hell are you talking about, Liam?' Madeleine looked puzzled, afraid. It was obvious from his words that they'd met before, but she had no idea of where and when. 'Had ... had we met before?'

'Yes, Maddie. Yes. We met at school. But you didn't like me back then, did you?'

'Liam, I ... I have no idea what you're talking about.' She continued to stare at him. Had they really met at school? She was still unable to remember him. 'You ... you must have changed. I really, really don't remember.'

He kicked at the wall, making the whole wooden structure of the summer house shudder. The beam above her head creaked and moved, allowing the rope to loosen, and her foot touched the floor, making it easier for her to stand. She waited for him to turn away and looked up to assess the rope. It was still secure, still held her tight, but at least now she had just a small margin of allowance. It was just enough to give her some hope of escape.

'I watched you from a distance, Maddie. I watched for such a long time,' he said. 'I used to watch you every day. I'd wait till every other person had left the corridor and watch as you went into your class, take your seat and take out your books. But each day you'd ignore me, pay me no attention and then finally, when I'd lost all hope, you smiled at me. Just once, you looked across and smiled. I was so happy. I felt sure you liked me and spent the rest of the summer waiting for you to speak to me, but you didn't.'

Realisation hit her as Madeleine remembered the boy who used to wait in the corridor. Everyone used to comment and wonder why. But now she knew. She remembered him, the dark rimmed glasses, the hair that looked far too long and a head that appeared much too big for his shoulders.

'Ah, now you remember.' He pushed her face to one side. 'Don't look at me.'

'I do remember. I'm so sorry, I didn't know, I didn't know you were waiting for me to speak,' she said as once again the rope twisted and tugged at her wrists. 'We were so young, Liam. I never meant to hurt you. I didn't even know who you were. You have to believe me.'

'I DON'T HAVE TO BELIEVE ANYTHING!' he screamed, stamping across the room and away from her towards the door. The door opened and light flooded the room. The smell of burning wood drifted in giving her the same uncomfortable feeling she'd had when she'd been trapped in the hall.

'Liam, what's the fire for? What are you doing?'

He walked back into the room carrying a bucket of fluid, which he sprinkled around the room. 'I'm preparing your death. I sentenced you to die by fire and die by fire you will. You see, once I decide how it will happen, then that's how it must be. You really shouldn't have escaped the first time, should you?'

Madeleine screamed. A high-pitched scream left her lungs and failed to stop. She could smell the fluid as he came close. Watched as he took a ladle and used it to throw the liquid at the floor, the curtains and the old pieces of furniture that surrounded her.

'Liam, please. You can't do this. You love me, think of the times we had.' She tried to think of things they used to do together, but couldn't and it suddenly occurred to her that their time together hadn't meant so very much at all. Their days had been an existence, a daily monotony of getting up, going to work and going to bed.

He rummaged in his pocket, pulled out a box of matches and began taking them out of the box, one by one. He lit one, then blew it out and placed it back in the box, making Madeleine stop breathing with fear. Slowly walking closer and closer to where she stood, he waved the box in her face. 'Which match will light the fire, Maddie, darlin'?'

'Liam, I'm begging you, please don't do this. Think of Poppy.'

'Ah, the brat. I should have killed her too. Perhaps I will. You see it on the news all the time, don't you?' He laughed in her face. 'But I couldn't decide if you'd go crazy with torment, need me more or push me away. I had it all planned, she'd have drowned in the garden pond, the one which is bottomless, or it just feels that way when you're sinking through the water, deeper and deeper, weighed down, unable to breathe. If only I'd decided before now, how you would feel.'

She was terrified. Her whole body shook with fear. She wouldn't allow him to hurt Poppy. There had to be a way to stop him, she had to escape. Images of her daughter filled her mind. The soft blonde curls, her tiny petite frame, and the beautiful way she'd smile, cock her head on one side and say please all at once.

Liam took the bucket of fluid with him and walked out through the door. She looked up at her wrists; saw the blood, the damage that the ropes had done. But it didn't matter. She didn't care how much she hurt herself, didn't care about her own pain. She pulled at the ropes, stood on her toes in an attempt to loosen the beam further, but blood poured from her wrists as the nylon cut deeper and deeper each time she moved.

'Stand still,' Liam growled as he stamped back into the

room. 'How dare you try to escape?' He walked behind her. She felt his hands pull her hair to one side.

She tried to spin around. 'Liam, don't. Please, don't. What are you doing?'

'Don't look at me,' he spat the words as he looked down at the floor and forcibly grabbed hold of her, his nails digging into her cheek as he turned her face away from him.

A cover went over her eyes and was pulled tight behind her head. She kicked out to where Liam stood, connected and heard him scream.

Then, there was a shout.

'ARMED POLICE. FREEZE OR WE WILL SHOOT.'

Maddie froze as she heard Liam laugh behind her, then the soft sound of him opening the matchbox, followed by a loud piercing bang.

Then there was silence as a loud thud hit the floor. Her blindfold was removed and the weight of her body was lifted off her feet. She felt her wrists being untied and found herself clinging to Bandit whose arms supported her.

'It's okay. I've got you.' His voice was trembling with fear and she could see the torment in his face; he'd just lived through Afghanistan again and again.

A police officer walked directly to them, felt Madeleine's pulse and picked up his radio. 'Get me a couple of ambulances as soon as possible. I've got one female patient, and one male deceased.' She heard the word deceased. It was distant and vague, yet for a few moments, the meaning didn't penetrate her mind.

All she knew was that she felt safe. Bandit held her in his arms and it was exactly where she wanted to be.

Chapter Fifty

Madeleine covered her eyes to shield them from the early morning sun as it burst through a slit in the bedroom curtains. She placed the diary on the table and lay quietly for a few moments before peering across to where Bandit slept. Smiling, she inched her body between the crisp white sheets in a determined effort to close the gap between herself and her naked lover.

Sleeping together was still very new, but she was certain that she'd never tire of watching him sleep. She loved the steady rise and fall of his chest, his deep, slow, untroubled breaths and the way he always seemed to curl his body around hers in a caring and protective state. He almost looked childlike in his sleep, yet he was still her hero. He'd saved her, found her when she'd needed him the most and had been protecting her ever since.

Pushing the sheet down to uncover his back and torso, Madeleine began to move her fingertips up, over and through the thick dark hairs which randomly covered his firm back. Each circle was firm, pronounced and seductively administered until she felt him stir beneath her touch.

'You awake, my hero?' she whispered as her hand moved down, lingering tentatively just below the sheet.

'Mmmmm, what do you have in mind?' he said as he pushed himself up against the pillows.

She laughed and knelt up before him, straddling his knee.

'Oh, no you don't.' He turned her onto her back, moved his body weight over hers.

Madeleine didn't need to be told twice. She felt the chill of the room as the bed covers fell from the bed. She watched Bandit's eyes grow dark as he looked over her naked body.

She stared longingly and lovingly at him. The deep volcanic sparkle of his eyes shone back through the darkness as his mouth took over hers. Pushing deep inside her, their bodies began to move as one, rhythmically together in pace and tempo. A soft scream of ecstasy left Madeleine's lips as a crescendo of shock waves passed between them both.

'I love you so much,' Bandit whispered in her ear as he pivoted above her. He looked directly into her eyes and Madeleine could feel the passion radiating from them.

'Not more than I love you,' she said, pouting as she ran a finger down his stomach in a soft but definite teasing motion, stopping just before she got to his thigh.

'Keep that up and you know what you'll get, don't you?' His hands were on each side of her ribs, the tickling began and Madeleine squealed.

'Mummy, guess what?' Poppy shouted as she burst in through the door. 'Nom Nom's going to make me pancakes, says I can have honey and chocolate sauce.'

Bandit moved to one side of the bed, grabbed his boxer shorts and discreetly pulled them on under the sheets. He smiled at Poppy and while she chatted endlessly to her mummy, he pulled on his trousers and jumped out of bed. 'Now then, Poppy, did I hear you mention pancakes?'

Poppy bounced up and into the bed and like a small and cunning chameleon, she cuddled into Madeleine.

'Mr Bang'it man, do you want some pancakes too?' she asked as Madeleine found herself being inched closer and closer to the edge of the bed.

'Hey there, missy, are you pushing me out?' Madeleine said as she began poking her daughter who squealed before she immediately picked up a huge white pillow and began thrusting it in Madeleine's direction.

'So, you want to pillow fight, do you?' Bandit shouted as the three of them tossed pillows around the bed; feathers flew up and around the room and Poppy shrieked with delight.

'Argghhhhh, Mr Bang'it man, stop, stop, we have to go down. Nom Nom won't have any pancakes left!' she shouted as she ducked down behind Madeleine.

Bandit ran to the door. 'Come on then, let Mummy get dressed. I'll race you to the kitchen.'

Chapter Fifty-One

March 1st, 1964

I haven't written in my diary for so many years. My days and years have been busy looking after my Eddie, but today my Eddie died. He's finally out of pain and no longer feels the torture of war that he's struggled with for most of his adult life.

In the end, Father had refused to let Eddie and I live at the hall. In his eyes we were not married and he said that only I could come home, but Eddie could not be with me. Our only choices had been living with his mother and Edward Arthur, or moving to the summer house, the house that Eddie had built for us. So, we chose the summer house. It was cosy at first and we made the best of it. Even though I'd sneak through the tunnel and take food from the kitchen whenever I could. Cook would make me pies and make sure they were hot for me to take home. It was easy to do and I didn't mind the walk, but then, after my parents died in 1954, I moved back to the hall and took my Eddie with me. After all, I was the only surviving Ennis, and whether Father liked it or not, the hall now belonged to me and to me alone.

But with it came no joy. I was sad that they were all gone. Baby Rose had been taken by the scarlet fever, Jimmy had died in the war and Mary had died in childbirth and then, one after the other, my parents were taken. I never thought I could feel any lonelier, but now my Eddie has gone too.

I long to see Edward Arthur, but I haven't seen him for years. He goes by the name of Arthur now and he left the gatehouse the moment he turned eighteen. He joined the air force, and from what Eddie's mother has told me, he has followed in his father's footsteps, even though he'd had no idea who his father had been.

I'm now all alone in a house full of memories. I'm the keeper of the house now, the one who has to look after it until the next keeper comes along and for that reason some of its secrets need to be lost. I can't bear the thought of the tunnels and I've asked that they both be bricked up today on the twentieth birthday of my son. It's a sad day although it should have been happy, but the last thing I want is for anyone else to travel through the memories that I have and if the tunnels are sealed, the boy, who's now a man, won't feel obliged to visit.

The tunnels had acted as a portal in time, a way for Eddie and I to meet in secret. I remember walking through them as a teenager with a huge smile on my face, just knowing that my Eddie was waiting at the other end. I remember kissing in those tunnels, and they had formed the perfect passage to our love nest on the night my son had been conceived.

The second tunnel was one that Eddie and I hadn't used so often, but had formed the perfect way for my boy to come to the summer house in the early days, and then to get to the hall once I moved back. Eddie's mother used to accompany him at first, it had been a good excuse for her to visit her own son, but after years of hope, Eddie still didn't know her and after a while, she'd bring my Edward Arthur to the entrance of the tunnel and return hours later to take him home. Of course, he thought he was just a visitor to the house, a child that came to play with the toys, eat creamed scones and visit the strange couple that lived there. But then he grew up and the visits became less, until one Sunday he didn't come at all.

Madeleine stood holding onto Bandit for support. They'd walked to the kissing gate to look at the house from a distance, as crisp white snow began to fall and cover the drive. It reflected back at them like a sparkling diamond carpet. A twenty foot Christmas tree stood in the huge Victorian window, antique baubles and lights hung from every branch, while the amber firelight glowed and the look and warmth of the house stared back at them.

'So, Emily finally took Eddie home to Wrea Head Hall?' Bandit whispered as though trying not to break the moment. He pulled Madeleine closer to him and kissed her lightly on the mouth.

'She did. She looked after him for so many years, but she never wrote in the diary again, not until he passed away in 1964.'

'Don't you think it's both lovely and sad, all at once?' Bandit said as he pulled himself up to sit on the wooden gate. 'The war broke him in two, it broke their love in two, their family in two, but she must have loved him so very much and asked nothing in return.'

'What do you think happened to Emily?' Madeleine asked. 'Father said he'd bought the hall from her back in 2007. Do you think she's still alive?'

Bandit stared into space, and gave a knowing nod. 'Do you know what, I think she might be.'

Madeleine smiled and they both stood for a moment, thoughts of Emily and Eddie running through their minds, until Bandit lifted his hand to Madeleine's face and dropped a kiss on her lips. 'I bought something for you.'

He pulled a medium sized box from his pocket.

'What ... what is it?'

'Well, you'll never know unless you open it now, will you?' He laughed and pushed the box towards her.

Taking the box, she carefully lifted the lid to reveal a tiny gold locket, identical to the one she'd lost, the one her father had bought her so many years before and she closed her eyes as her breathing slowed. She opened the locket to reveal a tiny picture of her father on one side and a similar sized picture of Poppy on the other.

'I'm afraid both Nomsa and Poppy are in on the surprise. She took the photo of Poppy for me and they're both dying to know if you like it. I thought Poppy would have burst by now with excitement.'

'I love it,' Madeleine said as she looked up. There was something deep within his eyes, something soft, caring and trustworthy. It was a look that made Madeleine feel safe, excited and overwhelmed all at once, a look she wanted to hold onto forever and it was then that she knew that the decision she'd made some weeks before had been the right one and she reached under her coat to pull out a gift of her own.

'I bought something for you too.' She passed him the box and watched as he opened it. A deep blue, leather bound diary stared back at them both. 'I thought it was about time we started a diary, you know, write down some memories of our own,' she whispered nervously as she urged him to open it. Inside the front cover was an envelope and Bandit's volcanic eyes began to sparkle.

'Is it for me? What is it?' He smiled nervously, taking the envelope from inside.

'Well, you know I said that on Christmas Eve the new owners of Wrea Head would be announced?' She watched as he nodded. 'Well, that's the announcement. I thought you'd like to read it first.'

She saw the colour drain from his face as he tentatively, with shaking hands, opened the envelope. He read the words, re-read them and then looked up.

'But ... but this says ...'

Madeleine nodded. 'It says that we are both the keepers of Wrea Head Hall. This house is part of your heritage, it's only right that it should be yours too.'

Chapter Fifty-Two

Darkness had begun to descend and dusk now surrounded the house making the Christmas tree lights shine up in the huge Victorian window and the amber lights of the log fires glow from within.

Every trace of the fire had now been extinguished and new decor adorned each room throughout, putting an end to the damage that surrounded the house and to the people within.

Jess's romance with Jack had moved forward. She now had a permanent smile on her face and a date for the wedding had been set. With this in mind, she'd finally moved the last of her possessions to the hall and was living there on a permanent basis. Not wanting to leave Jack for a moment longer than she had to, she'd quit her job on the cruise ships and had begun working at the hotel.

Bandit had been back to see his regiment. The marines were now helping him and giving him counselling for his stress.

And Madeleine, she had everything she wanted. She had Bandit, she had Poppy, Jess and she had her friends. She smiled, wondering what more a woman could ask for, just as Nomsa flew through into the dining room with her hands waving above her head in true Nomsa style.

'I hope Bandit isn't going to be long, Maddie. He needs to hurry himself up. That turkey, I won't allow it to spoil and oh, wait till you see the roast potatoes, they're browning off beautifully. Now, where is that boy?'

Madeleine supressed a giggle. Everything at Wrea Head was as it should be and she walked around the table and straightened the cutlery and glasses. She looked up at the clock and her stomach twisted with excitement. Bandit would arrive any moment with his father, he was finally bringing him home for good and everything had to be perfect.

Jack appeared at the door. 'Bandit's on the telephone for you, Madeleine. Wow, that table looks awesome.' He grinned from ear to ear and Madeleine knew that he was looking forward to the feast, just as much as everyone else, because tonight, they would all eat together. It was a tradition her father and Josie had begun and a tradition she had every intention of keeping up.

'Hi, what's wrong?' She felt nervous, Bandit never phoned.

'I have a surprise for you.' He sounded excited and Madeleine began to laugh.

'Another surprise, come on then. Tell me what it is.'

'Nope. All I can say is that my suspicions were correct and we need to lay another place at the table.'

Madeleine looked at the phone as suddenly Bandit was gone.

Madeleine took her place at the table and smiled as both Nomsa and Bernie continued an argument about who cooked the best roast potatoes, Hannah and Ann sipped their champagne and chatted excitedly, while Jess and Jack looked lovingly into one another's eyes. Poppy, on the other hand, thought that if she sat really quietly, no one would notice Buddy, who sat patiently by her feet, waiting for treats.

Madeleine sighed with admiration as Bandit walked through the door, pushing his father's wheelchair into the dining room, to take his rightful place at the head of the table. The childlike look of wonderment on his father's face brought a tear to Madeleine's eye.

But the seat beside him remained empty and Madeleine couldn't help but feel nervous and wonder what the surprise was that Bandit had in store.

'Ladies and gentlemen,' Bandit began as he stood next to his father and looked at everyone at the table. 'Today, I'd like to introduce you to two people. First, my amazing and brave father, who I love so very much. Today, he takes his seat at the head of the table, a place he should have taken many years ago,' Bandit paused and kissed his father gently on the cheek. 'And the second person I'd like to introduce you to is ... a lady who's cared for him, loved him and sat by his side at the nursing home for many years.' He walked to the dining room door, opened it and took the hand of a tiny, frail old lady. 'Ladies and gentlemen ... I'd like to introduce my grandmother, Miss Emily Ennis.'

Thank You

Dear Reader

Thank you so much for reading *House of Secrets*. I really enjoyed writing this book and do hope you enjoyed following Madeleine and Bandit through the smiles and heartache that they both went through to find true love and I'm sure that you'll agree, they both deserved it.

I'd like to think that anyone reading this book would want to go and stay at Wrea Head Hall themselves. Experience the hotel in all its glory, see Bandit's gatehouse, the greenhouse that stands in the grounds and take a hike through the woods to go and find the summer house, or sit on a cold winter's night by the inglenook log fire. (Just as I do many times a year.)

Like all other authors, I've been on quite a writing journey and I still find it surreal that my novel is now real, that's it's 'out there'. With that in mind, I'd love to know your thoughts and I'd be delighted if you'd take just a few moments to leave me a review.

Please do feel free to contact me anytime. You can find my details under my author profile, or come and look for my author page on Facebook, I'd always be happy to hear from you.

Once again, thank you for reading my debut novel, it was a pleasure to write it for you..!

With Love

Lynda x

About the Author

 Lynda, is a wife, step-mother and grandmother, she grew up in the mining village of Bentley, Doncaster, in South Yorkshire.

She is currently the Sales Director of a stationery, office supplies and office furniture company in Doncaster, where she has worked for the past 25 years. Prior to this she'd also been a nurse, a model, an emergency first response instructor and a PADI Scuba Diving Instructor ... and yes, she was crazy enough to dive in the sea with sharks, without a cage.

Following a car accident in 2008, Lynda was left with limited mobility in her right arm. Unable to dive or teach anymore, she turned to her love of writing, a hobby she'd followed avidly since being a teenager.

Her own life story, along with varied career choices helps Lynda to create stories of romantic suspense, with challenging and unpredictable plots, along with (as in all romances) very happy endings.

Lynda joined the Romantic Novelist Association in 2014 under the umbrella of the New Writers Scheme and in 2015, her debut novel *House of Secrets* won the Choc Lit's *Search for a Star* competition.

She lives in a small rural hamlet near Doncaster, with her 'hero at home husband', Haydn, whom she's been happily married to for over 20 years.

Follow Lynda on:
Twitter: @lyndastacey
Blog: http://lyndastacey2912.wordpress.com
Website: www.Lyndastacey.co.uk
Facebook: www.facebook.com/Lyndastaceyauthor/

More Choc Lit

From Lynda Stacey

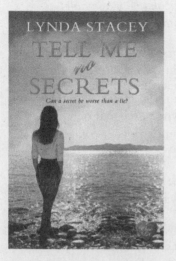

Tell Me No Secrets

What if you couldn't escape your guilt?

Every time Kate Duggan looks in a mirror she is confronted by her guilt; a long, red scar reminding her that she was 'the one to walk away' from the car accident. Not everyone was so lucky …

On the surface her fiancé Rob is supportive – but the reality is different. He's controlling, manipulative and, if the phone call Kate overhears is anything to go by, he has a secret. But just how dangerous is that secret?

When Kate begins work at a Yorkshire-based firm of private investigators, she meets Ben Parker. His strong and silent persona is intriguing but it's also a cover – because something devastating happened to Ben, something he can't get over.

As Kate and Ben begin their first assignment, they realise they have a lot in common. But what they don't realise is that they're about to bring a very dangerous secret home to roost …

Introducing Choc Lit

We're an independent publisher creating
a delicious selection of fiction.
Where heroes are like chocolate – irresistible!
Quality stories with a romance at the heart.

See our selection here:
www.choc-lit.com

We'd love to hear how you enjoyed *House of Secrets*.
Please leave a review where you purchased the novel
or visit: **www.choc-lit.com** and give your feedback.

Choc Lit novels are selected by genuine readers like yourself.
We only publish stories our Choc Lit Tasting Panel want to
see in print. Our reviews and awards speak for themselves.

Could you be a Star Selector and join our Tasting Panel?
Would you like to play a role in choosing which novels we
decide to publish? Do you enjoy reading women's fiction?
Then you could be perfect for our Choc Lit Tasting Panel.

Visit here for more details…
www.choc-lit.com/join-the-choc-lit-tasting-panel

Keep in touch:
Sign up for our monthly newsletter Choc Lit Spread for
all the latest news and offers: www.spread.choc-lit.com.
Follow us on Twitter: @ChocLituk and Facebook: Choc Lit.

Where heroes are like chocolate – irresistible!